One day Persephone is an ordinary high school junior working at her mom's flower shop in Athens, Georgia. The next she's fighting off Boreas, the brutal god of Winter, and learning that she's a bonafide goddess—a rare daughter of the now-dead Zeus. Her goddess mom whisks her off to the Underworld to hide until Spring.

There she finds herself under the protection of handsome Hades, the god of the dead, *and* she's automatically married to him. It's the only way he can keep her safe. Older, wiser, and far more powerful than she, Hades isn't interested in becoming her lover, at least not anytime soon. But every time he rescues her from another of Boreas' schemes, they fall in love a little more. Will Hades ever admit his feelings for her?

Can she escape the minions of the powerful god of Winter? The Underworld is a very nice place, but is it worth giving up her life in the realm of the living? Her goddess powers are developing some serious, kick-butt potential. She's going to fight back.

Praise for *Persephone*

"This story will completely suck you in. . . . This book is the first of a trilogy and I can't wait to see what's in store for these amazing characters.
—Amazon Top Reviewer, Melissa Groeling, Author of *Beauty Marks*

"*Persephone* is a fun, imaginative, smart retelling of my favorite myth, fusing modern culture with a rich world of magic. I had such a great time reading this.
—Amazon Top Reviewer, Molly Ringle, Author of *Persephone's Orchard*.

"From the first paragraph, I was enthralled with this story. I read it all in one sitting and enjoyed every minute of it. What a great spin on a Greek myth! Move over Rick Riordan!"
—Amazon Top Reviewer, Rita Webb, Author of *Daughter of the Goddess*

"I enjoyed Hades and Persephone's sweet romantic relationship. Persephone has her flaws, but she is likable and learns along the way. The author's writing is descriptive and entertaining. I am looking forward to the next book."
—Rebecca Foote @ Paranormal Muse

"Everyone needs to check this book out, I can't rave enough about it, Bevis is definitely a new talent to keep an eye out for, I give this 5/5."
—Sarah Brown @ Head Stuck in a Book

"I found this book to be a fun and fast paced adventure through Greek mythology with a modern twist."
—Stephanie Ward @ A Dream Within a Dream

Other books by Kaitlin Bevis

Persephone

Daughter of Earth and Sky

The Iron Queen

Persephone

The Daughters of Zeus Series
Book One

by

Kaitlin Bevis

IMAJINN

ImaJinn Books

This is a work of fiction. Names, characters, places and incidents are either the products of the author's imagination or are used fictitiously. Any resemblance to actual persons (living or dead), events or locations is entirely coincidental.

ImaJinn

ImaJinn Books
PO BOX 300921
Memphis, TN 38130
Print ISBN: 978-1-61194-622-2

ImaJinn Books is an Imprint of BelleBooks, Inc.

The Daughters of Zeus trilogy was originally published in ebook-only by Musa Press.

ImaJinn Books was founded by Linda Kichline.

We at ImaJinn Books enjoy hearing from readers. Visit our websites
ImaJinnBooks.com
BelleBooks.com
BellBridgeBooks.com

10 9 8 7 6 5 4 3 2 1

Cover design: Debra Dixon
Interior design: Hank Smith
Photo/Art credits:
Girl (manipulated) © Ipb | Dreamstime.com
Face (manipulated) © Javiindy | Dreamstime.com
Texture (manipulated) © Olgakorneeva | Dreamstime.com
Frame © Liudmila Metaeva | Renderosity.com

:Lpol:01:

Dedication

To my daughter, Isabella Elise Bevis.
I've been working on Persephone all her life,
and she's been very understanding for a toddler.

Chapter I

"PERSEPHONE . . ."

I hunched over, doing my best to ignore the sound of my name being whispered on the wind. It curled around me in a sensuous breeze. Once I would have turned around, tried to find whoever said my name. Now I knew better. There was no one there. There was never anyone there.

Too bad I hadn't figured that out before the whole school began to think that I was crazy.

"Persephone . . ."

I was starting to think they were right. I could feel someone watching me. Their eyes bored a hole in the back of my neck and crawled over my skin. The hushed sounds of my classmates did little to make me feel safe. Fabric swished as they shifted and moved. Nails scratched skin, lips smacked, and someone breathed too loudly. Above it all Professor Homer spoke with quiet excitement. Rare in teachers, but he was still new.

Something brushed against my spine and I twisted around, heart in my throat, only to see the innocent branches of the bushes swaying in the wind.

"Is everything all right, Kora?" Professor Homer's glasses glinted in the sun. He shielded his eyes with his hand, brown eyes crinkling in concern.

"Sorry." I shifted away from the bush and faced Professor Homer. He waited for Rachel and the twins, Jessica and Ashley, to stop giggling before continuing the story.

I ducked my head to ignore their laughs and whispers. The air around me stiffened, ice cold. No one else noticed. My breathing slowed, and I forced myself to stay rooted to the ground, as solid and unmoving as the gray trunk of the oak tree in front of me. It took every fiber of my being not to squeeze my eyes shut.

Please don't see me.

The thought was as illogical as a deer praying not to be spotted by a hunter. I was already in the hunter's sights.

"Are you okay?"

I jumped at the sound of Melissa's whisper; her hazel eyes remained riveted to Professor Homer to fool him into believing she was paying attention. He narrowed his eyes in her direction, not missing a beat in the story he was telling the class.

It's not real, I reminded myself, and latched on to the distraction she provided. I gave Professor Homer an innocent smile, touching my thumb to my chest to sign I was fine to Melissa. We'd learned American Sign Language years ago to share secrets, but ASL wasn't often discreet. To learn another "secret" language, we'd signed up for Latin.

It hadn't taken long to realize vocabulary wasn't the focus of Latin class. No, we had to learn about declensions, cases, conjugations, and sentence structures. No wonder the language was dead.

Professor Homer tried to keep it interesting by mixing in classical education and mythology. Since tomorrow was the start of winter break, and two-thirds of our classmates were taking make up exams, we were taking what he called a "mental health day."

He leaned against the trunk of the oak tree, brown loafers peeking out from beneath the cuffs of his tailored pants. A yellow legal pad full of scrawled notes was propped haphazardly against the tree trunk.

A shift in his tone caught my attention. He rolled up the sleeves of his blue dress shirt, moving his hands as he told the story. He leaned forward, voice becoming ominous.

"Oreithyia danced upon the river bank, unaware she was being watched."

A cloud passed over the sun, bathing the class in sudden shade. Goose bumps rose on my arms as the temperature plummeted. I flinched when a gust of wind knocked over the legal pad with a thump. The yellow pages fluttered open, sending loose scraps of paper floating toward the lake.

"Suddenly, the God of Winter, Aquilo, more commonly known by his Greek name, Boreas, swept her away in a cloud and . . ." Professor Homer faltered at the sight of the escaping papers. "Married her."

I rolled my eyes. At sixteen, it wasn't as though Melissa and I were clueless about what happened to poor Oreithyia. Beside me, Melissa nodded as though I'd spoken aloud.

Professor Homer continued. "For nearly a century afterward, the people of Athens traced their lineage back to Oreithyia and Boreas, claiming to share the blood of the gods. Can anyone tell me what's special about this myth?"

"It explains winter, right?" Rachel's voice drew my gaze past Andrew to where she was perched on the opposite end of the short stone wall our class was using as a bench, flanked by Ashley and Jessica.

"Right!" Professor Homer smiled, and every girl sighed. "The ancient Greeks and Romans didn't know why the seasons changed, so they came up with this myth to explain it. Every year, on the anniversary of Oreithyia's abduction, it grows colder for the length of her captivity."

Andrew raised his hand. "And this is the best they could come up with the explain winter?" he asked without waiting to be called on. "Seems like something as drastic as seasons changing would get more than one myth."

Professor Homer shook his head. "I'm afraid this is all they've got for the *why* of Winter, but there were some pretty interesting festivals and celebrations that took place during the winter months."

I tuned out Professor Homer's overview of Roman holidays, my thoughts turning instead to Oreithyia swept up into that cold cloud. A chill crept up my spine. I hated winter. Luckily I lived in Athens, Georgia, where winter was rarely serious until late January and over by April.

"What is with you today?" Melissa asked when the class broke up.

"That shirt looks really good on you. You should wear purple more often." I stalled, reaching down to gather my things. I didn't know how to put my paranoia into words without sounding crazy.

"Thanks." Melissa's narrow cheeks flushed against her olive-colored skin. She gave me a wry look to show she wasn't oblivious to the fact I'd avoided the question, but to my relief she didn't press me further. "Do you want to eat here?"

"That's a great idea!" Rachel piped up, passing behind Melissa. "It's so beautiful out." Before we could stop her she called the twins over. Melissa gave me an apologetic look.

A yellow page landed at my feet. I plucked it from the ground, and walked to where Professor Homer was gathering stray pages before the wind could snatch them away again. I knelt to help him.

"Don't you know it's a half-day?" He placed a wrinkled page in the middle of his legal pad. "Shouldn't you be fleeing this awful place?"

I inclined my head toward the parking lot. It was just visible over the hill, but even from here it was clear it was gridlocked by soccer moms picking up their kids. On full days the lower school got out earlier than we did, but half-days messed everything up. "I don't think anyone is getting anywhere fast."

"Smart girl." He smiled, meeting my eyes. His pupils dilated, brown eyes disappearing into black. I looked down at the papers. The last time I'd seen that, the eight-year-old I'd been paired with for the tree decorating ceremony had professed his love for me in front of the whole school. I'd been humiliated!

Professor Homer's hand brushed mine when we reached for the same sheaf of paper. He jerked his hand back as though he'd been bitten by a pit viper and sprang to his feet. "Could you rescue what's left of these and drop them off before you leave? I'll be around for a while this afternoon."

My nod proved unnecessary as he was already receding in the distance toward the circle of white buildings on the horizon. I felt the eyes lingering on me and gulped, finding myself alone at the edge of the lake. As I grabbed the rest of the papers, my hand paused over a yellow page, one half submerged in the water, flakes of frost climbing up the other half.

"What the hell?" I closed my eyes and shook my head. I really was crazy if I was seeing frost on this perfect sunny day.

"Hey, Kora!" Melissa called. "You gonna eat or not?"

"Yeah." I rose to my feet, turning so I didn't have to look at the lake. A crackling sound came from the water, and I quickened my pace until I reached the stone wall. I smiled in thanks at Melissa for remembering to call me by my middle name. It was easier to say and a lot more normal than my first name. Melissa and my mom still called me Persephone, but they'd both known me since birth, so I let them get away with it.

"Did you see that look he gave you?" Jessica asked.

I gave her a thanatotic glare, shoved the papers in my purse, and sat next to Melissa. Behind us a trio of seniors evidently came to the same conclusion about the parking lot and starting throwing a football between them.

"I bet you get an A in his class." Ashley snickered.

"Would you mind dropping those papers off in *my* room?" Rachel mocked, her voice breathy as she waggled her eyebrows.

"Oh my God! Would you all shut up?" Melissa snapped. "That is *not* what he meant."

"Sounds like someone's jealous," Jessica teased.

"Yeah," Melissa shot back. "And it's not me."

Persephone. The name curled around me, whispered on the wind.

I swallowed hard, checking to see if anyone else had noticed. They sat in an awkward silence, too angry at one another to hear voices in the wind. Melissa pulled her lunch from her giant leather purse, splitting half of it with me without a word. Neither of us offered any to the twins or to Rachel. Offering them food would either be construed as an invitation to eat lunch with us or to complain about their weight, and we didn't want to offer them either.

Rachel pulled sunscreen out of her purse and squeezed it into her hands. "What?" she asked when we all looked at her. "Just because it's December doesn't mean I won't burn." She rubbed it onto her pale legs, stopping when she reached her barely legal Soffe shorts. "So, Kora, that's all you're going to eat?"

"Why?" I glanced down at the whole grain roll, carrots, celery, pomegranate seeds, and blueberries. "What's the matter with it?"

"That's, like, zero points." Ashley's voice was layered with false sympathy.

"She means there's not many calories there," Jessica explained. Her brown hair was chopped short in a pixie cut to distinguish her from her twin's longer hair. "Mom's dieting again, and she's labeled every package in our house with a black marker so she knows how many points they are." She rolled her eyes.

"Yeah, you should eat meat or cheese or something," Rachel added.

"I'm a vegan." It wasn't an animal rights thing; I'd been this way all my life. My mom and I just preferred to eat things that came from the ground.

Rachel shook her head and pulled out her phone. "Here. I'm gifting you an e-book that deals with your problem."

"What problem?" Melissa's eyes flashed.

Rachel let out a deep breath through closed lips that puffed her red bangs into the air. "Kora." She spoke haltingly, as though she didn't want to continue, but her eyes glittered, telling another story. "You don't have to starve yourself to lose weight. I mean, the amount you've lost already isn't healthy."

All ninety pounds of Melissa's thin frame quivered with anger. "Oh?"

"You're different." Jessica waved her hand. "You're taller. Kora, you're like, what, four-ten?"

"Five foot."

"Exactly."

"Is that what you guys were whispering about during class?" I asked, incredulous. "My problem?" I put the word in air quotes.

"What?" Ashley wrinkled her forehead, and then laughed. "No, some idiot freshman asked Joel out this morning and got completely rejected. It was brutal." She giggled. "You should have been there."

"Oh." I really was paranoid. No one had been talking about me, and no one was watching me at all. It was probably all in my head. My shoulders loosened, and I allowed myself to relax.

"Don't change the subject, Kora. You don't have to be afraid to ask for help." Rachel's voice was so sugary I felt ill.

I took a big gulp from my water bottle to avoid protesting. Instead I let Melissa chew them out, her voice tight with anger.

I *did* eat, just not big meals. I liked to snack throughout the day. I hadn't *done* anything to lose weight. My body slimmed down and toned up of its own accord after I turned sixteen.

I heard soft laughter on the breeze, the sound so cold I shivered. The hunter's eyes bored holes in the back of my neck. I rubbed it, wondering if I should tell someone about the feelings I'd been having.

Tell them what? I wondered. *That someone has been following me? Sorry, Mom, can't describe them because I've never actually seen this person. It's just a feeling.*

"Hey!" Melissa waved a manicured hand in front of my face. "Where did you go, Pluto?"

"Sorry." I blushed as I wondered how long she'd been trying to get my attention.

"Did you remember to bring the tickets for the Orpheus concert?"

"Are you ready to go backstage?"

"No way!" Melissa exclaimed and let out an ear-piercing squeal, pumping her fist into the air. "No way!"

"How did you get tickets?" Ashley folded her legs under her and leaned forward. "It's been sold out for months!"

I shrugged. "My mom managed it somehow."

"That's in Atlanta, right?" Jessica asked.

"Yeah. We're staying in a hotel." Melissa managed to keep the smugness from her voice, but I could still tell she enjoyed the importance of that statement.

"By yourself?" Rachel asked in disbelief.

"Our mom would never go for that." Ashley shared a look with her sister.

I suppressed a grin. My mom trusted me. Unlike most parents, if I told her I was going to follow her rules, she believed me. "I'm going to have to work at my mom's flower shop every minute of the break to make up for this, but it's completely worth it."

"Absolutely," the girls agreed.

"I want that big cardboard cut-out of him they have in the mall for my birthday." Jessica's cheeks turned pink when we turned to look at her. "Oh come on, who wouldn't want to wake up to *that* in their bedroom. That man is a god."

Rachel snickered and started to say something, but something behind me caught her attention. Her eyes widened. I heard my name carried on the wind, felt the piercing stare, then gasped as something hit me from behind hard enough to force the breath from my lungs. I fell forward, gasping. Melissa's hands shot out to me. Rachel and the twins cried out in surprise.

A shadow fell over me.

Chapter II

I KNEW I WASN'T crazy! I didn't have time to wonder if insanity might be preferable before I felt hands grip me from behind.

"Are you okay?" It was Joel. He picked up the ball and threw it back in the general direction of his friends. "Don, I told you to be careful where you're throwing that thing!"

"I'll live," I managed, simultaneously relieved that this guy wasn't the creepy name whisperer and annoyed at the prospect that I might still be losing my mind. I pushed myself off the ground and sat up, hands moving automatically to fix my hair.

I found myself staring into dazzling blue eyes. He shot me a confident grin and held out a hand. "I'm Joel."

The introduction was pointless. I knew who he was. Everyone knew who he was. Unlike most of the boys at this school who'd been here since preschool, he'd transferred here for his senior year. I'd seen him around but never worked up the courage to talk to him.

When I didn't say anything or accept his extended hand, his smile faltered. "Persephone, right?"

"Kora," I corrected. Melissa's sharp elbow dug into my side. "Um, and this is Melissa." She shot me an annoyed look and then gave a pointed look at his extended hand.

Right. I flushed and gripped his hand. I felt a pinprick of pain when static electricity zinged through my fingers with an audible pop.

"Hey, Melissa." He gave her an easy grin and swept his blond hair out of his face.

Her cheeks colored. "Hi."

"I'm Rachel." Rachel thrust her hand at him. I jerked back when her hand came close to grazing my face. Her voice prompted the twins to chime in with their names. Joel nodded, but didn't spare them a glance.

"Didn't I see you at the last game?" he continued when it became obvious I was too tongue tied to speak.

"She doesn't go to the games." Jessica scooted closer to Joel.

"Yeah," Ashley chimed in. "No school spirit, I guess."

"But I'm at every game." Rachel fluffed her hair, as if that was always what she'd been planning to do and Joel hadn't left her hanging. "I saw you make the final touchdown. I've never seen anyone run that fast."

Melissa gave them all a scathing look. "Kora, I'm going to go get my stuff. I'll meet you at the car. And weren't you guys just saying that you were running late?"

"No," Rachel said.

Melissa's cheerful voice belied her death glare. "Yes, you were."

They got the hint and left. I could have killed Melissa. I didn't know what to say to guys! There was an awkward silence and then I stood.

"I should get these back to Professor Homer." I clutched the yellow papers in my hand and started toward the Lampkin Building.

Joel was beside me in a flash. "I'll walk you." He didn't sound confident anymore. He sounded self-conscious. "I mean, um, if you don't mind."

I smiled. "I don't mind."

We made our way down the cobblestone path woven through a trail of magnolia trees and harvest maples with bright red leaves.

"So . . ." Joel trailed off when we reached the classroom. "About the football, I'm really . . ."

"It's fine," I assured him.

He hesitated. "Hey, I was wondering, did you wanna go—" He touched my hand. I glanced up at him, meeting his eyes. His pupils widened and he broke off mid-sentence.

He leaned toward me. I backed up and met the door of the classroom. I hadn't realized how little space there was between us before.

"I . . . um . . . I should go," I squeaked, fumbling behind me for the doorknob. I opened the door and practically fell into the classroom.

Confusion marred Joel's features. "Right. I'm so sorry." He turned bright red. "See you," he muttered before retreating down the hall.

Like most classrooms at Athens Academy, the door from outside opened straight into the classroom. Sunlight flooded the room from the floor to ceiling windows. I waited until Joel was out of sight before I turned to find Professor Homer.

He was sitting at his desk behind the glass wall separating his office from the classroom, red pen dancing across some unfortunate student's paper. I walked past the posters depicting ancient Rome and laid the papers on his desk, moving the Colosseum paperweight on top of them so they wouldn't fly away. He gave a distracted wave, hunching forward over the paper. His pen made an angry red slash across the page. I hoped it wasn't mine.

I ducked into the bathroom on my way to the car, frowning. It wasn't like Professor Homer to just wave a student off. He didn't even tell me to have a nice vacation. I gulped, wondering if it really was my paper he'd been grading. Was my translation of *The Aeneid* so awful he couldn't even look at me? I closed the stall door, pushing the sliding lock into its bracket. I was calculating what failing my final would do to my grade when I heard Jessica laughing.

"What would he even see in her? She's just so weird." The door slammed and I jumped. "I don't get why she tries so hard. And have you looked at her eyes? They have to be contacts, right? Nobody has eyes that color."

"What about her hair?" Ashley asked.

There was a second of silence and I could imagine the three of them looking at each other. "Bottle blond," they said in unison.

Are they talking about me? My eyes were green, but I'd never noticed anything unnatural about them. They were the color of a new blade of grass, just like my mother's. I touched a lock of my honey-blond hair. They couldn't be talking about me. My hair color hadn't changed in the last thirteen years. My mom would have a fit if I dyed it.

"That's not the only thing about her that's fake." Jessica snickered. "I heard she had work done over the summer."

Definitely not me, then.

"She acts so innocent, too! Melissa's practically her guard dog." Rachel's voice echoed through the bathroom. "It's sickening."

"I heard she's with Professor Homer," Jessica said.

"Ugh. Do you think they've ever done it on that couch?" Ashley asked. Professor Homer's room was famous for having a leather couch next to the bookshelf.

"It's so wrong of her to lead Joel on," Rachel said.

"You want to know something gross?" Jessica asked. "She's probably doing Professor Homer right now."

The girls squealed, and Jessica continued. "They're probably on that couch doing—"

I flushed the toilet, drowning out whatever gross thing she said next. I forced myself to take a deep breath and open the speckled gray stall door, restraining myself from throwing it open.

I met their stares, not looking away until they dropped their gazes. With measured steps, I moved across the gleaming white tiles until I reached the sink and washed my hands. I wanted to break the silence, but why make it easier for them?

Proud my hands weren't shaking, I dug a brush out of my purse and fixed my hair, and straightened my blue peasant dress, turning to make sure I looked okay from behind.

The girls stood in the doorway as if made of stone. I looked at them and kept my arms by my side instead of crossing them like I wanted to.

Jessica mustered up the courage to speak, her voice indignant. "You—"

"I was using the restroom. Maybe next time you want to spread garbage in a public place, you'll be more careful."

"I'm sorry." Rachel tripped over each word. "We shouldn't have said—"

"No, you're not. You're saying that because you got caught."

Ashley rolled her eyes. "Oh, like you and Melissa don't talk about us when we're not around."

"I don't think about you at all when you're not around. Were you planning to keep me in here all day?" They looked at me, confused, and I motioned behind them. "The door."

"Oh." Jessica let out a nervous laugh. "Oops." They moved out of my way and I left, quickstepping to avoid the door slamming on my heel.

WHEN I REACHED my yellow bug I slammed the door so hard the white gerbera daisy fell out of its vase on the dashboard.

"What happened?" Melissa asked. Her seatbelt was buckled and she had Facebook pulled up on her phone. How much time had I wasted listening to that garbage?

I shook my head and scooped my daisy up with a smile. It was hard to stay angry in my car. My mom had bought it for my sixteenth birthday last March, and I'd used my meager paychecks from the shop to add the daisy rims to the tires and the flower cut outs to the brake lights. I even had a wildflower license tag that spelled my name.

"Well?" Melissa asked after we turned out of the parking lot.

"Can you call our moms and let them know we're on our way? I don't want to waste another minute, and they won't talk to me if they think I'm driving."

"I already did. They said to drive safe."

"Always." I turned onto Timothy Road. "Ugh. You will not believe what I overheard!"

My recap of the conversation lasted until we got to Highway 316, and Melissa's colorful descriptions of our classmates and what fates she believed should befall them took up the remainder of the forty-five minute trip to Atlanta.

She fell silent when Highways 75 and 85 merged and a wall of semi-trucks converged on either side of us. I wished I could just stay in the slower moving right lane, but it kept turning into an exit lane. I stayed in the middle lane for safety, keeping what I felt was a reasonable distance behind another intimidating semi-truck. A red convertible squeezed in front of me, followed by a black SUV.

"Seriously?" I gripped the wheel.

"I think you have to follow closer." Melissa's voice was quiet with tension. I inched forward and almost got sideswiped by a yellow taxi that didn't bother with a turn signal. "Or not."

A huge gust of wind hit my car, pushing it to the left toward the left lane. A blue Civic honked, steering out of our way.

Melissa shrieked and I clung to the steering wheel, trying to keep the car in our lane. With an audible *thunk*, the wind pushed us from the driver's side.

"What's happening?" Melissa yelled.

"It's the wind!" I clung to the wheel as a gust propelled the car forward. I resisted the urge to squeeze my eyes shut as we closed in on a black SUV.

"Why isn't it affecting the other cars?"

I was too busy trying not to hit the other cars to notice how they were being affected. I gritted my teeth and flipped on my hazard lights, dodging into the right lane seconds before colliding with the SUV. A silver Prius had no choice but to brake and let us over.

"Bricks," Melissa muttered. I gave her a tight smile. Melissa always joked that she was going to keep a pile of bricks in the car to chunk at bad drivers. Not a bad idea, but with our luck they would just blow back onto my windshield.

"One lane down," I announced. "Two to go." My knuckles ached from gripping the wheel as I tried to keep control of the car and waited for the other drivers to let me over.

"Can't they see the hazard lights?" Melissa flipped off a white Dodge Ram roaring past us.

The wind slashed across the windshield, leaving a trail of frost in its wake. I screamed as the car careened out of control and skidded onto the shoulder.

Chapter III

HORNS HOWLED. I slammed on the brakes just before hitting the concrete pylon of an overpass.

Melissa and I stared at each other, panting. "Is that ice?" Her hand shook as she pointed at the windshield.

I nodded, reaching for the door handle. "No." Melissa spoke fast. "Don't get out."

"Someone could be hurt." I glanced behind us to the center of the highway.

Not a single car had been caught in our wake.

"Let's take this exit and get the hell out of here." Melissa leaned forward as if she could make the car go.

Trembling, I put the car into gear and waited for an opening back onto the highway. We crept forward the twenty feet to the MLK exit. "When we get off, map the way to the hotel?"

Melissa nodded, instructing my phone's navigator to avoid highways. We drove in silence until we pulled into the hotel parking lot. My legs were shaking when I climbed out of the car. I took a deep breath to calm my nerves.

"We can't tell our moms about that," I said. "They'll never let us drive anywhere again."

Melissa looked troubled but nodded. "Persephone, what was that?"

I shook my head and shrugged. "Just the wind, I guess. Why didn't you want me getting out of the car?"

"Um, because it's a huge freaking highway. People have gotten hit changing their tires."

"Oh." I grimaced at the thought.

"Plus the fact your car was just singled out by a force of nature." Melissa's voice was dry, and for once I couldn't tell if she was being sarcastic or serious.

I laughed, the sound coming out higher than I'd like. "That's not possible. I'm sure the others were affected; you might not have been able to tell. They were all huge SUVs." I patted my car. "This is a light-weight."

"There was ice."

"It's December."

"It's seventy degrees!"

"Maybe they were having a Christmas party over at the CNN tower? The wind could have picked it up from the roof . . ." I trailed off, realizing how little sense that made. "There's a logical explanation."

"I don't doubt it." Melissa fell silent until we found our room.

I turned and met her eyes. "Stop being creepy. Let's just drop it, okay?"

Melissa sighed and opened the door to the hotel room. "I still can't believe your mom went for this."

"It was her idea!" I smiled at her in thanks for dropping the subject and inhaled the chemical scent of carpet cleaner and stepped into the humid room. "I still don't know how she pulled it off."

Melissa's boots left impressions in the wheat-colored carpet. She dropped her green book bag next to one of the queen-sized beds with a *thunk*, then crossed to the window and pushed aside the marble-patterned curtains.

"Maybe she's got a boyfriend or something and just wants some time alone." I grimaced at the idea, setting my daisy-patterned duffle bag on the bed. "I'm surprised your mom went for it."

"You know she'll do anything your mom asks." Melissa struggled with the cream curtain liner and pushed it aside, revealing thick white blinds. She sighed, pulling the string until the blinds parted in the center, folding up like my closet door. "Finally." Sunlight streamed in through the window.

"Nice parking lot." I peered past her out the window, grinning so she knew I was joking. I preferred the naked window to the thick stuffy curtains. A view of the parking lot was still better than suffocating in a windowless room.

"To think we could have gone our whole lives without witnessing this marvelous sight." Melissa spun to face me. "We need to get ready."

We spent the next hour making sure we looked perfect in case Orpheus saw us. I pulled on a black dress I'd borrowed from Melissa and groaned when it brushed the top of my knee. "I hate being short! On you, this was practically indecent."

Melissa ran a brush through her hair. "Yeah, but I didn't pull off that neckline half as well."

I tugged the square neckline up self-consciously then twirled, laughing as the skirt rose into the air. I'd loved "spinny" dresses since I was seven.

"Oh my God!" I came to an abrupt halt. "I look seven!"

"You do not!" Melissa's reflection stepped next to mine. "Twelve at least."

I narrowed my eyes at her reflection. *She* didn't look seven. Her legs seemed to go on for miles under her tight-fitting black skirt. Four delicate black chains hung from her neck, each longer than the last, until they reached her waist, glinting darkly against her flowing purple blouse.

"You look great." I smiled at her.

"Aw, you too." She handed me a pair of black strappy heels. "Let's go."

We walked across the street to the Tabernacle, alternatively poking fun at each other and giving compliments the entire way. A part of me felt cool and grownup as we joined the throng of people pressing against the stage.

It was loud and claustrophobic, but the moment Orpheus came out on stage all of that changed. Our energy converged with the energy of the crowd. We screamed, jumped, and danced to his songs. I felt energized and exhausted.

My hair was a mess and I was sweating when we pushed our way backstage, but I didn't care. Orpheus was there, drinking a bottle of water while his band packed up around him.

When he looked up I gripped Melissa's hand and she squeezed back hard. He did a double take and walked over, an average looking woman trailing behind him.

"Hello." He sounded tense and looked stiff and uncomfortable. The way he was standing in front of the woman made it seem like he was protecting her. "This is quite an honor. Pleased to meet you, Persephone."

I blinked, captivated by his golden eyes. "Kora," I corrected. "And this is Melissa. How did you know my name?"

"Your mother told me all about you."

"You know my mom?"

His eyes darkened. "I suppose it would be more accurate to say I know of her. Last night was the first time we'd spoken."

Mom had arranged all this one night before the concert? I glanced around and noticed we were the only fans backstage. What had she said to him? How had she contacted him? And how would a rock god like

Orpheus know of a flower shop owner from Athens, Georgia?

My confusion must have shown on my face. Orpheus studied me with an intensity that made me uncomfortable. He stared at me for a long moment then nodded like he'd come to a decision.

"You really are just a kid, huh? Look, I'm sorry. It was a long show, and I can get a bit . . . edgy when I get too tired. It's always great to meet a . . ." He paused, eyes searching mine. "Fan?"

I beamed at him. *He thinks meeting me is great!*

"This is my wife, Eurydice," he said, motioning to the woman behind him. "She's also my manager." He put his arm around her shoulder and gave her a smile that melted my heart. "I'd be lost without her."

She waved, obviously used to the crestfallen looks of teenage girls at her introduction. "It's nice to meet you."

As we exchanged pleasantries I studied her, trying to see what had drawn Orpheus to this nondescript woman. Her voice was deeper than I would have imagined from a woman with such a slight build. Her dark skin was marked with freckles, and her gray eyes were narrow and squinty. She dressed casually, in jeans and a T-shirt. My feet ached when they saw her comfortable looking sneakers, reminding me why I hated heels.

In the best of circumstances this woman would be called plain. Standing next to her, Orpheus shone like the sun. His unmarred bronze skin seemed to glow with health. His gold hair was pulled into a short ponytail, revealing his rectangular face. He wore his trademark black sleeveless T-shirt, showing off his muscled arms—and oh God, I was staring.

"It was a wonderful ceremony," Eurydice said. I blinked, following her gaze to Melissa.

"It sounds like it. I want to get married on the beach." Melissa's voice was wistful.

Thank you, Melissa. Maybe they hadn't noticed my faux pas.

"Your time will come. I know mine did." Eurydice smiled, and in that instant I knew what Orpheus saw in her. Her entire face transformed, radiant with inner beauty.

"So you girls are from Athens?" Orpheus asked, squeezing his wife's shoulder.

As we made small talk I was able to come to my senses enough to wonder again why we were the only fans backstage. How had my mother pulled this off?

Before I knew it, Melissa and I were on our way out the door, loaded down with a surprising amount of autographed gear. I'd just reached the door when I felt a hand brush my shoulder. I turned around, surprised to see Orpheus and Eurydice behind me.

"I don't normally do this." Orpheus slid me a card with a hand-scrawled phone number written on the back of it. "But you're going to have questions. When you do, don't hesitate to call."

"I don't—"

"You will." Orpheus held the door open for me.

I walked out the door, starstruck. Melissa waited until the metal door slammed shut before asking, "What did he just give you?"

I brandished the card, a triumphant smile spreading across my face. "His number!"

Chapter IV

IT WAS COMPLETELY worth working my entire vacation, I reminded myself the following Wednesday when the phone rang again. I forced myself to take a calming breath. The air smelled green and raw. I closed my eyes and tried to pick out the individual scents of my favorite flowers. I'd found the sweet scent of daffodils, the heady fragrance of roses, and a soft hint of daisies when the phone trilled.

I swore under my breath. The flowers may have smelled relaxing, but the sight of so many of them stacked behind the glass door of the refrigerated room and waiting to be made into holiday arrangements was stressful enough without more last minute shoppers calling every three seconds. Worse, the seventy-degree weather I'd enjoyed last Friday had fled and it was getting cold.

"Demeter's Garden." Mom's voice was serene. "How can I help you?"

She grinned at me behind the front counter as she took an order over the phone. Her sleeves were rolled up and she had a smudge of dirt on her cheek that meant she'd been potting plants in the nursery out back earlier. It was magical watching seedlings burst forth from the earth, ripening under her green touch. It was like she could make anything grow any time.

She moved around the shop with the quiet grace and confidence of a queen. Would I ever feel that comfortable with myself? I sighed, retied my green apron, and inspected the work order in front of me. Daffodils and poppies. I could do that.

I frowned when I found a scribbled notation on the back of the ticket: narcissus. I glanced at the customer's name and saw it was one of our regular customers, Flora. I could imagine the conversation that had taken place during that order. Flora's shrill voice demanding those small white daffodils she'd seen in one of the other arrangements. Mom gently asking if she meant narcissus, a smaller flower frequently confused with daffodils, then the old woman insisting she knew what she was talking about until my mother wrote down the order and penciled in the correction later. For the record, the customer is never right.

"We've been busy," I remarked when she hung up the phone.

"Got to love the holidays." She laughed. "How's Melissa?"

I shrugged. "Busy making fruit bouquets. I think Mrs. Minthe sells as many fruit arrangements as we do flowers." Melissa's mother owned a shop in Watkinsville that made faux flower arrangements out of various fruits.

Mom started to comment, but the phone rang. "It's been ringing off the hook all day," she said after asking the caller to hold. "I'm going to take this out back and work in the nursery. Can you man the front?"

"Where's Chloe?" I asked, dreading the prospect of a customer demanding my attention. The shop was empty now, but I knew the minute Mom left my sight someone would walk in.

The phone beeped in my mom's hand, reminding her of the caller on hold. She gave it a harried look. "Making deliveries. I don't expect her back this afternoon." She tucked my hair behind my ear when I frowned. "The customers won't bite, I promise." The phone beeped again and my mother sighed.

"Go," I told her. "I've got this."

I waited for the heavy wooden door to close before working on the flower arrangement. We'd owned Demeter's Garden since before I was born, and it felt like my second home. I smiled, remembering that if I kept my grades up and got into the University of Georgia, it *would* be my home. Melissa and I were going to share the apartment above the shop.

I leaned against the counter and looked around the shop, imagining all the changes I would make when Mom retired. The shop looked as if it had been carved out of an oak tree. The rough floors, counter, and cabinets were all the same honey shade with dark brown spots showing up every few feet, like buttons. Glass doors with wood lining formed the walls, showcasing flower arrangements in their refrigerated glory. This time of year the arrangements in vases crowded the shelves. Potted plants hung from the rafters. Windows filled three walls of the shop, giving pedestrians an unobstructed view of our merchandise and allowing the shop to be filled with warm sunlight.

Mom and I called the shop "the fishbowl" when no one was around to hear. There was no hiding from customers peering in from the outside. If you arrived early to get some work done or stayed late to count inventory, they saw you. They knocked on the glass or called the shop to get their order taken right then. It drove me crazy.

The first thing I planned to do was hire someone to deal with all the customers. I loved making the arrangements, doing paperwork, and maintaining our website. I just didn't like dealing with people. I didn't handle confrontation well, and as friendly as most of our customers were, they always wanted discounts, or rush orders, or impossible flower combinations.

I turned back to the arrangement, running wires through the poppies and letting the arrangement take shape beneath my hands. I smiled at the completed project and wrote the card in flowing script, signing the name of Flora's husband, as usual. He never remembered the special occasions, so she bought her own flowers.

I bet Joel was the kind of guy who would remember to send flowers. *Not that it matters,* I thought, smiling as I placed the card in the center of the arrangement.

"How beautiful."

I jumped, spinning around to face the man on the other side of the counter. "I'm sorry?"

"The flowers." He gave me a strange look. "They're beautiful. Poppies and daffodils, right?"

I made a noncommittal noise, and he smiled as if pleased to have guessed right. "It looks great. You have a real gift."

"Thank you." I was sure my face was bright red. I'd jumped like the devil himself had patted my shoulder. Now this guy probably thought I was crazy too.

That would be a tragedy. His eyes were the precise shade of liquid gold as Orpheus'. With the exception of his angular face, short haircut, and leaner physique, he could be Orpheus. *I wonder if they're related.*

Horrified, I realized I was staring. "Oh . . . uh . . . how can I help you?" I tucked a wavy strand of hair behind my ear.

His eyes twinkled in amusement. My cheeks heated as I realized a guy as hot as him must be used to shop girls getting flustered for different reasons than being caught off guard. I glanced at the antique golden bell against the door, cursing myself for being so wrapped up in the stupid flowers that I hadn't heard it ring when he came in.

" . . . arrangement to be delivered next weekend," he was saying, leaning on the counter.

"Of course." I took a breath to pull myself together. I fished the pen and ordering pad from the pocket of my apron, gathering confidence from the familiar routine. "Can I get your first and last name?"

"Pirithous," he answered, spelling it for me. He looked down to read the name emblazoned on my chest. "Pleased to meet you,

Persephone," he said, pronouncing it Purse-a-phone.

I ground my teeth together. My mother refused to change the monogrammed name on my apron to Kora. It was getting to the point where I was thinking of getting it fixed myself.

"It's Persephone," I corrected. "Kind of like Stephanie. What's the occasion?" I held the pen poised over the paper.

He grinned and ran his fingers through his golden hair. "My mother's birthday."

My eyes widened as I realized why he thought I'd asked. With more emphasis than the situation called for, I wrote "mother's birthday" on the appropriate line to show him I'd been asking professionally, not fishing to see if he was single.

My face stayed red throughout the ordering process because Pirithous kept teasing me or misinterpreting my questions. I grew angry when I realized he was enjoying seeing me so flustered.

"I meant what I said, you know." He leaned so far over the counter I wondered how he kept his balance.

"Huh?" I replied articulately.

"You're beautiful. Do you . . . wanna grab a coffee sometime?"

Okay, I thought, *enough is enough.* Time to pull out the big guns. "Sorry. My mom won't let me date until I turn eighteen." Some guys didn't care that I was underage, but the ones that did always made faces like I'd just offered them rat poison.

I gave him an innocent smile and dropped his change into his open hand. Pirithous closed it as the cold quarters touched his skin. His fingers brushed against mine. He grinned and, for the first time since he'd walked in the flower shop, looked into my eyes.

His pupils widened and he quickly closed his eyes, looking away from me. "I don't believe it."

"No, really," I babbled, so fast the words ran together. "I just turned sixteen this March. My mom's a bit paranoid, but you can't blame her with the university down the street and frat boys all over town."

"He was right! A daughter of Zeus. I didn't think there were any left."

Speaking of frat boys . . . "Isn't it a little late in the semester for pledging?"

His hand wrapped around my wrist like an iron vice. "Let me go," he demanded, eyes glittering.

"After you!" I struggled to pull my hand free.

He laughed. "You have no idea, do you? What you are? What

you've done? Oh that's right, you can't lie. You're *really* sixteen." He shook his head as though in disbelief. "Even better. I thought he'd sent me on a fool's errand. Everyone knows Zeus is dead, but here you are—" his eyes glittered maniacally "—my chance at immortality."

I yanked my arm back but he didn't let go. Panic flooded my chest. "Are you high? Let me go!"

I struggled against his grip as he pulled me around the counter. "You're mine. I found you first. You belong to me!"

I grabbed the counter with my free hand. My fingers closed around a pen, and with more strength than I thought possible I slammed it into his arm.

He howled in pain and I ripped my arm free and scrambled back behind the counter. I yanked open a drawer, spilling the contents, searching for the small knife I used for cutting wires and flower stems. I caught a glimpse of the green handle and grabbed it.

"Stay back!" I waved the arrangement knife in his direction.

"Persephone?" my mother called, throwing open the storage room door. "Is everything—" She looked from Pirithous' bleeding arm to the knife poised in the air.

I moved between him and my mother. "I'm calling the cops!" I fished my cell phone out of my apron pocket.

That seemed to penetrate Pirithous' maniac rage enough for him to look up at me, eyes saturated with hate. "I'll be back for you," he hissed before running out the door.

"Like hell," I muttered, locking the door behind him.

Chapter V

TWENTY MINUTES later I was sitting at our computer watching the security feed replay for the police. I looked over at my mother. She looked so vulnerable curled up on the green papasan chair with her feet tucked under her. Her eyes were wide with fear as she watched the incident replayed on the monitor.

"I didn't hear a thing." I reached over and patted her hand, and her guilty eyes turned to me. "Not until he yelled."

I didn't know what to say. I'd never seen my mother afraid. She didn't get scared—she got organized. She juggled being a single mother, a small business owner, and having a busy social life with an ease I envied.

Seeing her frightened made me feel worse. My hands shook as I answered the questions the officers asked me before leaving with a copy of our security feed. My mother locked the door behind them and stood there with her back to the door, looking lost.

"Do you want to talk about it?" she asked.

I shook my head, kneeling to pick up the scattered flowers. "He scared me."

I started with surprise when my mother knelt beside me, picked up various objects from the floor, and put them in their proper place in the drawer. I hadn't heard her cross the room.

"Was this a frat prank, or do you think he was a psychopath? I mean, why would he come after me?" I thought of the feelings I'd had of being followed, and the strange snowstorm on the highway, and the meeting with Orpheus. I shook my head. "It just . . . Nothing makes sense anymore. Did you hear that guy? He said I was Zeus' daughter? And that I couldn't lie? You don't get much crazier than that."

I swallowed hard. If I really was going crazy, imagining voices and being paranoid, was that what I would be like? Assaulting random employees in flower shops?

I need to tell her. This wasn't just scary, it was serious. What if I got bad enough to hurt someone?

"I think he was disturbed." Mom gathered the business cards and put them back on the counter.

"Mom, I think I'm going crazy."

She blinked. "What?"

"Lately really weird stuff has been happening to me, and I know it's not real. It can't be real because no one else notices it."

She pulled the chair behind her and sat down. "What sort of things?"

It all came out in a jumble. "I've been having these weird feelings, and everyone acts strange around me. There's this thing that happens with their eyes and suddenly they don't act like themselves anymore. And the weather." I shook my head. The more I talked the stranger it sounded. "I don't want to go nuts and start attacking people."

"Oh, honey." She put her hand on mine and drew me to the chair beside hers. "You're not going crazy. This is my fault. I thought I'd have more time to tell you, more time to prepare you."

"Tell me what?"

She closed her eyes and took a deep breath. When she spoke, the words seemed to fall out of her mouth against her will. "You're a goddess. The first new deity born in over a—"

"Mom, I'm serious," I said, annoyed at her for taking this so lightly.

"So am I. I was going to wait until you graduated. Build up a support net of people who would understand, but if you're already coming into your powers, I've waited too long."

My forehead wrinkled incredulously. "You actually believe this?" There was no trace of humor in her voice.

She gave me a level stare and continued talking. "You had to act normal and fit in to be safe, and that would be much more difficult if you knew you weren't human."

Not human? My head was spinning. It was genetic. Of course it was genetic. Crazy ran in families. "Mom, I think we should call someone. Tonight was stressful, but—"

"This isn't a nervous breakdown, Persephone. You are a goddess."

She seemed to change every time she said that word. It was like she was less my mother and more something else. Her expression grew more detached, her eyes somehow got older, wiser. Looking at her, there was nothing comforting about her that said *mom*. This was something else. Something powerful.

Something scary.

No. This was insane. Everyone secretly wished they were special.

But in all my dreams of discovering I was a superhero, or a witch, or maybe even a princess, I'd never gone as far as *goddess*. That was too pretentious. Only seriously disturbed people thought they were gods. The words my mother had spoken weren't some tolerable fantasy that could be indulged; they were dangerous.

"Stop saying that! If I were a goddess, I'd have powers and could have blown that guy away!"

"We aren't as powerful as we used to be. Most of the remaining gods are those who were associated with nature. People still believe in and fear the world around them. We are lucky, Persephone. As the Goddess of Nature, my position is fairly secure."

"You think you're the Goddess of Nature?" I interrupted in disbelief.

"I primarily preside over agriculture."

I thought of our shop. "Like Demeter?"

"I *am* Demeter, or Ceres to the Romans, or hundreds of other names depending on the time or culture."

"Of course."

She sighed, looking old and weary as she studied me. "In time you will come to terms with your divinity. For now, all you need to know is that you've been discovered, so we have to leave."

"Wait!" I cried, alarmed. "Leave? Leave where?"

"Athens. We have many places we can go—"

"Like moving? We can't, Mom! I'm halfway through the school year! What about the shop? What about our home? I can't leave Melissa—"

"Melissa will come with us, of course."

"How? Mind control? I doubt Mrs. Minthe will be okay with you taking her daughter!"

I had to do something before she did something crazy, like putting our house on the market or kidnapping my best friend. I glanced over at the phone, wondering who you were supposed to call when your parent went crazy. Was that a 9-1-1 thing, or should I Google the local psych ward? What would happen to me if my mom had to be committed?

"Minthe is one of my priestesses. She will go where she is told. Melissa is your priestess, and she needs to be with you."

"Uh huh, sure thing, Mom."

"As for school, you have an eternity to finish your education. I hope we'll be settled by the end of the break, but if not—"

"Eternity?"

"Yes, dear. You're immortal."

I laughed. "Of course. How silly of me. An eternity in high school—what could be better?" My eyes widened as she emptied the cash register and headed to the back room where we kept the safe. "What are you doing?"

"Persephone, we have to leave here! There's a reason you're the first full deity born in thousands of years. It wasn't safe before, and this place is no longer secure."

"If you're a goddess, can't you just, like . . . *smite* anyone who comes against us?" I tried to reason with her as she tucked all the shop's cash into her purse. "If we can't do anything special, why would anyone come after us?"

"Because you're a daughter of Zeus."

I stifled a hysterical giggle and waited until I was sure I could speak. I knew if I laughed right now I would never stop. "Mom, don't be gross. If you're Demeter, then Zeus would be your brother, not to mention he was married." She looked at me as if trying to figure out the relevance of that statement. "To someone else!" I waved my hands, frustrated. "You really expect me to believe you had an affair with your brother?"

My mother took a measured breath. "It doesn't work like that. We were created, not born. Genetically we have nothing in common with each other. Brother and sister are human titles for the relationship we have with each other. And marriage is different to gods. Humans have a much narrower moral code—"

"Rather shortsighted of you to raise me as one then."

"Nothing I do is shortsighted. If you'd like, we can discuss the different customs and moral standards between gods and humans on the road. We have a long drive ahead of us. Now get in the car."

I decided to humor her. It was either that or take her seriously, and I couldn't handle that. If I treated this like a joke long enough, maybe she would crack a smile, or laugh and admit she was just messing with me. It could be true. Mom had a horrible sense of humor. "I suppose Mount Olympus is a rather long drive. But hey, I've always wanted to meet my dad."

"The majority of the gods died thousands of years ago when Olympus fell."

Okay, I was done humoring her. "Mom, I'm only sixteen, I wasn't around a century ago, much less thousands of—"

"Of course not. I couldn't let you come into the world back then," she said, catching my hand. "Those were terrible times. I waited to have you until I knew you would be safe. I cursed my priestesses with immortality so I would always have worshippers—"

"Doesn't sound like much of a curse."

"And when the time was right, I arranged for Melissa to be born. I'll curse more priestesses for you over time."

"Well, thanks for that."

My sarcasm was lost on her. "As a child of Zeus, you're especially blessed." She released my hand and turned to take a last look around the shop. "You will be successful in anything—"

I couldn't listen anymore. I bolted out the door and dashed into the parking lot. My mother had lost her mind to a delusion of freaking Greco-Roman proportions. This was my fault. I'd brought home too many of Professor Homer's myths.

I fumbled with the keys, watching the door of the shop for my mom. My car roared to life before she got the door opened. I slammed my car into drive and tore out of the parking lot, narrowly avoiding the tree in its center. My cell phone rang and I silenced it, throwing it in the back seat. I turned the radio on when I turned onto Lumpkin Street.

When Five Points disappeared from my rearview mirror I let myself cry. What was I going to do? I didn't know a lot about crazy people. Was this the first step before my mom went on some kind of murderous rampage? Oh my God, would she take my suggestion to smite people seriously? I had to warn Chloe not to come back to the shop.

I reached for my phone instinctively before remembering it was in the back seat. I glanced in my rearview mirror. The screen was still lit up, indicating a call was coming through. I remembered Mom saying Chloe wasn't coming back after the deliveries. I'd just have to hope that was the case.

The stores and traffic faded behind me, replaced by trees and winding roads. I realized I'd driven toward Melissa's farm. I needed to warn her in case my mom really did try to kidnap Melissa. Mrs. Minthe could help me. She could tell me what to do.

Chapter VI

ORPHEUS' LATEST album blared out of my speakers as my bug tore down Hog Mountain Road. *What if she's not crazy,* a voice in the back of my mind whispered. I laughed. Was this how it started? Voices disguising themselves as your own thoughts? She had to be crazy.

I gripped the steering wheel. If I began to believe my mother's claims of divinity, my world would unravel! If she were telling the truth it would mean everything I knew about myself was a lie. My mother, and even Melissa, the two people I trusted more than anyone else in the world, had lied to me my entire life.

No. I would rather believe my mother was crazy. They had pills to fix crazy. Trust was harder to repair. Lives were harder to rebuild. I couldn't move away! This was the only home I'd ever known. I'd fix this somehow.

It makes sense.

"Shut up!"

Unbidden images flashed through my mind. Eyes disappearing behind enlarged pupils. Frost creeping up yellow legal pad pages. Ice slashing across my windshield. Orpheus handing me his card.

Orpheus . . . I turned my head to look at my phone, perched tantalizingly on the back seat. I swore, turning my attention to the road. A deer darted across. I didn't even slow.

Was this what he'd been talking about? No way. *You've never even been sick,* I reminded myself. Gods couldn't get sick, could they? The other kids at school got sick all the time, colds, allergies, something.

"And the feeling of being watched, Persephone?" I deflected. "Got an answer for that? This is textbook crazy. I mean, I'm even talking to myself."

Pirithous did mention someone sending him.

I wanted to put my hands to my ears, but the damn steering wheel demanded my attention. I sang as loudly as I could but the voice within me would not be silenced.

I heard Melissa's voice. *"You know she'll do anything your mom asks."*

"You're going to have questions."

"No!" I stabbed at the dial, turning up the music. Gravel crunched under my tires when I pulled into Melissa's driveway. I didn't even have time to knock before Melissa opened the door and threw herself into my arms.

"Your mom called and told us what happened! Are you okay?" She pulled me into the house before I could formulate an answer.

All that reckless driving and I'd gone exactly where she'd expected. Go figure. "What did my mom tell you exactly?"

"She said some guy found out what you are and tried to take you!"

Found out what you are! My hope that this was all a crazy theory of my mother's was being ripped from my grasp. "What do you mean by that?"

"He found out that you're a goddess."

I couldn't breathe. The world spun. I was slipping and sliding sideways, unable to regain my balance.

"Persephone!" Melissa yelled as I swayed on my feet.

I took a deep breath, forcing the sparkling spots to slowly slip away. I stumbled away from Melissa and back onto the wooden porch. "Not you, too."

"I'm sorry. I wanted to tell you, but your mom wouldn't let me." She reached out to steady me.

"Stay away from me!" I retreated down the stairs and to my car. Melissa shouted after me but I ignored her. I needed to get out of here. I needed to think, to process everything that had happened. The drive passed in a blur that I couldn't remember, and I found myself at Memorial Park.

I made my way to my usual picnic spot; the flowers and trees and flowing water fountain in the middle of the sparkling lake always calmed me down. My stomach growled, reminding me that I'd skipped lunch in all the confusion. I dug in my purse for my stash of snacks and pulled out a plastic bag full of pomegranate seeds.

I walked past the playground to the rock garden, spreading my daisy-patterned blanket out on top of the bleached grass. Wildflowers grew, tricked into bloom by the mild weather. My breath caught when a crane took flight from the scrub bushes near the wooden bridge spanning the lake. I ate a pomegranate seed and tried to think. I needed a plan.

My red-stained fingertips reverently clutched the card Orpheus had given me. Did my mom think he was a god? Mom had said something about building a support net. Maybe that was why he'd acted so weird around me.

But Melissa believed my mom. What did that mean?

My hands shook as I held the card. If one more person believed her theory, I'd know. I'd know I wasn't going crazy, that something was legitimately different about me.

I didn't need to look at the card to dial the number. My heart threatened to beat free of my chest as the phone rang.

"Hello?"

My mouth went dry at the sound of his voice.

"Hello?" He waited a beat, sounding irritated now. "Is anyone there?"

I hung up. I couldn't ask him if I was a god! He'd think I was crazy! Or worse, he'd know that I wasn't.

This was ridiculous. If I was a goddess, I should be able to do something. If I couldn't, I wasn't. No need to drag anyone else into this.

"I can't believe I'm even considering this," I muttered.

My hair whipped across my face as a breeze picked up around me. I sat up and placed my hand on the cool, dark earth before me, feeling energy thrumming through the soil. I closed my eyes and concentrated on making something, anything, happen.

I felt a tickle against my palm and jerked forward, eyes flying open. I nearly fell face first in the dirt when a bright green stem unwound itself between two of my outstretched fingers. I scarcely breathed as red petals unfurled themselves into a tiny red poppy.

I gasped. I had powers! I was a goddess! I wasn't crazy, Mom wasn't crazy. Melissa, Orpheus, it was all true. *Wasn't it?*

"I'm not hallucinating, am I?" I touched the flower, feeling the silky petal brush against my hand. The wind pushed me forward forcefully. My bag of pomegranate seeds blew over, spilling around the poppy. My dress flapped against my ankles as chills shot across my skin. I heard crackling and spun around to see the ground freezing around the flower.

The frost crept toward me. The branches above me stretched toward my face, ice inching along the branches. I heard a loud snap and a massive branch broke from the tree and hurtled toward my head.

I screamed and stumbled backward. The branch crashed in front of me, scraping my legs. I ran for the parking lot as fast as I could. The frost closed in, surrounding me. I'd never been claustrophobic, but as the frost cut off my escape path with a solid white wall, I panicked.

Fog rolled in, like cold death, cutting off my view of the park. It curled around me, brushing against my face, arms, and legs. I turned back to the tree and ran faster, my dress tangling between my legs as the fog and icy wind blew against my skin.

The parking lot is the other way! my mind screamed. The other way was cut off by a mountain of ice. I felt as if I was being herded. *By ice?*

I slipped on the icy ground, falling face first into the frost. Ice crept up my toes and along my legs. I thrashed and screamed. I felt the fog becoming a solid mass above me, pinning me to the ground. The ice piled around me. *Am I going to be buried alive?*

I dug my nails into the frigid snow in front of me and tried to claw my way out of the frosted death trap. I was so panicked I didn't feel it when my nails broke against the impenetrable wall of ice, leaving red crescents of blood welling up on sensitive skin. A hysterical sob worked its way out of my throat as I gouged red lines into the ice. The ice was above my knees, snaking its way up my thighs. I shivered.

Shivering's good, I reminded myself. *It means your body hasn't given up . . . yet.* The cold was painful, like a thousand little knives pricking my skin. A violent tremor went up my spine, sending waves of pain through me.

"Help me!" I screamed, knowing it was futile. I was going to die here.

Except I couldn't die. Could I? Mom said I was immortal, but was that all-inclusive? Did I have a weakness? Was snow my Kryptonite? If I got hurt, would I heal or would I be trapped in an injured body in pain forever?

I suddenly didn't know if immortality was a good thing or a bad thing. The cold hurt. I was kicking, screaming, and clawing my way out of the frost, but for every inch I gained a mountain piled around me. I thought I heard a man's laughter on the wind, the sound somehow colder than the ice freezing me into place.

The ground before my outstretched hand trembled. The shaking increased. The earth lurched beneath me. The surface cracked and the sound was so loud that for a moment all I could hear was high-pitched ringing in my ears. The ground split into an impossibly deep crevice. My voice went hoarse from screaming as I peered into the endless abyss, trapped and unable to move away from the vertigo-inducing edge. A midnight black chariot, drawn by four crepuscular horses that looked like they'd been created out of the night sky, surged from the crevice. I ducked my head into the snow with a frightened whimper as they passed over my prone body.

The fog around me dissipated as the ice melted away from my body.

Terrified, I sprang to my feet, stopping when I was eye-to-eye with one of the frightening horses pulling the chariot. For a moment I could do nothing but stare into its huge, emotionless eyes. A strangled whimper tore from my throat, and the horse snorted at me.

They weren't black; they weren't anything. They were an absence of color and of light, a nauseating swirling void. They hurt to look at. My head ached, and my stomach lurched in mutiny. I clenched my fists and turned to the driver.

His electric blue eyes met mine, and he seemed to see everything I'd done and everything I'd ever do. I had the strange sensation I'd been judged and found wanting. No way this guy was human. His skin could have been carved from marble; his hair was the same disorienting black as the horses. A terrifying power emanated from his tall, statuesque frame.

I couldn't speak. I couldn't move. His ebony cape billowed behind him as he marched toward me. At the grasp of his hand I snapped back to life and jerked away from him.

"We have to get out of here."

"Let me go!" I yelled, yanking my arm away. He closed in on me, pushing me toward the chariot. I struggled against him, shrieking with rage when he picked me up and slung me over his back like a sack of potatoes.

I punched his back, kicking my legs. "Let me go! Someone help me! Help!"

I recalled the instructor of some self-defense class long lost in memory reminding me dead weight was harder to carry than a thrashing captive. My body rebelled at the idea of going limp so I pushed aside his cape, pulled his shirt up and raked my torn and ragged nails across his bare skin. His hands jerked in surprise and I slid off his back and onto the hard ground.

My breath left my body as I hit the ground with enough force to make me dizzy. With strength I didn't know I possessed, I scrambled away, clawing at him as he pulled me back.

"Enough!" he shouted. "We don't have time for this! I have to get you out of here!"

"No!" I yelled. Did he really just expect me to go *Okay, strange creepy man, I'll get in your scary chariot of death. No problem.*

His furtive gaze took in the empty park, and he swore in a voice as smooth as silk. "I'm sorry."

My eyes widened in surprise as his lips pressed against mine. I went wild, hitting and scratching and pushing for all I was worth. He didn't budge. He exhaled, and I sank lifelessly into his arms.

Through a haze, I felt myself being lifted and carried away. I tried to open my eyes, but they were too heavy.

"You handled that well, Hades," a woman's sarcastic voice intruded on the fog of my thoughts. "You know what might have made it a bit easier?"

"I'm sure you're going to tell me."

Hades? I struggled harder against the heaviness of my eyes. *The* Hades? Lord of the Underworld, Hades?

Crap!

"A simple 'I'm the good guy' might have—"

"You think I'm the good guy, Cassandra?" He laughed.

"How about 'I'm here to rescue you'?"

"I didn't say that?" He placed me on a soft surface. "I need to talk to Demeter, tell her what almost transpired here. Could you—"

"You're not going to return her home." It was a statement, not a question.

"Gods help me, Cassandra, I thought you were kidding."

"You know I don't joke about my . . ."

I tried to listen, but their conversation wasn't making any sense and my mind wasn't up to decoding their nonsense. I thought of my picnic blanket, poppy, and pomegranate seeds. What had happened? Had that freak ice storm been a consequence of using my powers? Something nudged the back of my brain, calling ancient myths and legends forward, but my mind banished those thoughts and surrendered to blissful darkness.

Chapter VII

I FELT LIKE I was lying on a cloud made of silk. I frowned, eyes fluttering open. *My* bed was not this comfortable, and my sheets were not made of silk, satin, or whatever this shiny, slippery stuff was. I sat up, looking around the room, disoriented. It looked like my room but richer somehow.

I climbed off the loft bed. The moment my feet touched the cool wooden floor, memories rushed through me. I gasped as I recalled the earth freezing and the chariot exploding from the ground. I traced my tingling lips with my fingertip. He'd kissed me! Well, sort of.

I felt different, lighter somehow. For the first time in my life I'd woken up without any pressing needs. I wasn't hungry or thirsty, nothing ached; I felt exhilarated.

It was unnerving. My hands shook and my heart raced so fast I thought it would beat out of my chest. I gulped, remembering the man who'd taken me. I unclipped my phone from my waistband. It was four-forty-four. I'd been out for over six hours? I tried to call 9-1-1, but couldn't get a signal. I walked through the room, keeping an eye on my phone. No luck.

I studied my reflection in the full-length mirror hanging on the door. The fabric of my white dress was somehow unmarred by my struggle in the park. The scratches on my legs from the ice were gone; I didn't have any bruises from the fall or so much as a hair on my head out of place. I checked my nails, expecting them to be torn, ragged, and bloody. They were perfect. I frowned, studying them closer. My clear polish had even been restored.

Only my lips were different. They were as red as a pomegranate and tender to the touch.

"What the hell?"

I was surprised to find the door wasn't locked. I opened it and stepped into a huge hall that looked as if it was carved from ebony. Not a single fingerprint marred the gleaming surface or silver trim. The floors formed a checkerboard of black and white marble. I glanced up, curious if the ceiling was made of marble as well, but couldn't tell because it was so far above my head.

I memorized every detail, searching for something that would help me identify this place to the cops. I couldn't think of a single building in Athens this tall. Had he taken me to another city? How long had I been out? I checked the time on my phone again: four-forty-four.

Must be broken. It would be more surprising if it had made it through the entire ordeal unharmed, but as I scrolled through the screen everything seemed responsive.

I took slow, careful steps, knowing in a cavernous hall like this my footsteps would be amplified. I didn't see any light fixtures and wondered how the corridors were illuminated. The hall was neither dim nor bright; the light just . . . existed.

I heard raised voices. *That sounds like Mom!* I ran toward the voices and paused outside a half open door, peeking in uncertainly.

" . . . should have just let Boreas have her?" Hades' voice boomed through the small room, echoing off the wooden wall panels.

My mother—I paused; it wasn't my mother. It was an image of her, bleached of color. As her form wavered, a red tapestry became visible behind her then vanished as she solidified. Her lips were tight in anger.

"Of course not! But what you did was—"

"Nothing short of a miracle, Demeter. Perhaps you should be thanking me for bothering."

"It's *why* you bothered that frightens me, Hades." She gave an exasperated wave of her hands. "What you did was—" She broke off with a sigh. "You could have just sent for me. I could have—"

"Done absolutely nothing," Hades snapped. The soft glow of the lamps played over his face. The whole room was tinted red from the lampshades. "You barely have the power to swat a fly."

"But you—"

"She would be better off dead!" Hades thundered. "Don't you get that? None of you saw Oreithyia after he had finished with her, just me! I practically had to drown her in the Lethe to wash those memories away; there is nothing left of her! Is that the fate you would prefer for your daughter, Demeter? Because that's what would have happened had I sent for you instead."

"Am I . . . dead?" My voice was shaking as I walked into the room. Silence descended on the room as they both stared at me. I felt like an insect being examined in a jar. I took a deep breath and straightened my back so I was standing at my full height, clenching my fists so my trembling hands didn't give away my fear. I raised my chin and met Hades' stare with what I hoped was a bored expression on my face, but what probably looked more like a deer caught in the headlights.

"Persephone," my mom breathed, her face relaxing. "Thank goodness you're all right."

I tried to tear my gaze from Hades to look at her, but it was hard. I'd never seen anyone that looked like him. Movie stars, models, they paled in comparison, and as terrified as I was that I'd died, I couldn't seem to look away from him.

Seriously? He might as well be the devil. With that comforting thought I jerked my head to the side and looked at my mother. "Am I dead?" I asked again, suppressing the panicked edge in my voice. Being dead would explain a lot.

"You're not dead." Hades spoke, yanking my attention back to him like a rubber band. His lips curved in a sardonic smile. I got the distinct impression that he'd enjoyed my struggle to look away. "Thanks to my intercession."

I narrowed my eyes in disgust. So he was one of *those* guys. "So I'm supposed to thank you for knocking me out and dragging me here against my will? Where am I, and how do I get home?"

"Hey, I saved you!" Hades looked back and forth between my mother and me. "No good deed, huh?"

"It didn't feel like I was being rescued, it felt like an abduction! You kissed me!"

"About that . . . ." My mother glowered at Hades.

"Can it, Demeter. That was the only way to get her down here and you know it."

"Where is *here?*"

"You're in the Underworld." Mom's voice was gentle. "But you're not dead. Hades has made it possible for you to travel between planes."

"Oh," I said, nodding like I understood. "Can I go home now?" I glanced at Hades and added a grudging "Please?"

"You may come and go as you please, but I don't think that would be wise. You've caught the attention of the god Boreas. He attempted to subdue you, but I was able to intervene. Next time you may not be so lucky."

"Next time?" I didn't like the sound of that.

"Boreas isn't easily dissuaded once he sees something he wants," Mom explained. "He's the God of Winter, so his power is at its peak right now. But we can take precautions to keep you safe until winter has passed."

"The best precaution you can take is to leave her with me," Hades interjected. "No god can come after her in the Underworld."

"Can't you do something?" I asked my mother. "I mean, you're the Goddess of Nature, right? Doesn't that kind of give you reign over winter?"

"His domain is over the elements of winter, not the life that persists during his reign. It is best when we work in harmony, but balance has long since been lost. Winter destroys life. Death always has more followers than life." She glanced meaningfully at Hades. "People are frightened by it. For our purposes, fear translates to worship. Boreas was difficult to control when there was balance—"

"Difficult!" Hades snorted. "That's an understatement, to say the least."

"So he's done something like this before?" I asked.

"To an Athenian princess of uncommon beauty called Oreithyia," Hades recounted in clipped tones. "Though she paled in comparison to you."

"Well, of course, she was human," my mother said.

I blinked in surprise. Was that disdain in her voice? I was so shocked by her disgust for the species with which I most identified, I almost missed the rest of the story.

"She was dancing by the Ilissos River when Boreas descended upon the clearing, freezing everything in his wake," Hades continued. "He captured her within a cloud for his own personal use until her death months later. He dumped her back into the Ilissos like nothing had happened. You, my dear, would not have the luxury of dying."

"Oh," I whispered. I looked to my mother who was staring at Hades with an unreadable expression on her face.

"She can stay in the Underworld," Mom said, "each winter until Boreas either moves on or she comes into her powers."

"So be it," Hades agreed.

"Wait a minute!" I protested. "Don't I get any say in this?"

"Not really," Mom replied. "As your mother—"

"You lied to me my entire life, and now you're playing the mother card?"

"I said you were welcome to leave at any time, and I meant it." Hades' voice rose to drown ours out. "No, Demeter." He cut off my mother's protest. "I'm not holding her here against her will."

"Thank you." I tried not to sound surprised.

His electric blue eyes seared into me. "Before you make a decision, let me show you something."

"No." Mom's voice was stern.

"I won't sugarcoat this, Demeter. She needs to make an educated choice."

A thin dark-haired girl entered the room as if by some unspoken signal. She was leading a hunched, trembling figure carefully.

"Oreithyia." Hades sounded gentle. "I'd like you to meet someone."

The small figure looked up, and I barely stopped myself from gasping.

"Hello." The word was slow and careful, as though she wasn't sure of the language. Her face was void of emotion, and seemed to change as I watched. Her features shifted in and out of place as if they couldn't quite align themselves. After a moment, she resembled me. The blank expression on my face had me shuddering.

"Oreithyia," Hades murmured, "can you tell Persephone a little about yourself?"

Her empty eyes met his. "Myself?" She tested the word then stared at the floor, face blank. "I'm Oreithyia?"

"Yes."

She smiled at him, her face shifting to his features. If Hades was bothered by the unusual reflection he didn't show it. "I like to dance." A smile lit her face. I saw a glimpse of the beauty she had been, then her vision clouded and her features began to shift.

Hades nodded, and the dark-haired girl led her away.

"Eternity, do you understand? For her, an eternity of *that* was better than any trace of a memory of her time with Boreas."

I felt sick to my stomach. "I have conditions." My voice was weak and brittle.

Hades raised an eyebrow. "Aren't you the entitled one?"

I gathered my confidence and looked at my mother. "We aren't moving."

"Pirithous—"

"Is mortal, and you are a goddess. Do whatever you have to, but I'm not leaving Athens."

Her eyes glittered in challenge. "I don't know what you think has changed in the last twenty-four hours, but I am still your mother. You'd better modify that tone, young lady."

I glared at the floor, unwilling to meet her eyes.

She waited until she was sure I wouldn't object before continuing. "I will do everything in my power to ensure we can stay in Athens." I looked up at her, and she gave me a small smile. "I know you're angry with me right now, but you can't believe I want to see you forced to leave our home."

"Thank you," I said, relieved. "This solution is short-term at best. I want to be able to defend myself from any future threats."

"Your powers won't develop until—"

"I know, but I want to know how to use them when they do. In the meantime, some self-defense training—"

Hades laughed. "That wouldn't make a dent against Boreas."

"It slowed you down." I motioned to the scratches decorating his angular face.

"*I* wasn't trying to hurt you."

"Whatever," I said, irritated. "Pirithous is human. So are all those other creepy guys . . ." I trailed off when I saw my mother's alarmed look. "In any case—" I made an effort to inject respect into my tone "—I'm sure you've got no shortage of dead ninja warriors or something down here. I don't expect to turn into some type of gladiator, but I want to be able to protect myself."

I saw a glimmer in his eyes when he nodded. I'd like to think it was respect, but most likely it was amusement. "Anything else?"

I stared at him in surprise. The scratches were gone! *Seriously, Persephone? That's what surprises you about this whole situation?* I had a point. I was in the Underworld, talking to a god. Self-healing wounds shouldn't really be a surprise at this point.

"I'd like to know who is still around . . . topside?" I shot my mom a questioning look. How pathetic was it that I didn't know what to call my own realm? She nodded at me, so I continued. "I don't want to accidentally get anyone else's attention when I go home."

"That can be arranged. Is that all?"

"Um . . ." I felt dumb asking, but it was important. "How long is winter?"

"From the winter solstice to the spring equinox."

I gave him a blank look and he sighed heavily. "This year it's December twenty-first to March twenty-first. Midnight to noon."

"Three months. I can do that." My head snapped up as a thought occurred to me. "Time runs the same here as it does in the living realm, right?"

Hades gave me an incredulous look. "Beg pardon?"

"When I go back it won't be like thousands of years have passed, right?"

He raised his eyebrows and shook his head. "Um . . . no, no danger of that."

"And he can't come down here? You're sure?"

"Unless he dies or is invited by me. He's no threat to you, either way."

"So he can't do anything to hurt me down here?"

Hades exchanged glances with my mother. "He can't have much power left."

Mom shook her head. "Even if he does, I don't think he would risk making an enemy of you." She gave me a reassuring smile. "You're as safe as you're going to get, hon."

I studied the two of them. The psychotic serial rapist was afraid of pissing off Hades? What kind of a world had I stumbled into? "How do I know you're telling the truth?"

Hades shot my mom a look I couldn't read. "She doesn't know?"

"She didn't even know she was a goddess until this morning."

"Oh, so that's why she was flaunting her powers in an open field. By the Styx, Demeter!"

"She needs to be able to blend in!"

"I'm sure Boreas would have appreciated that particular ability."

I looked back and forth between the two of them. "I don't know what?"

"Gods can't lie." Hades spoke in clipped tones. "You really didn't know?"

"What do you mean, gods can't lie?" I motioned to my mom. "She lied to me every day about being human. That doesn't make any sense."

"Oh, we're very good at misleading. We just can't speak words that aren't true. It could unravel all of creation."

I blinked. That sounded serious.

"If I tell you you're safe, you're as safe as you can possibly get, okay?"

I jumped when Hades put a hand on my shoulder. My eyes met his and my heart dropped to my stomach. No one should look that good.

"You can trust me, okay?"

There was something in his expression that made me believe him. "Okay. I'll stay."

"It's settled, then," my mother said. "Persephone will stay here for the winter, but Hades . . ." Her voice took on a sharp note. "If you so much as lay a hand on—"

"Please!" Hades scoffed. "She's a child even by mortal standards. What I've done means nothing."

"What you've done?" I asked.

"When I breathed my essence into you—" I blinked, remembering the odd kiss "—it gave you the ability to enter the Underworld without dying, and return from my realm unscathed." He hesitated. "It also marked you as my bride."

"*What?*" I yelped. I had to be dreaming. No, I'd wrecked my car when Melissa and I were driving to the concert. I was in a coma somewhere having insane dreams. Pirithous, the goddess thing, the ice attack, it hadn't been real. *That makes so much more sense.*

"It means nothing." Hades looked flustered. "In title, you are my wife, and queen of this realm, but it means nothing. Much like Zeus and Hera's marriage." He sent a pointed look in my mom's direction.

I pinched my arm, frowning when it hurt. Maybe dreams *could* hurt you when you were in a coma. I could be stuck, forever wondering if anything was real until I lost my mind.

Mom held her chin high. "I'd like a moment alone with my daughter."

"But of course." Hades bowed mockingly and departed from the room.

My mother waited until his footsteps faded down the hall before speaking. "I can't imagine how hard this is for you."

My shoulders slumped. "I'm not this creative." I couldn't dream up something this crazy. I'd failed every creative writing assignment my teachers had ever thrown my way.

Of course now that I thought about it, that might have something to do with my inability to lie.

"What?"

I blinked back tears. "Mom, I'm scared."

"I know, but you're safest there."

Saf*est*, not *safe*? I stared at my mom, wondering what else she wasn't telling me. *I can't trust her.* The realization made me sick. If this was really happening, if I wasn't lying in a coma ward somewhere, then she'd never been honest with me, whether she could lie or not.

"I know, but—"

"Once you come into your powers, you won't have to hide anymore."

"What powers? I'm a goddess, but what can I do?"

"You'll be able to do so many things. You're spring. Everything is new again in the spring; the plants, the animals—"

"I can control animals?"

She frowned. "No, that's another god. Think more along the lines of plants."

"I could end world hunger!"

"I'm actually Goddess of Agriculture, and believe me, the earth grows enough to feed everyone. Humans just haven't learned to share."

I stared at her, deflated. All I could do was make pretty flowers bloom. "I don't want to stay."

"I know, but the time will pass before you know it. I'll work everything out with your school." She smiled at me. "I love you, Persephone. You're my entire world."

"I love you too, Mom."

She smiled and her image flickered again. "I have to go. If you need me, Hades knows how to do this." She motioned to her flickering image. "But it takes a lot of power, so . . ."

I stared at her in disbelief. I was really going to be alone down here. "I can't talk to you or Melissa or anyone on the surface?"

"You can, it's just costly. Power's all that's keeping us alive, hon. We have to be careful. But if you need me, we can do this, or dream walk, or—" She flickered out, then back in. "I'm sorry, I have to go. I love you." She held her palm up. I held my palm up to hers, and for a brief second I could almost feel her hand against mine. Then my mother was gone.

I sank to my knees and cried.

Chapter VIII

I HEARD A HESITANT knock on the door and quickly wiped the tears off my face. "Come in!" I looked at the door, expecting to see Hades. I was surprised when a dark-haired, waif-like teenage girl entered instead. My eyes focused on the unicorn rearing up toward the full moon on her purple T-shirt, surprised to see something I recognized in this strange place.

"I'm Cassandra," she said cheerfully, offering me a hand.

I took it, and she hauled me up to my feet. "You've had a good thirty minutes to feel sorry for yourself. Now it's time to look around your kingdom."

I bristled, opening my mouth to tell her off, but changed my mind. However angry I was, Cassandra wasn't the one who should be left dealing with the fallout. I looked her over—she couldn't be much older than me. Maybe I didn't have so much to complain about.

After all, I was still alive.

"I'm Persephone." I'd considered introducing myself as Kora, but I didn't want to stay down here long enough to justify someone calling me by my nickname. "And yeah, I guess I'd like a tour."

She led me down the hall, stopping at a set of black double doors across from the room I'd woken up in. "This is my room." She threw the door open.

The chamber had a living room with a long hall branching off to what I assumed was the bedroom. I gaped as I took in the posters of anime characters plastered to the walls, the picture windows overlooking an unfamiliar skyline, and fixed upon the huge flat screen television hanging on the wall, surrounded by a comfortable wrap around leather sofa.

"Nice! I didn't know you guys got TV down here." This might not be as bad as I'd thought. At least I wasn't going to fall behind on all my favorite shows.

"Every trend eventually dies," Cassandra explained with a grin. I nodded as though that made perfect sense, and she laughed. "I'm kidding! We have access to almost everything you guys do. It's just separate. We can call or message each other, but the living are strictly off limits." She gave me a mischievous look. "Otherwise we might cause a lot of trouble."

I got the feeling when she said *we*, she meant *her*. I grinned back at her. I kind of liked this girl.

She ushered me out, closing the door behind her.

"Does everyone live in here?"

"In the palace? Nah. The souls mostly live in the suburbs. The palace is just for a few special people. Like Moirae, Charon, Thanatos, visiting deities—oh, and now you, I guess. I'm kind of an advisor to Hades, so he keeps me close at hand."

I nodded, digesting the knowledge that I was standing in some kind of castle. Advisor? Judging by the posters in her room, Cassandra hadn't been dead for more than five years. I doubted she was an advisor to Hades. Maybe she was his girlfriend? If so, she was taking this whole marriage thing really well.

"Suburbs?" I asked, seeing Cassandra eyeing me expectantly.

She laughed. "We'll get to those later."

She led me through the palace, pointing out the impressive dining hall. The entertainment suite surprised me—complete with a computer, big screen television, and every video game console I'd never known existed. It just didn't go with the ancient decor.

"He gets bored." Cassandra shrugged. "Eternity is a long time."

I followed her down yet another long hall, trying to remember all the twists and turns and rooms we'd gone through. "Can I get a map of this place?"

Cassandra just laughed and led me up a winding staircase to a tower. I blinked, taking in the glass walls overlooking a picturesque landscape. I stared at the sky, blue as forget-me-nots. Splashes of fuchsia flowers bloomed against the emerald green grass. Dazzling aquamarine rivers wound their way through lavender mountains.

"I thought—"

"That is would be all underground and cave-like? Yeah, that's a common misconception. Everything that dies comes to the Underworld. It's a separate realm, and it's huge. It would take eternity to see it all, but from here I can give you the highlights."

"Okay." I was in complete awe of the beauty of this place. I didn't see the sun, but felt the sensation of sunlight flooding through the windows.

"So that—" Cassandra pointed at one of the beautiful rivers winding its way through the landscape "—is the River Lethe. Don't drink the water, bathe in it, or even touch it."

"Why?" I gazed longingly at the translucent water and pressed my hand against the cool glass. I've always hated swimming, and all the water I'd ever drank came from a faucet, but something about the sparkling water called to every fiber of my being.

"You'll forget things. Sometimes when a soul comes here, their death was traumatizing, or maybe their whole life sucked. This river gives them a chance to forget the things that would otherwise haunt them."

"Like Oreithyia?"

Cassandra hesitated. "She's an extreme case. There are different levels of memory loss. The Lethe can take away all memories associated with a singular event or person, or wipe away their entire lives, and everything in between. Some memories go deeper than others. Boreas knew she would be coming here so he . . . made it difficult. He doesn't like to be forgotten."

I didn't ask how. I was having a hard enough time dwelling on what could have happened to me. I didn't need further details.

"We also use it on people who've done bad things in life," Cassandra continued. "We take away all their memories, and they serve in the palace or around the Underworld until their sentence is up."

That didn't seem like much of a punishment. "Why?"

"For most people, their circumstances contributed to whatever crime they committed. This gives them a blank slate. When they finish their sentence they can live the rest of their afterlife in peace. Of course it doesn't work like that for everyone, but between me and Moirae we can usually tell who should go straight to Tartarus."

I didn't want to hear anything about Hell. It was bad enough it was so close by. "Who's Moirae?"

Cassandra smirked. "You'll meet her later. Anyway, the point is, don't drink from the Lethe."

I nodded, staring at the Lethe. I wished I could forget the last forty-eight hours, but that wouldn't change anything. I would still be here and Boreas would still be—

My head shot up. "Could we give that water to Boreas? Make him forget he ever saw me?"

She shook her head. "It doesn't work on deities. You haven't grown into your divinity yet, but when you do you'll be immune too."

"Oh," I said, disappointed.

"That was a good idea, though," Cassandra said encouragingly. After a moment's pause she pointed above the Lethe. "Do you see that mountain up there? That's Olympus."

"I thought Olympus was supposed to be in the sky."

"It fell thousands of years ago when people stopped believing in the gods. Most of them died then. They live above the Elysian Fields on their mountain now."

"Could I meet them?"

Cassandra shrugged. "You can't go into the Elysian Fields, but the gods get bored easily. They may come to you. You're new and interesting."

I wasn't sure how I felt about that. So far, having the gods take an interest in me had been nothing but trouble. Cassandra turned me to the left and pointed at another river.

"That's the Styx, and you see those houses over there?"

I nodded.

"Those are the Asphodel Fields. I call them the suburbs."

I could see why. Pastel-colored houses lined the streets, with postage stamp green lawns surrounded by picket fences. "It looks nice."

"Pretty much everyone ends up in the Asphodel Fields. You have to be really awesome to end up in the Elysian Fields, and really horrible to end up in Tartarus. Most people live normal lives, and live a normal afterlife."

"It's not what I pictured." I thought back on the Divine Comedy essay I'd written for English class.

Cassandra leaned against the glass wall. It was so clean it looked as if there was nothing stopping her from falling through the bright blue skies. "The Underworld's just like the living realm, only more peaceful. We still have stores, but no money changes hands. People had things they loved to do up there, and now they can do it down here without any pressure."

"I wouldn't want to work in my afterlife." I stretched. "I'd relax and . . . well, I don't know what, but I wouldn't work."

"Well, the people sentenced to the Lethe do most of the work, but the shops are run by hobbyists. Most people don't want to do anything resembling work at first," Cassandra said with a smile, "but eventually they get bored and start learning how to do new things or perfecting a skill they already had."

"I guess." I wasn't convinced. "Can I meet Charon?"

"Maybe later. He's on the other side of the river right now. See his little boat? The new batch of souls should arrive with him soon." She pointed to a speck bobbing on the Styx.

I peered closely at the River Styx. In the center was a small island of trees. I could just barely see a long, wooden, canoe-like boat gliding around the island.

"Anyway," Cassandra continued, "there's a few other rivers beyond the Styx, but you have no reason to visit them. If you go past the suburbs you'll run into a river made of fire called the Phlegethon; that marks the boundary to Tartarus."

"Sounds like a great place for a swim," I muttered.

Cassandra laughed. "It's not as bad as you'd think. There's a fail-safe, so it doesn't burn the souls on this side of the river. It actually feels pretty cool." She paused, considering. "But then I am already dead. No telling what it would do to you. Anyway, you can go anywhere in the suburbs, the palace, and the gardens, but no matter where you are, stop when you get to water."

I almost wanted to object—who was Cassandra to tell me where I was allowed to go?—but I suppressed the feeling. Beyond the river of fire was Hell. Not a place I wanted to go sightseeing. I didn't want to risk touching the Lethe, and if I recalled correctly, Cerberus, Hades' three-headed monster dog, guarded the other side of the Styx. If Cassandra said an area was off limits, I didn't intend to take any chances.

"Okay. I think I can handle that."

Cassandra beamed. "Great! Now let me show you the coolest part of the Underworld." She led me back down the stairs, through the palace, and opened a set of double doors with a grin. "This is the throne room."

I stepped inside and stared in awe. It was massive and carved entirely from white marble. At the center of the round room were two thrones cut from a solid black stone I couldn't identify. Two small chairs of the same material sat off to either side.

"Wow," I whispered.

"I know. You never get used to it. The court of the dead is held here about twice a week. Moirae hangs out over there." She motioned to a chair on the left of the throne. "I'm over there." She indicated the chair to the right. "You and Hades will be right here."

I looked at the thrones. Surely they wouldn't have added a throne for me. I wasn't really queen, and I'd been here for less than twelve hours. But why have two thrones? Cassandra hadn't hesitated before pointing to her usual spot, so it wasn't as if *she* typically sat there. I wondered at the mentality behind having an empty seat beside you for all eternity. Who would want the reminder that they were alone?

I mulled that over while I followed her back to the hall with the bedrooms. I caught sight of a man making his way down the long hallway. "Who's that?"

Cassandra followed my pointed finger and narrowed her dark eyes. "Hey you!" She jogged through the entertainment room to the hall.

I followed closely behind her, studying the man. Something was off about him. He was tall, wearing robes the same disorienting black I'd seen on Hades, but that wasn't what stood out to me. Light seemed to bend around him, as though he was sucking it out of the room.

"Reapers aren't allowed down here." Cassandra frowned. "How did *you* get clearance?"

"From Thanatos. What about you? Do you have clearance?" he asked in a snide voice.

Cassandra bristled. "I live here."

"Ah yes, Hades' pet soul. I almost forgot. What about her?" He motioned to me.

"None of your business. She belongs here, you don't. So shoo!"

"I'm Persephone." I was determined to be polite, no matter how snide he sounded.

Cassandra sighed. "You don't have to talk to him."

"I'm Zachary." He gave me an appreciative once-over. "You must be new here."

"I am." I made myself meet his eyes. It was hard to look at him directly; my eyes kept getting distracted by the strange bends in light around him. "Nice to meet you." I extended my hand.

"No, Persephone, don't!" Cassandra reached out to block the Reaper's hand. His fingers brushed mine and I fell to my knees screaming. Fire laced through my veins. Something ripped inside of me, trying to break free.

"Shit! She's alive?" Zachary sprang away from me, hands in the air.

"Yes, she's alive, you idiot!" Cassandra yelled. She knelt beside me. "Hades!"

I gasped. My arms were crossed over my chest, gripping my shoulders to hold myself together. My vision swam. I doubled over, my head nearly touching the stone floor.

"What happened?" Hades appeared in front of me. He knelt beside me, a frown marring his otherwise perfect face. He touched my shoulder and I cried out. Something within me shifted and suddenly the pain was gone.

I stared up at him, breathing hard. "What—"

Hades was already on his feet, turning on the Reaper. "What are you *doing* here?"

"I didn't know she was alive, I swear!"

"I didn't ask if you knew she was alive, I asked what you're doing here."

"What happened?" I asked Cassandra when she offered me her hand and helped me up.

"Reapers collect souls and bring them to the Underworld," she explained.

"Thanatos sent me. I was getting the list. I'm really sorry." Zachary met my eyes. "I didn't know you were alive."

That horrible feeling had been my *soul?* I stared at Zachary in disbelief. He looked terrified. I followed his gaze to Hades.

"It was my fault. I shook his hand. I didn't know that would happen."

Cassandra rolled her eyes. "He shouldn't be here at all, and he knows it. You should be able to walk around freely in your own palace."

"Her own . . ." Zachary paled. "Oh shit. I mean, I'm really, *really* sorry. I didn't know we have a queen."

I opened my mouth to correct him, but Cassandra squeezed my hand.

Hades looked at Cassandra, then back at Zachary. "Go find Thanatos and bring him to me."

Zachary stumbled away, apologizing with every step.

"You okay?" Hades touched my shoulder and looked me over.

I nodded, shaken. Hades looked concerned, so I cleared my throat and climbed to my feet. "I'm fine." To my embarrassment I felt myself leaning into his touch. I snapped out of it and looked at Cassandra. "Why did you say this was my palace? I'm just visiting—"

"Nope, you're the queen," Cassandra corrected cheerfully. She glanced at Hades. "You want Persephone to have lots of exposure. She needs to be seen by everyone."

"What did you see?" Hades sounded alarmed.

"See?" I asked confused. My eyes widened as I made the connection. "Wait, you're *the* Cassandra?"

She gave me a tightlipped smile and nodded before turning back to Hades. "Nothing concrete yet. I just know Boreas is still looking for her."

Hades leaned against the wall, brow furrowed in thought. "Do you think he'll give up if he finds out she's here?"

Cassandra shrugged. "I can't be sure. But there's no way he can get down here. As long as he doesn't have reason to believe she'll return to the surface, I don't see why he would bother."

"But he may cause trouble on the surface to lure her up."

She shrugged. "Anything is possible at this point."

"What do you mean?" I demanded "And I *am* going back. In three months, remember?"

"I'm already counting the days," Hades replied dryly. "Unfortunately, you'll be back next winter." He looked at Cassandra. "I'll contact Demeter and tell her to keep her guard up. She can warn her people."

"Boreas can't be stupid enough to think we'd let the queen leave her realm," Cassandra pointed out.

Hades didn't look convinced. "Well, Brumalia is coming up. That's as good a time for a marriage announcement as any. If Boreas has spies here, they'll see her."

"*She* is standing right here!" I snapped. "I'm not sure I want to play queen. And spies? I thought I was safe here."

"You're not playing queen," Cassandra began.

Hades cut in. "You are safe—"

"Someone just tried to rip my soul out of my body!"

"It was an accident, and your soul wasn't going anywhere. You're a goddess, remember? In a couple of years you'll be able to shake hands—" he gave me an incredulous look "—with Reapers all day without any problems. You are safe from Boreas and his spies. It's the rest of the surface I'm worried about. Boreas knows I intervened, but he's not going to jump to the conclusion that my next step was marrying you and bringing you here."

"True," Cassandra said. "Hades has gone millennia without getting married. Why would he choose to share power now? Boreas is probably looking all over Athens for you now, and your people aren't exactly used to winter."

I blanched, thinking of everyone I knew up there. "What will he do when he can't find me?"

"He'll go after people you know and make them tell him where you are." Cassandra's voice was gentle.

"How does he know who I am? Or who I know?"

"He knows," Hades replied. "He's never got along particularly well with your mother, so it's only natural he'd keep close tabs on her whereabouts. I imagine he's been watching you for quite some time, waiting for you to develop enough of your abilities to survive your abduction."

I sucked in my breath, realizing the paranoid sensation of being watched hadn't been so crazy after all. How long had he been lingering in the shadows waiting for the right time to take me?

"He's been watching me?"

My voice was shaking. Hades' eyes went wide and he shot a look at Cassandra. She shook her head and stepped back, arms in the air in an "I surrender" motion. "I'm dead, remember? I don't do comfort well."

Everything I thought I'd imagined was real. I shuddered, thinking of all the times it had felt like something was right behind me.

A hand touched my shoulder and I jumped.

"It's okay." Hades' voice was reassuring. "He's not going to find you here."

I swallowed hard. "If no gods can come down here—"

"Most," Cassandra interjected.

I froze. Hades shot her an annoyed look. "You're not helping." He returned his attention to me. "Without my permission. And that's a one-way trip. The only gods who can go back and forth are you, me, Thanatos, and Hecate."

"I haven't seen Hecate in years," Cassandra mused. "She's still avoiding Moirae. Hermes used to be able to cross realms, but he died." She returned Hades' death glare. "Fine, not helping. Got it."

"So how could he have spies?"

Hades sighed. "Anytime I leave the Underworld, it creates an entrance to this realm. Generally only gods or gifted humans can see it. Humans cannot enter except by death, and gods cannot enter except by invitation."

"So how—"

"Demigods." Cassandra chimed in. "They kind of fall into a gray area."

"Which is why all entrances lead to Tartarus," Hades explained. "That in itself is enough to dissuade most of them. Furthermore, they can't cross the river if they fall below a certain moral standard. Since Boreas is one of the few gods out there still reproducing, it stands to reason he has some spies among us."

"They wouldn't dare attack you. Hades is a fierce god." Cassandra rolled her eyes when Hades grinned. "Sort of. No one is going to touch you if they think they would have him to deal with afterward. He does have the unique ability to kill you and *then* torture you."

Hades chuckled, and the sound sent shivers down my spine. "Of course, we're being excessively cautious. Once Boreas knows you're spoken for, he should simply move on. However interested he is in you, you're not worth taking on a god of my caliber."

"Uh, thanks." I grimaced. "I feel safer already. If you're such a powerful god, why do you let spies in your kingdom?"

Hades gave me a savage grin. His footsteps echoed in the large room when he walked over to his throne. "I've got nothing to hide. Let them see how far they've fallen. And in this case it serves our purposes." He sobered. "Nonetheless, you'll need a guard. Do we need to add dance lessons into your—" he suppressed a laugh "—combat training?"

His voice was so smug I was tempted to punch him in the face. I liked him better when he was worried about me and being comforting. Not when he was being an arrogant jerk. "Melissa and I took cotillion classes a couple of years ago."

Hades snorted. "Of course you did."

"Shut up!"

His eyebrows shot up. He pushed off the throne and straightened his spine. The air seemed to grow heavy and darken, crackling with an electric charge.

"Shut up?" he demanded. "Have you forgotten who you are speaking to? I rule a third of creation! I am the most powerful god left in this world, and I will not be ordered about by an infant!"

I saw Cassandra's throat bob as she swallowed hard. She stared at the ground fiercely. A part of me felt like diving underneath the throne and hiding like a small child, but something deep within me responded to his show of power.

I straightened my back, tilted my chin up, and narrowed my eyes at him. "Wow, it is shocking you weren't already married. Look—" I cut him off before he could speak. "I appreciate your saving me and going through all of this effort to make sure the people I care about are safe, but that doesn't give you the right to mock me or to yell at me. Got it? I may not rule a third of creation—"

"Actually—" Cassandra interjected, but a withering glare from Hades cut her off.

"See to it she's prepared for the ball. I have much to attend to."

"Wait a minute!" I protested. "What the hell is Brumalia?"

"*Now*, Cassandra," Hades growled.

"Sure thing. We were just wrapping up our tour." Cassandra grabbed my hand and hustled me down the hall. "Bye now!"

Chapter IX

CASSANDRA LED me through the rest of the tour fast, but I didn't mind. I was too busy seething with rage at Hades. I didn't know what it was about him that set me off, but something just made me want to wipe the self-satisfied smirk off his face.

Cassandra had an amused grin the remainder of the tour, and I wondered what she wasn't telling me. Instead she filled me in on Brumalia. In the Underworld, it was kind of like a combination of a Christmas party and New Year's ball with a keg party thrown in. Cassandra explained people in the living realm used to celebrate it until the Anglo-Saxons combined it with their holidays.

"Luckily, there's no need for sacrifices, because everyone is already dead." Cassandra's voice was too cheerful.

I stared at her, horrified.

"I'm kidding, Persephone. Hades was never into sacrifices." She stopped before a door, and I realized we were at the same room I'd woken up in. "This is, of course, your room."

I shuddered.

Cassandra frowned and opened the door. "Something wrong?"

"It's a little creepy," I confessed. "It looks kind of like my room at home, but . . . different."

"Oh! You must have been thinking about your home while you were asleep. The room decorated itself accordingly."

"The room can read my mind?" I twirled my hair around my finger and backed away from the door. "That's weird."

"Not exactly," Cassandra said, walking over to my window. "It just kind of . . . molds itself to what you want. What kind of afterlife would this be if you had to spend all your time in a place you weren't happy with? Home is the most important . . ." She trailed off, looking at the blank windows behind the curtain. "Yeah, this is creepy. Let's redecorate."

"There's nothing outside!" I cried, alarmed.

"What would you like to be out there?"

"I can decorate anything, any way I want, just by thinking about it?"

Cassandra grinned. "In this room, sure. Go for it."

A smile formed on my face. This was going to be fun.

"ENOUGH!" CASSANDRA laughed, flopping down on my bed. "We've been at this for hours! It looks perfect; can we move on?"

I looked around, unconvinced. I'd traded out the loft bed for a huge king-size bed. At home I liked the loft bed—there was something comforting about being in the air—but it didn't feel the same here. I also switched my pink comforter out for a white down blanket, added a canopy of sheer billowing fabric to the bed, and added identical curtains to the large bay window.

I moved the curtains aside and sat on the window seat, turning my back on the view of the flower-filled meadow to look at the rest of the room. I'd chosen a cherry shade of hardwood flooring with a matching dresser, nightstand, and bookshelf. A flat screen television was fastened to the green wall.

The closet was my favorite part. Cassandra lent me a thick stack of magazines to look through and figure out what I wanted to wear. All I had to do was think of an outfit I liked, and it would appear in my closet.

"What did you want to do?" I wasn't anywhere near done, but it was nothing I couldn't do on my own. Cassandra was clearly bored.

"Dinner. I'm starving."

"You eat?"

"Well, fine. I'm obviously not starving. It's just an expression. Yes, we eat. All the same foods you do." She affected a voice reminiscent of Hades. "Meals are important rituals to the souls. It grounds them in the familiar and provides a wonderful opportunity to socialize."

"He doesn't talk like that!" I laughed.

Cassandra giggled. "Just get him started on what he thinks is best for the souls. He's all about making everyone feel right at home. Oh gods! He reads these stupid psychology books and just spouts off random psychobabble. It's awful!"

I snickered. "Okay, so you can eat. Can we order pizza or something?" I realized the question was foolish. But decorating put me in a great mood. My mind danced with thoughts of pizza, movies, and maybe popcorn for later.

"We typically eat in the main hall. With Hades."

My mood crashed. "Oh. Uh, is what I have on okay?" I smoothed my dress, wondering why I cared.

"Yeah, you look fine. I'll show you where we go."

DINNER WAS AWKWARD, mostly because I finally got to meet Moirae. The "Fates" were embodied in this schizophrenic woman. She was middle-aged and average height, average build, average looking—brown hair, brown eyes, brown skin so light she could be any ethnicity. She referred to herself as "we," and apparently had three voices vying for attention in her head at any given time. The past, present, and future; the young, middle-aged, and old; and the maiden, mother, and crone in one. Good times.

I sat next to Cassandra, and she moved me to an ornately carved wooden chair to the immediate right of where Hades would sit, heading the table. The banquet hall was surprisingly homey. I'd been expecting something as grandiose as the throne room. The floor was divided into wooden squares. The wooden paneled walls had sporadically placed paintings depicting different gods.

Feeling out of place, I squirmed in my seat, watching as everyone else gathered around the table. Moirae turned in her chair to glare at me.

"It's her," she hissed, then nodded in agreement with herself.

"Persephone," I said helpfully. "Pleased to meet you."

"*You* are the reason we're down here."

I looked at Cassandra for clarification and she shrugged. Leaning over, she whispered, "There's a reason Hades keeps me around. She may be able to see the future too, but I'm way easier to talk to."

When I nodded in agreement, eyes wide, Cassandra laughed. "Okay, that's not the only reason. She can't see anyone who's been marked."

"Marked?"

"When a god gives someone a blessing or a curse, it interferes with their fate. They drop out of Moirae's sight. She can't see gods, either; that's why Hades needs me."

I nodded again, amazed at how badly I'd misjudged Cassandra. She was without a doubt the most important soul in the underworld. No wonder she felt comfortable taunting Hades; her position here was completely safe.

I turned back to Moirae. I was dreading the answer, but had to ask, "How am I the reason you're down here?"

"We are the fifth generation of Fates. We took our sisters' place before the fall of the gods. Hecate, your mother, and you are meant to release us and be the sixth generation of Fates. Instead, you will choose to remain in the realm of the living. Hecate with her witches, your mother with her foolish crops. And you . . ." She sneered. "What will you do while shirking your duties?"

I blinked. "I . . . uh . . . what? I haven't even come into my powers yet!"

"You will."

"There's something to be said for a self-fulfilling prophecy," I muttered, shaking my head. If she wanted to be mad at me for something I hadn't even considered doing yet, fine. I wouldn't have to feel bad for not stepping up as the next Fate later. Good. I didn't want to be a Fate.

"Making friends already?" Hades asked. I looked at him in mute appeal, and he grinned. "Persephone, allow me to introduce you to everyone. You've met Moirae, I see." At my nod he continued. "This is Charon, my ferryman; Thanatos, God of Death; his twin brother Hypnos, God of Sleep; and Aeacus, Rhadamanthus—"

"Call me Rhad," he interjected.

"—and Minos, my judges," Hades finished.

I nodded as each man stood in turn. I knew some of the names from school, but seeing them matched up with actual faces was unnerving.

"And this is my—" Hades broke off and cleared his throat. "May I present my wife, Persephone."

I moved to stand as they had for me, but Hades put a firm hand on my shoulder, keeping me in place. They all bowed then returned to their seats. People dressed in white robes served the food. I wondered if they were the people who drank from the Lethe. Dinner chatter began on the far side of the table, seeming to revolve around Charon recounting his day on the ferry.

I stared down at the white tablecloth, trying to remember which of the silver utensils I needed to use for the first course. A silver plate was placed before me with a fried pink oyster mushroom served with grapefruit. It was topped with an orange nasturtium blossom.

"So . . ." I turned to Moirae, who glared daggers at me, and quickly turned back to Hades. "Uh, what did you do today?"

He looked surprised by the question. "It's barely been an hour since I last saw you."

"It's called small talk," I snapped. "You should try it some time."

He sighed. "Fine. I spoke with Hestia about your history lessons, arranged for you to begin self-defense lessons with Charon—"

"What?" Charon piped up from his end of the table. "When did that happen?"

"Just now," Hades said around a bite of chicken. "I'm multitasking."

"Why does she need to learn self-defense?" Aeacus asked.

I popped the flower into my mouth, savoring the spicy flavor. I wondered how they'd known I was a vegan. Everyone had something different on their plates. Maybe it was just a cool Underworld trick, like the rooms decorating themselves.

"You're going to have Charon teach her?" asked Thanatos. "He won't be able to shut up long enough to teach her a single move. I'm way better at self-defense."

"Not everyone can kill someone just by touching them," Hypnos pointed out.

"You'll be busy guarding Persephone any time she leaves the palace." He looked at me. "You're perfectly safe in all but the public areas of the palace. Only certain souls can enter the living quarters. Just stay out of the public sections, the ballroom, the front lobby, the banquet hall, and the court room, unless either myself, Cassandra, or Thanatos are with you."

"Hah!" Thanatos laughed at Charon. "You may be the self-defense guru, or whatever, but I'm the one people want around if there's any *real* trouble." He looked at Hades. "I'm going to need to recruit more Reapers to cover my shift."

"What?" Cassandra snapped. "You have too many Reapers already! One of them nearly killed Persephone today." She saw my eyes widen and sighed. "Fine, not nearly killed. Gods, you deities need to learn to appreciate a good exaggeration."

"I'm well aware of what happened this afternoon." Thanatos yawned. "And since my Reapers are banned from the living quarters, that means I have to distribute the list. If I'm also expected to act as a guard, then I'll need more Reapers to keep things moving smoothly."

"And last week?" Cassandra asked. "What was the reason then?"

"You guys won't believe who I met on the ferry today," Charon said from his side of the table.

"Who?" Minos asked.

"Okay, you guys remember that movie with the . . ."

I didn't get to hear the rest of his sentence because Thanatos drowned him out. "More people are dying every day. I need help."

I shifted closer to Charon, but couldn't hear him over Cassandra.

"Bull! You only had a handful of Reapers during *the plague!*"

"And maybe a tenth of the population," he retorted.

"How many do you need?" Hades asked.

Cassandra sighed loudly and sat back in her seat. Heads shook around the table, and I caught more than a few amused grins. Cassandra seemed to be the only one who was bothered by the Reapers.

"A hundred?"

"You get fifty. And keep them out of the palace, would you?"

Thanatos grinned and took a bite of his steak. I studied him closely. He wore black robes, grim-reaper style. His dark hair was pulled back from his narrow face. His dark eyes met mine from across the table and I gulped, staring hard at the soup before me. I didn't want Death shadowing me. I glanced at his twin brother, Hypnos. He looked just like Thanatos, only his robes, eyes, and hair were grey. Not old-people grey; more like the color of smoke.

Charon laughed. "Give us a week, Thanatos. Persephone will be able to kick your bony ass across the Styx."

The table erupted into cacophony. Everyone was talking over everyone else, adding wagers and jesting with each other. Lethians deftly ducked between the dueling deities, serving the main course. A plate of corn-filled phyllo tulips and eggplant topped with tomato sauce was put in front of me and I took a nervous bite.

"You're on!" Thanatos replied. He gave me a devilish grin. "One week, Persephone."

"That's okay," I squeaked. I didn't want to go hand to hand against Death.

No one heard me. Hades' eyes glittered in amusement. He gave me a look that said *see what you started?* as plainly as if he had spoken.

"I'm also trying to clear my schedule to teach you about your abilities." Hades smiled wryly. "And I've still got to prepare for Brumalia. You're keeping me busy."

"I'm sorry. I don't mean to be any trouble."

He chuckled. "Don't apologize. It's a welcome diversion."

"Then thank you."

"You're welcome," he said, seeming pleased.

"Well, since no one else is asking," Charon called from the end of the table, "I suppose it's up to me. Hades, when did *you* get a wife?"

Everyone laughed. "You miss everything." Cassandra snickered.

"Damn those needy souls," Charon joked, sliding an easy grin my way, his gray eyes twinkling. "So what happened? Hades sweep you off your feet?"

"You could say that." I glanced at Hades. I wasn't sure what I was allowed to disclose.

"See, I had this vision—" Cassandra began.

"Always visions with you," Thanatos groaned.

"—that Persephone was in trouble. So I calmly told Hades—"

"If by calmly you mean bursting into the throne room shrieking like a banshee," Hades teased.

"I do not *shriek*," Cassandra said indignantly.

"Yelled, then." Rhad's white teeth gleamed against his midnight-dark skin.

"Whatever. Anyway, Hades took off—"

"Since when did you have visions about the living?" Hypnos interrupted.

"Two living deities were involved," Cassandra said. "These days that's unheard of."

"Two?" Minos asked, stroking his gray beard. "So you must be . . ." He trailed off, looking at me speculatively.

"Goddess of Spring," I supplied.

There were murmurs of approval from around the table.

"You're a new one." Hypnos sounded intrigued. "How old are you?"

Cassandra smacked him over the head. "Heathen!"

"Back to the story," Charon said impatiently. "What was happening topside?"

Hades took over then, recounting the story dramatically. Anytime he made himself sound too heroic Cassandra put him in his place. I looked around the table with the fresh realization that this group wasn't just a collection of souls or subjects but a trusted inner circle.

"Well, Persephone, it's great to meet you." Aeacus straightened his dark robes.

I nodded at him. "Thank you."

"Don't you worry any about any demigods," Charon said. "Anyone who comes down here with the intent to do you harm will regret it."

"Ah yes," Cassandra teased. "Charon could do something really helpful, like hit them with an oar."

"Hey! *I'm* the self-defense guru! Remember?"

"He could always talk them to death," Thanatos said.

"Cassandra could shriek at them." Hades snickered.

I laughed despite myself. For the rest of the meal, Charon grilled me about life among the living. I was surprised my voice wasn't hoarse by the end of the meal.

No one lingered after the meal. Everyone had too much to do, I supposed. Even Cassandra waved goodbye and slipped away down one of the endless hallways.

I walked back to my room but paused outside the door. I wasn't sure I could handle this. I'd followed in the footsteps of the dead, befriended a prophet, been attacked by a snowstorm, married the King of the Underworld, found out I was a goddess, and stabbed a guy with a pen all in one afternoon. I was terrified of what tomorrow might bring.

I walked back the way I came, idle thoughts of enjoying the entertainment center filling my mind. I'd created a television in my own room, but the thought of being in a place I decorated with my mind was just too much to handle right now.

Across from the entertainment suite, a half opened door beckoned. I could see a wall of books. A library? Cassandra hadn't shown me that. *What do they read in the Underworld?*

I walked into the library, fingers trailing along the spine of the books while I read the titles. I didn't recognize anything, but that didn't surprise me. I laughed when I reached a section of psychology, self-help, and parenting books. Cassandra hadn't been kidding.

A loud thud drew my attention. I heard Hades swear and turned to see him bending to pick up what looked to be an ancient book.

"Can I help you?" he snapped.

"I . . . uh . . . I was just checking out the library." The look on his face told me that was the wrong answer.

"This would be the entrance to my private living quarters. Not a public library."

I flushed. "I'm so sorry. I didn't know."

"Do you have a problem with your own rooms?"

The condescending tone of his voice washed the apology right out of me and let in a torrent of anger. "I was under the impression I could go anywhere I pleased."

"How presumptuous."

I glared at him. "Whatever. So sorry to intrude on your precious solitude. Here, I'll just—"

He laughed then, startling me.

"Are you bipolar?" I snapped.

Still chuckling, he shook his head.

"Then what's so funny?"

"You, actually." I narrowed my eyes at him as he continued. "You're such a curious mix of humanity and divinity. I've just never seen anything quite like it."

"Well, as much fun as it's been to entertain you—" I spun on my heel when I realized I didn't have a way to finish that sentence, and moved to leave the room.

"Stop." Hades laughed. "Really, I'm sorry if I've offended you. You're more than welcome to browse. I get—" he paused—"defensive, I suppose, when I'm around too many people. It's become understood that after dinner I prefer to be left alone."

A biting retort died on my lips as he motioned me to the shelves. "I understand." I bit my lip as I searched for a familiar book. "So that never goes away?"

"What?"

I tried to explain. "I used to love being around people. I always wanted to be right in the thick of things. But lately . . ." I trailed off, careful to select the right words. "I just want to be left alone. Not always, just . . . I can't take so much—"

"It never goes away," Hades confirmed. "Not for us. We're made for solitude, I'm afraid. Well," he amended, "except Zeus. He was always more like the humans than the rest of us. Most of the deities can't even stand each other's company after a while."

"Why not?"

"Because we're not human." Hades set his book down. "Their lives are over in a blink of an eye, so they surround themselves with noise and . . . life. They throw themselves into everything they do with all their energy, and it is exhausting to watch. The dead calm down after a while. Except Cassandra."

I smiled. I'd known her less than a day, and I already knew *calm* was not a word that could ever be applied to her.

"Unfortunately, most of the souls we'll interact with are new."

"It must suck for you to have to stay down here." Hades looked confused, and I rushed to clarify. "Well, you drew, like, the short straw or something, right? I just meant that—"

"I *chose* the Underworld."

"Why?"

"The same reason your mother chose the earth or Poseidon the sea. I was drawn to it. I didn't have to deal with all the problems of Olympus, and I could help people down here."

"Help people?"

"You're surprised I care? I helped create this species, Persephone. I'm invested."

My heart gave a strange thump when I heard my name uttered from his lips. Damn it, I was staring again! I shook my head to clear it. "So you help them when they die?"

"People are vulnerable after death. They're confused and frightened. I help them find a place here."

I hadn't thought of that. Even after Cassandra showed me the suburbs, I hadn't truly contemplated the fact that people *lived* here. It was just too strange.

"That's nice. You're not what I expected as ruler here."

"How do you mean?"

"You seem to care about your people, and the way Cassandra and the others talk to you . . ." I smiled, remembering the lively dinner. "You don't treat them like subjects."

"I'm a god. I don't have to rule through fear or intimidation. That's a mortal weakness."

"Tell that to my Latin teacher. The myths don't portray you guys as friendly."

Hades shrugged. "There was more competition back then. The gods were already fading, and they were desperate to outdo each other and stay alive."

I thought about that. What wouldn't I do to stay alive? And how much more frightening would impending death be to an immortal?

"Cassandra and the judges were always volunteers, but the others could have retired when Olympus fell. Hypnos and Charon died long ago. Thanatos is one of the only other gods left in the Underworld who's still alive, and just barely. People fear death, but in reality what they fear is the uncertainty of their afterlife. That worship gets channeled to me."

"So why did they stay?"

"Because we're friends," Hades said as though that explained everything.

Maybe it did. I would do anything for Melissa, and I knew she would do anything for me. The most tedious and boring classes were fun as long as she was there. We had a lifetime of memories bonding us together. Hades had known his friends since the beginning of time.

"They're your family."

Hades laughed. "No. Goddess lesson number one: Fear the family."

"My mom—"

"Was a wonderful mother to you, I'm sure. But she still deceived you at every turn." He waved off my protest. "Consider yourself lucky. Our father tried to eat us. We all grouped together and killed our parents. Instead of drawing us closer, we spent the next few millennia ripping each other apart. Families think they know what's best for you. Your friends let you figure that out for yourself."

He looked down, blue eyes boring into mine. "The people who sat around that table tonight are my friends. Not my subjects, not my employees, not my family. I'm not that kind of god, and I'm certainly not that kind of king."

"Uh-huh," I murmured, staring into his eyes again. "I uh, mean I'm glad." I shook my head to clear it, again. He smiled, and I felt my face grow hot. "Um, thank you for letting me look at your books."

"My pleasure."

Chapter X

COLD. I COULDN'T move, could barely breathe. Couldn't scream. I felt heavy, trapped, terrified. The cold snaked its way up my torso, crushing my chest.

Where are you?

My mind rebelled against the foreign thought. I could feel something, someone, flipping through my mind, looking for answers.

The library. Hades' voice. *My pleasure.*

Frustration and rage coursed through me, but it wasn't mine. Footsteps in the distance. I didn't know what would happen when they reached me, but I knew it wouldn't be good.

A hand brushed against me. My blood ran cold.

"No!" I bolted upright. My breath caught in my throat. I was in bed; it was okay. Just a bad dream.

Nightmares make sense, I rationalized. I'd been through a lot; my brain was just trying to process it all. First Pirithous, then Boreas attacking me? I had a right to be traumatized. Plus, what kind of goddess would I be if I couldn't handle a silly nightmare?

I climbed out of bed and walked over to my closet. I was down here for better or worse, and I should make the best of it. It was my winter break, after all, and like any other girl on vacation I was going sightseeing.

I chose a flowing yellow skirt with a white lace blouse reminiscent of an outfit I had from home before setting off for the Asphodel Fields.

I winced when Thanatos fell into step behind me. "You don't have to do this."

"Yeah, I do." He grinned. "It's my job, remember?"

"Aren't you busy, like . . . killing people?"

He shook his head. "I don't kill people. People die, and I collect their souls. Well, I have my Reapers collect their souls. I rarely leave this realm these days."

"So why are you making new Reapers?"

"I only make a personal appearance when someone is killed by a god. That doesn't happen much anymore, but people will always find new ways to kill each other. Did you know that every second someone dies?"

"Forty thousand men and women every day," I quoted, uncomfortable with the knowledge.

"Every day," said Thanatos. "More Reapers allow for crazy things, like weekends off and reasonable hours. My Reapers are just souls, you know? They deserve the same respect as any other being. Labor laws aren't only for the living."

"They don't look like souls," I said, remembering with a shudder.

"They're blessed. They can go out into the world and come back. Just like demigods." He saw my worried look and added, "They're completely under my control. I get the list from Moirae every day and divide it amongst them. They go, they come back. I'd know if anything else happened."

"No free will?"

"Plenty of free will. No privacy. Still, it's not hard to recruit—who wouldn't want to visit the living world?" He studied me carefully, and I took a deep breath as homesickness filled me with longing.

"No one," I whispered. "How can you possibly choose?"

"They have to meet a few requirements. They can't know anyone in the living realm." At my confused look he laughed. "That only takes a few decades. They can't have drunk from the Lethe. Demigods get preferential treatment." Thanatos shrugged. "Outside of that, it's just like any job interview."

"If they're just souls, why does Cassandra hate them?"

Thanatos smirked. "You caught that, huh? They can be pretty full of themselves. They think they're special, and Cassandra caught wind of that. It really pisses her off when she finds them wandering around the palace."

His eyes twinkled in a way that made me think the Reapers popping up every time Cassandra entered a public area of the palace wasn't coincidence. "You're messing with her!"

Thanatos winked at me. "Yeah, sorry about the whole . . . soul thing. I think Zachary was more shaken up than you were."

I doubted that. "Does it always hurt so much?"

Thanatos tilted his head, considering. "It's hard to tell, what with the pain of people dying and all. I've never had a soul complain about the process. It probably hurt you because your soul's tethered so strongly to your body. It didn't have a way to leave." Thanatos gave me an easy grin. "Where are you headed?"

"A coffee shop in the suburbs."

"Breakfast with Cassandra?" he guessed. A smile broke across his face when I nodded. "She has excellent taste in food."

The Asphodel Fields closest to the palace were designated for the new or active souls. The longer souls stayed in the Underworld the further out they would spread. Most preferred peace and solitude to the crowded suburbs around the city.

Thanatos escorted me to a sidewalk café that looked surprisingly like a Starbucks.

"Over here!" Cassandra waved from a table on the edge of the sidewalk.

"Good morning." Thanatos flashed Cassandra an insincere looking grin.

She scowled at him. "Just her. You can sit somewhere else."

Thanatos shrugged and grabbed another table, settling in with a cup of coffee and a book. It was still early, so there weren't too many souls out and about. There were a surprising number of Reapers. Thanatos handed them each a page from his book when they approached his table.

"Morning!" Cassandra's voice was bright and cheerful. She held out her hand and a thick black organizer materialized. My eyes widened when I saw that every hour on the open page of her schedule was filled with tightly scrawled notes. "We've got a busy day today."

I eyed her coffee cup with suspicion. I wasn't a fan of coffee, but if the stuff they served down here gave me even a modicum of Cassandra's energy, I'd take it.

Cassandra launched into the schedule, and I waved down a soul wearing a green apron.

"Can I have whatever she's having?"

The waitress gave me a sympathetic look. "It won't help, dear."

I sighed. It had been worth a shot. "Soy hot chocolate?"

"Coming right up."

I turned my attention back to Cassandra.

"Okay, so we attend court every afternoon." Balled up straw-paper flew past Cassandra's face. She shot a glare at the table of nearby Reapers. The paper vanished the moment it hit the ground. "Moirae and I pass judgment, separating out the few souls who'll go to Tartarus and the Elysian Fields, and then we take any who deserve or chose to the Lethe to drink. Then Minos will explain the rules of the Underworld and take the souls on a tour. That's where you and Hades come in. When

Minos returns with the souls, introduce yourself, and send them on their way."

"That's it?"

The waitress set a cup of steaming hot chocolate on the table in front of me.

A piece of straw-paper landed in it.

"Sorry!" one of the Reapers called.

I plucked out the paper and took a cautious sip. Perfect.

Cassandra ignored the Reapers. "It rarely goes that smoothly. The souls want to talk, mostly just trying to get sent back, and they're not stupid. They know that Hades is their best shot at getting back."

"Can he? Send them back, I mean?"

Cassandra hesitated. "That's complicated. I've never seen it done, but Hades swears that if the conditions are just right, it's possible."

"So are you and Hades . . ." I trailed off, poking my fingers through the holes of the black, wrought-iron patio table. I somehow couldn't picture Hades dating. Cassandra took a sip of her latte, looking at me expectantly. " . . . together?"

She choked, grabbing a napkin and pressing it to her lips. "*What?*" she exclaimed, half laughing, half coughing up coffee. "Gods, no! I'm dead! And taken. But even if I wasn't . . . *Hades?*" She gave a mock shudder, crumpling her napkin up. "No, we're *just friends.*" Her look turned crafty "Why?"

"Does being dead matter? I mean, you're corporeal here, and it's not like you're a zombie."

"It matters," Cassandra assured me. "I could be with any soul I wanted, but a living being? That would just be weird."

"Well, not anyone topside, but down here there doesn't seem to be any difference between us."

Cassandra chewed her bottom lip. "It's not that." She watched the shop owner across the street sweep the sidewalk as she tried to formulate her answer. "It's just . . ." She sighed. "Look, he's a god, for one. Once bitten, twice shy." She ignored my puzzled look. "Things between gods and humans are weird."

"Zeus didn't seem to think so."

"Zeus had sex; he didn't have relationships. Either way, the humans were never better off for having gotten involved with him. Even without the whole god problem, or it being Hades, he's alive. I'm not. That's a huge barrier."

"How?"

"It just is. When we die, something about us changes. Our society would never work if it didn't, not to mention our non-economy. The drive the living have to always do more, get more, and conquer more dies with us. We've got our memories, the same basic thoughts, but inside we're different. You'll be able to feel a difference between souls and gods if you stay here long enough. We're just *different*. It would never work between me and Hades."

"Okay." I couldn't help but laugh at how flustered Cassandra looked.

She glared at me and took another sip of her latte. "Anyway, why did you ask?"

"I was just curious."

She nodded, and I was surprised she accepted that as truth so readily. At school an exchange like this would have resulted in me being grilled mercilessly, but she knew I couldn't lie. How had I not realized that before?

"Let's go shopping," Cassandra said, nudging her plate to the center of the table.

She showed me all sorts of stores where people made beautiful things for the sake of doing something they enjoyed. I browsed the jewelry stores and the handmade clothes.

I could shop for fashions across time. My hand skipped over a blue Victorian gown and stopped on a green tunic. In school, wearing something like this would be ridiculous, but here people would just assume I was from Ancient Greece.

"You going to get anything?" Cassandra asked, taking a sip of her coffee.

"Not today." I tucked the tunic back into the rack. I was comfortable in my own era of clothing.

"All right. Well, I have to head back to the palace. Do you remember the way back?"

I nodded. "I'll be back in time for my history lessons with Hestia."

Cassandra grinned. "Good girl. I'll see you in court."

I watched her leave, and then meandered through the shops, doing my best to ignore Thanatos. It was weird shopping with a guy following me. As the light from the sky grew stronger, more souls and Reapers crowded the shopping square, so I made my way out to the riverbank. I avoided the Lethe; I didn't trust myself not to do something stupid like fall in. Instead I walked along the Styx back toward the castle, watching Charon's little boat move along the bank.

"You're not afraid of me, are you?" Thanatos asked when he caught up to me.

"Why?"

"You keep speeding up when you see me behind you."

"Sorry." I slowed down.

Thanatos fell into step beside me, his dark robes seeming out of place against the vivid colors of the Underworld. "I'd forgotten."

"Hmm?"

"What it was like to frighten someone."

"I find that hard to believe. I mean, you're Death!"

He smiled. "No one down here has any reason to fear death. They're all immortal or already dead."

"I'm sorry if I've been rude."

"Don't be. I wouldn't want a guard following me either. It's kind of condescending, really."

"I'm glad someone sees it. I mean, don't get me wrong, I appreciate the protection, but I thought I was *supposed* to be safe down here. I'm not safe enough to walk to a coffee shop by myself?"

Thanatos nodded, pushing his hands into the pockets of his robe. "Tell you what—don't think of me as a guard. Just think of me as a friend. We're just walking together, okay?"

I smiled. "Okay."

We reached the palace, and our footsteps echoed on the marble floors. "I'll be around if you need me," Thanatos reminded me. I waved, heading to my room for lessons with Hestia.

She arrived right on time. The goddess was soft-spoken and diminutive. After looking askance at my papasan chair with her smoldering gray eyes, she created a side room for our lessons that contained a simple wooden table and two wooden chairs. The most interesting thing in the room was the fireplace.

She took one of the seats, motioning for me to take the other. In her soft voice she gave me a brief rundown on all the living gods and proceeded to tell me the history of the gods of Olympus. She spoke for precisely one hour and fifty minutes, leaving ten minutes for questions.

I had a splitting headache by the time I got to the throne room. It didn't help that I was nervous. Rhad and Minos had already taken their seats. Their voices rose and fell in murmured conversation. Moirae glared at me and sat in her chair with a huff. I ignored her and waved to Cassandra.

"Where's Hades?" I asked.

"Here." Hades appeared out of thin air at his throne.

"You have *got* to teach me how to do that."

He grinned, and the carved wooden doors set in the intricately carved stone arches burst open. Aeacus led more souls than I could count through the door.

"Now we're back to the throne room," Aeacus said. "You've met Moirae, of course, but now allow me to present the rulers of the Underworld: Lord Hades and Queen Persephone."

I stood and smiled. My gaze traveled over the court. I was vaguely aware of Hades speaking. There were men and women of every age and ethnicity. Their style of dress made it clear they were from all over the world. They watched Hades with rapt attention. I'd expected tears and panic, but except for a few souls fidgeting anxiously, they stood there calm and collected in the face of their deaths. My gaze kept getting caught on the children.

"Say something," Hades hissed.

"Can they all understand me? English, I mean."

He gave me an odd look and signaled to Cassandra. She launched into a speech warning about the dangers of the Lethe as Hades whispered, "Everyone you've met so far isn't speaking English. All speech at its base carried universal meanings. Death is the universal translator."

"I'm not dead. How can I understand them all?"

"Uh, you've always been able to. You're a goddess."

"No, I can't."

Hades sighed. "Yes, you can."

"I've taken foreign language classes—"

"Demeter let you—" He sighed as Cassandra began wrapping up her speech. "Which language?"

"Latin."

"That's mostly written, and there aren't any native speakers anymore."

"So if the person speaking isn't—"

"Look, can you just say something so we can go?"

"What should I say?" My heart hammered in my throat and my mouth went cotton-dry. What could I possibly say to a bunch of dead people? Sorry you're dead? Abandon all hope? Welcome to hell? Good news, we've got cable?

I clamped my lips shut. Oh God! What if I actually said something like that in front of all these people?

Hades sighed again.

"Do you need a paper bag or something?" I snapped.

Hades shot me a murderous look, and I realized all the souls were looking at me. I spoke without thinking. "Thank you, Cassandra. I hope you all enjoyed the tour." *Yeah, Persephone, I'm sure they enjoyed the postmortem tour.* "Um, have a happy afterlife."

Minos jumped in before I could make a bigger fool of myself. "Does anyone have any concerns they would like Lord Hades or Lady Persephone to address?"

Aeacus led the souls without questions from the throne room. I was relieved to see most of the children go with him. As I suspected, the souls who stayed had been the ones fidgeting throughout the speeches, waiting for their chance to speak. They clamored for our attention. I could sum up their requests in three words: *put me back.* Unfortunately they used far more than three words. They each told heartbreaking stories.

"You *have* to let me go back," a man in a black tuxedo was saying.

"I'm sorry, but I won't do that." Hades sounded sincere, but it didn't escape my notice that he didn't say that he couldn't do it, just that he wouldn't.

The man must have noticed as well. "I'll give you anything. I've got money, lots of money, and I've got—"

"You can't buy me off." The compassion was gone from Hades' voice.

The man shifted gears and looked at me. "Please," he whispered. "I have to go back."

I looked at Hades, then back at the soul. "I can't—"

"No!" he shouted. He rushed forward, ignoring the judges' shouts. "You can't say no to me, no one says no to me! I—"

Hades flicked his fingers when the man reached my throne. He flew backward, hitting the throne doors with a thud.

"Minos," Hades said in a calm voice, "please see to it that this gentleman gets settled."

I stared at Hades wide-eyed. "Is that code for something?"

Hades gave me a look. "No, it's not *code* for something. The man just died. Bargaining and anger are part of the process. He'll be fine. Next!"

By the time it was over, Hades was gripping my shoulder, keeping me in my seat until the last soul left the room. When his hand left my shoulder I bolted out of the throne and ran for the door.

Hades waved Thanatos off and followed me as I fled from the

palace. "It gets easier," he said when I finally came to a halt in the center of the castle gardens.

"How?" I gulped, blinking back tears. "I mean, there were *children*, and they all wanted—" I couldn't finish.

He opened his mouth, closed it, and ran his fingers through his hair. "You get used to it. Those people, they're upset for the moment, but when they adjust—"

I made a strangled laughing sound.

"I'm serious," he said. "Follow me."

I hesitantly trailed him through the courtyard. He led me to the edge of the suburbs where the new souls milled around looking out of place.

"What—" I began.

"There." He pointed at an elderly man rapidly approaching the group, calling a woman's name.

An older woman turned, her eyes widening when she saw the man. A wordless yell erupted from her lips and she ran to him and leaped into his arms. He spun her around, laughing.

"See?" Hades said. "It gets better."

"Thank you," I whispered.

He nodded and walked back toward the palace. "See you at dinner?"

I nodded. Thanatos came and took his place beside me when Hades stopped at the group of children gathered near the new souls and knelt to their level, speaking animatedly.

I watched in disbelief as worry and fear left their faces. They smiled when he produced some candy from his pocket and sent them clamoring toward a large playground with adults surrounding it. The adults watched the children with expressions ranging from hope to dread. Were they people who'd always wanted kids, or parents looking for their children? What would that be like, watching every day, half hoping you could see your children again, half terrified because it meant their lives would be over?

I watched the playground for a long time, waiting until each child was claimed.

Chapter XI

"THERE YOU ARE!" Cassandra exclaimed, dragging a gorgeous blond woman with her. "Persephone, Helen. Helen, Persephone. Come on, we've got a lot to do."

"Like what?" I followed her back to my room.

"Helen designs the best dresses, and we have to go over everything you'll need to know about the ball tomorrow."

"I'll be out here if you need me," Thanatos reminded me.

Helen and Cassandra were babbling to one another at the speed of light about fabrics, colors, and cuts. All I knew about dresses was that they came from the mall. "I think I may need you," I whispered to Thanatos in trepidation.

Thanatos grinned at me. "No way in hell." He winked as my door closed.

Designing a dress didn't take long in the Underworld. Helen tapped my shoulder, and I was wearing a princess cut gown. She frowned and made adjustments here and there, tapping my shoulder each time.

"Are you Helen of Troy?" I asked. Her golden eyes warily turned to me and she nodded.

It was strange being in the same room with the face that launched a thousand ships. She was pretty, but it wasn't her face that stood out to me. It was her hair. It was a beautiful shade of red and blond that combined to make a golden color I'd never seen before. It fell down her back in luxurious waves. I'd never had a problem with my hair before. I considered it to be my best feature, but seeing Helen's hair, I was jealous.

"You have pretty hair!" I blurted out. My eyes widened, horrified I'd spoken aloud.

"Thank you," she said warmly. "Want to try it out?"

"Huh?"

A floor-length mirror appeared in front of me and I glanced into it, startled to see my hair the same golden tone. I stared at the two of us standing side by side in the mirror, and something about the reflections bothered me.

In a flash I knew what it was. "You look like me!" I reverted to my blond shade. "I mean, not the hair color, obviously, but we look alike."

"We do share a father."

I was momentarily dumbfounded before I remembered: Helen of Troy was a daughter of Zeus.

"Okay, we're done here." She tapped my shoulder, and I was wearing a pair of black shorts and sleeveless blue t-shirt, made of thin waterproof material.

"What?" I looked at my outfit dumbfounded.

"Time for your self-defense lessons." Cassandra grinned.

Helen smiled. "I'll be by tomorrow night, right before the ball."

They'd hardly left when Charon entered my room.

"Good afternoon," he called in his jovial voice. "You ready to learn how to kick ass?"

He walked me through basic self-defense moves. I remembered most of it from the class I'd taken a few years ago. Charon reviewed how to escape different holds and grabs.

"Can I meet some of the heroes?" I asked when he wrapped up the lesson.

"Sorry, sunshine. Most heroes choose to drink from the Lethe. They tend to have tragic lives. Now they can finally rest."

"Oh."

He laughed at the obvious disappointment in my voice. "Who were you hoping to meet?"

I flushed. "I was a fan of the Hercules show when I was younger."

"He had a show?" Charon raised his eyebrows. "I only caught the cartoon."

"I loved that cartoon!"

"Don't let Hades hear you say that." Charon laughed. "Or that you're a fan of Herc."

"Why?"

"There's been bad blood between those two ever since Hercules stole Hades' dog."

"Cerberus? The myth called that a *loan*."

"It was. But Hercules never brought Cerberus back, and now he's drunk from the Lethe so he can never tell Hades where to find him."

I blinked. Everything dead came to the Underworld. If Cerberus had never returned . . . "You mean there's a three-headed dog running around on the surface?"

"Your guess is as good as mine. You seem to have a pretty firm grasp on the basics, so let's see how you do."

"Do? Like . . ." I struggled to remember the word. "Sparring?"

"Yes."

"With you? Today? I only just started. You and Thanatos weren't serious about that bet, were you?"

"No, Thanatos isn't an idiot. He wouldn't dare lay a finger on you, and neither will I."

I raised an eyebrow. "Why not?"

"You're Hades' wife."

I flushed. "Not really, we're just—"

Charon waved a hand. "Doesn't matter. No god in their right mind is going to lay a finger on you unless they want to start a war. We need someone Hades can safely channel his anger at if you get hurt."

"I don't think I'm ready for—"

"You're not human. Humans have fight-or-flight instincts. We have only fight. We weren't designed to be afraid of anything. We created the food chain, so that arrogance is hardwired right into our DNA. You have better instincts for this than you think you do, and the only way I can evaluate that is to see you in action."

"Wait. Better instincts? So because I can make flowers bloom, I'm hardwired to do battle?" I laughed.

"Not every god was lucky enough to get powers," Charon pointed out. "So don't knock yours. Every god is blessed with better reflexes and a touch more strength than the average human." He frowned. "It was a much more notable difference before humanity discovered vitamins."

"I'm not strong." I wished I could claim otherwise, but some heavy doors gave me trouble. I had no delusions about my strength.

"Not yet. You haven't grown into your powers. We're not talking super-strength, anyway; it's a pretty tiny boost. And it does correlate to height and build, so chances are while you'll be stronger than someone else your size, you still won't outmatch most humans."

"Oh."

"So let's see what we've got to work with." Charon snapped his fingers.

Before I could ask what he meant, a man grabbed me from behind. I threw my head back like I'd been taught, but instead of breaking his nose, my head bounced harmlessly off his chest.

I slammed my foot down, causing him to grunt in pain. His grip barely loosened but it was enough to twist free. I spun to face him and froze.

The figure before me was a bent and twisted husk of a man. His skin was gray, bleached of color, and gaunt. I could make out each bone in his face. His eyes sparked with hatred and he came toward me with a guttural growl.

I sprang backward. "What is he?"

"This is Bob," Charon said, his cheerful demeanor seeming out of sync in the same room as the man before me. The thing cut Charon an irritated glare and Charon shrugged. "Not Bob? Meh, no one actually cares what your name is. Bob here is one of the residents of Tartarus. I told him if he could beat you I'd consider letting him out on good behavior."

I remembered what Charon had said about needing a safe target for Hades if I got hurt, and my eyes widened. Before I could respond, Bob surged forward, and I scrambled to get out of his path. I wasn't fast enough, and he caught me in my shoulder. I stumbled, and his hand flashed out, wrapped around my neck, and slammed me into the wall.

I pried at his hand but his grip didn't weaken. My vision blurred. I kneed him in the groin and he dropped me with an angry yell. I kicked his knees. He fell to the ground. I rolled to my feet, but his hand wrapped around my ankle and gave me a vicious tug. I fell, my head striking the exercise mat hard enough to see stars. He pinned me to the ground. I squirmed beneath him, trying desperately to escape his grasp, and suddenly the weight lifted off me.

"Bye, Bob," Charon said, snapping his fingers. Bob vanished. "Okay, so here's what you did wrong." Charon launched into a lecture.

I slowly rose to my feet, watching Charon with disbelief. "You're not letting him go, are you?"

"I considered it." Charon's eyes were bright with mischief. "And then I realized I don't have the power to authorize something like that. Lighten up, Persephone. It wouldn't be Hell if they couldn't experience false hope. Can you run?"

"I am capable of running," I replied, confused by the rapid change of topic. "Sure."

"Fast, for long distances?"

I frowned. Every year in gym class we trained for the Presidential Fitness Award and ran a mile on the track. Melissa and I typically came in the bottom tenth of the class, but we'd never *tried* to do better. We'd run for a minute so our teacher couldn't say we hadn't tried and walk and talk the rest of the time.

"Maybe."

Charon shook his head. "That won't do. You need to run every day."

"Why?"

"Every technique I'm going to teach you is about getting away. If you can't run from your assailant, then it's a waste of time."

I thought of my nightmare last night and shuddered. "What if I can't get away?"

"If it's a mortal, you kick their ass. If it's anything more than a minor deity, you're screwed."

I frowned. "We have to have some kind of weakness."

"Yeah, our kids. You know that whole created-not-born thing?"

I nodded.

"When gods conceive, they give their children part of their power. Literally. From what I can tell, Demeter gave you a major chunk of hers, and Zeus probably just gave you your charming personality." He smiled at me. I narrowed my eyes at him, unsure whether to take that as a compliment or an insult. "Regardless of how much power a god gets from their parents, it was once a part of their parent, so their parents are vulnerable to them."

All the myths I'd heard where the parents were convinced their children were going to kill them suddenly made a lot more sense.

"That doesn't help you, though. You come up against a god, run the other way and pray they can't teleport."

With that cheerful thought, he worked out a training schedule for me. I was supposed to walk for five minutes, and then jog for thirty seconds, increasing the intervals of jogging time over the course of a few weeks gradually building up speed and distance. Charon helped me connect my phone to the Underworld's network and download a jogging app some tech savvy soul had created. He offered to help me create a room with an indoor track, but I declined in favor of finding one outdoors. I was still shaken by the fight and wanted to get as far away from Charon as possible.

The Underworld had no shortage of beautiful trails cutting through dense forests of elms, maples, pines, and oaks. Thanatos showed me a path that wound around a picturesque lake, bordered by live oaks draped with Spanish moss. I put on my headphones and started my playlist, letting the program guide me from walk to run.

I fell into the rhythm without any trouble, leaving my mind free to wander. I didn't like the idea of being defenseless against anyone. What if I couldn't run? What if Boreas could teleport? I paused with a sudden thought. Could I teleport? I'd have to ask Hades later, but if I could, was there even any point in building up running endurance?

Maybe insisting on self-defense lessons was silly. Hades seemed to think so, and Charon had pretty much just confirmed it would be useless if I were in any real danger.

Pirithous is human. He can still hurt me. People, guys in particular, had been acting strange around me. I hadn't felt safe in a while. It would be nice to know I could handle myself if some crazy situation came up. My mind flashed to Helen and I wondered if that was something we had in common.

I finished running and dropped by my room for a shower, changing into a green dress before heading to dinner. I left the table afterward with every intention of going to bed, but Hades pulled me aside for what he called Goddess 101.

"I thought you needed time for yourself after dinner," I said as he led me into his library.

"Who said this was going to take long?" He motioned for me to sit in one of the two high-backed leather chairs. "I can't know what you're going to be able to do, but we can make a few educated guesses. You're Zeus' daughter, so you most likely got the same thing from him he gave the rest of his children." He smiled at me. "Charm."

"Charm?" I repeated in disbelief. I thought back to Charon's compliment that I'd inherited Zeus' charming personality. "That's seriously something you can inherit?"

"Charisma, or whatever you like to call it. Something you said yesterday leads me to believe it's already taking effect."

"What do you mean?"

"At the height of his power, Zeus was . . ." Hades paused as if searching for the right words. "He was unstoppable. Everyone listened to him, and everyone loved him. The gods trusted him without question. Humans reacted to him by becoming jealous, possessive, aggressive, or enamored. Zeus brought out whatever was at their heart, their basest instincts. It was chaos."

My throat felt dry. "How is that *charm?*"

"If you can knock a person off balance, you can control them. Zeus thrived on chaos. The more irrational everyone around him became, the more he was able to control. That's not his only power, of course, but it's all he's ever given his children."

"Great," I muttered. "So that's what happened to everyone after last spring? That's a sucky power."

"Not if you can control it."

My eyes met his and I dared to hope. "Can I?"

"You're lucky. A demigod can't control their charisma. I don't need to tell you how careful you need to be with this ability. Humans are helpless against it. It won't work on the dead, but topside it is very powerful."

I shifted, uncomfortable with the idea of controlling people. "How do I turn it off?"

"We'll work on that, but first we need to go over what's going to happen tomorrow night."

I tensed, waiting for a lecture on etiquette. Instead, he took my hands in his and looked me in the eye, the expression on his face serious.

"The souls are going to worship you. It's only natural. You're their queen, and a goddess. If you begin to experience any headaches or discomfort—anything at all—tell me immediately."

I nodded, eyes wide. "Why?"

Hades started to respond, but a knock on the door cut him off.

"Hades." Hypnos opened the door. "My apologies, but I need your opinion for security tomorrow night."

Hades nodded, and Hypnos entered the room. "I'll see you at the ball tomorrow, Persephone," Hades said. "Have a good night."

I blinked at my dismissal and left the room feeling numb.

Chapter XII

"YOU'RE GOING TO be fine." Hades winced at the death grip I had on his arm. "We're going to walk through the door, they'll clap, we'll dance, and then you can follow me around while I make small talk. They're just dead people. Nothing to be afraid of."

If it had been any other time I might have laughed and told him how many things were wrong with his last sentence, but instead I shook my head. "It's not them. It's the people who might be alive that worry me."

"No one's going to hurt you." He studied me, eyes flicking back and forth over my face. "You're pale. Are you really that nervous?"

I shook my head. "I'm not sleeping well." I'd had a nightmare every night since I'd arrived in the Underworld. I shivered at the memory. They were getting worse.

"Why not?" Hades asked.

I opened my mouth to explain, but our names were announced and the doors burst open, revealing the largest crowd I'd ever seen. The applause were thunderous. My eyes scanned the room, pausing at the shadow-enshrouded Reapers. I hadn't realized there were so many of them. I scanned the mass of souls for Boreas' spies.

A Lethian gave us glasses of champagne and we raised them to the crowd. Hades and I took a sip and the crowd roared.

"You're popular," I muttered through a smile.

His grin broadened. "You seem surprised."

"No, it makes sense," I said, unable to resist a jab at his ego. "With a snap of your fingers, you could send them all to Tartarus. Even I would want to stay on your good side."

"I could send you to Tartarus," Hades teased.

"You're too frightened by my mother."

"There is that." He held out his hand. "Dance with me?"

Another Lethian took our glasses, and I took Hades' hand and let him lead me into a waltz. I studied Hades, reconsidering my jest. While I didn't doubt fear accounted for a large part of his worship, I knew there was more to it. The souls genuinely seemed to like Hades. From what I'd seen, he was a fair and just ruler, full of kindness and consideration for his people.

So why did he annoy me so much?

"There's too many people," I realized. "The spies could be anywhere."

"Just don't wander off with a demigod and you'll be fine."

"How will I know who's a demigod?"

"By sight. Halflings have ichor running through their veins." When I looked at him blankly, he sighed. "The golden blood of the gods?"

"I have gold blood?" I asked incredulously. *At this point, why not,* I thought ruefully. *Hell, I can probably fly.*

"Not in color," Hades clarified. "In essence. Though it does affect their appearance."

"How?"

"They look gold." At my disbelieving look he sighed again. I thought about offering him an inhaler, but he continued. "Gold hair, skin, eyes—they practically glow. Surely you've met a demigod, either here or on the surface. It's a useful marker we decided on long ago. Accidentally killing or cursing another god's child is rife with political complications."

"I'll keep that in mind," I said dryly. The ability to identify a threat made me feel safer. I let myself enjoy the dance, my pink dress swishing around my feet. The dress had an open back, and Hades' hand gently guiding me through the steps felt strangely intimate.

He looked good tonight. *Who am I kidding, he always looks good.* His tailored black suit emphasized his broad shoulders. His tie was the same blue shade as his eyes, almost neon blue. Human eyes were never that bright in color. I thought of my eyes. I'd always thought they were normal, but now I knew their unnatural brightness marked my divinity.

The thought raised a flag in my mind, dragging a half-forgotten memory to the forefront of my brain. Hades' hand shifted, sending shivers up my spine. Heat flooded my cheeks as I realized I'd been staring into his eyes the entire dance.

My mouth went dry. He led me through a turn, pressing my body against his. He cleared his throat, subtly adjusting our positions. To distract myself, I scanned the room, looking for gold eyes. The memory came back to me, and my back stiffened. Hades looked at me in concern.

"I'm an idiot." Gold eyes. How had I missed that, especially after seeing Helen? I'd seen the color before. "Pirithous," I whispered. "He's a demigod! That can't be coincidence, can it? Boreas attacked me the next day. What if that's his dad? He's a spy, and he's probably down here right now." I was feeling more panicked by the second.

"Your mother would have mentioned it."

"She only saw him from behind for a second, and then only on the computer monitor which is all messed up because of that vase I spilled last summer, and everything kind of looks blue, which is ridiculous—"

"Persephone," Hades interrupted gently.

"He said someone sent him! I just didn't listen because I thought he was crazy or I was in a coma—"

"A coma?"

"It makes a lot of sense if you think about it, except I'm not really creative enough to dream all this up. Ohmigod, Orpheus! He has gold eyes too! Oh, but he can't be working with Boreas, he tried to help me. Or did he?"

I closed my mouth with a snap. I'd been rambling a mile a minute like a crazy person. Thankfully no one seemed to have noticed. Or they were too polite to stare.

Hades ignored my random rant. "Even if either of them is down here, they can't hurt you. Demigods are harmless. They're barely more than gifted humans."

I nodded, trying to bury my fear.

Hades studied my face for a moment and sighed, motioning for our drinks. "Will you just try to have fun? It's the best night of the year."

"Fine." I sighed, mocking him, and took a sip from my glass. "Mmm . . . this is sweet. What is it?" I took a longer sip.

"Yours? Sparkling white grape juice." He grinned. "Did I mention that I'm afraid of your mother?"

I rolled my eyes and finished the glass. It didn't taste like any grape juice I'd ever had, but that wasn't surprising. Everything in the Underworld had a richer flavor. Hades made his way around the room, greeting the souls between dances. I stayed close, keeping an eye on the ballroom for any demigods. When another glass found its way into my hand I smiled. I could get used to having servants.

The next time Hades invited me to dance a grin stretched across my face. My teeth felt tingly, and all the dancing was making me dizzy. As he led me through the simple motions I gave him an appraising look.

"You look nice tonight."

Surprise flitted across Hades' face. "Thank you. You look lovely as well."

"I always kind of figured you'd be ugly."

Hades blinked. "Excuse me?"

I giggled. "Well, you know, in books and movies you're always, like, deformed or something crazy. You know, like a reflection of your soul?"

"Ah, I take it you mean my ugly and deformed soul?" Hades kept his voice light. He held me at arm's length and gave me a quick once-over. I felt a ping of power pulse through me.

"No. That's not what I meant." I touched my hand to my forehead, trying to make sense of my jumbled thoughts. "I don't think you or your soul is ugly. You're actually pretty hot."

Hades raised an eyebrow. "I see. Not so fast." Hades intercepted a champagne glass from a tall Lethian and studied the liquid carefully. After a cautious sniff he took a small sip, and his eyes widened.

"Something wrong?"

I jumped at the sound of Thanatos' voice. I hadn't realized he was behind me.

"Somehow Persephone was given ambrosia instead of grape juice," Hades replied.

Thanatos raised an eyebrow. "How much did she drink?"

"Is this a god thing?" I asked, growing annoyed. "Talking about people like they aren't standing right there? What's ambrosia? Some kind of poison?" The thought should have alarmed me, but I found it very difficult to care at the moment. Everyone looked so nice, and the music was so pretty.

"It's just a divine drink," Hades assured me. "It's not poisonous. Well, not in the traditional sense of the word."

"Do you think someone gave it to me on purpose?"

Hades frowned. "I can't imagine what purpose it would serve. It was probably just a mix-up, but Thanatos, would you mind interviewing the Lethians who were in charge of our drinks?"

"Sure. Did you want me to take her to her rooms?"

Hades stared at me, considering. "Do you drink? In the living realm, I mean?"

I shook my head. "I'm boring. Mom always asks me to promise her not to drink anytime I go out."

"Demeter does that?" Hades sounded surprised.

Thanatos let out a low whistle and shook his head.

My mouth dropped open. I couldn't lie. My mom wasn't lax. She didn't trust me. She just knew if I promised not to drink, I physically wouldn't be able to do it.

"That bitch!"

Thanatos snorted, and Hades raised an eyebrow.

"Water for her." He motioned to a Lethian for a refill.

When our glasses arrived, Hades tested my drink before passing it to me. "I've got her, Thanatos. Go on."

Thanatos studied me, looking so serious that I giggled. "Hades, she'll only embarrass herself. Let me get her out of the—"

"*She* is right here and *she* doesn't want to go back to her room. *She* wants to dance and have fun."

"Yes, Thanatos, you're being rude." Hades' lips twitched as though he was suppressing a grin. "See to the Lethians."

"I really don't think—"

"What exactly are you worried about?" Hades asked.

"You're a lot taller than Thanatos," I observed.

Thanatos met Hades' eyes with an unreadable expression on his face. "If someone got close enough to switch her drink—"

"To what end?"

"Compromise her judgment? Lower her guard? Should I go on? She's vulnerable."

"*She* is right here," I grumbled.

"Yes, you are." Hades grinned. "I need you to stay with me until you're safe in your room. Would you be willing to do that?"

"Sure."

Hades gave Thanatos a look. "Satisfied?"

Thanatos made a noncommittal noise and signaled a Lethian from the crowd.

Hades shook his head when Thanatos disappeared into the crowd. "He worries too much."

"You're not worried?"

Something flickered in Hades' eyes but it was gone before I could interpret it. "It was probably an innocent mistake. But still . . . I'd rather not have you out of my sight." He held out his hand. "Still want to dance?"

Time passed in a blur of color and light. People laughed and danced around us, the spinning arcs of the skirts making me dizzy.

"I can't dance another step." I giggled, clinging to Hades so I wouldn't trip and fall.

"Let's get some air." Hades led me out of the ballroom. The party was scattered all across the Underworld, but we found privacy in the grove of trees. The trees stretched into the sky, their branches arching and spilling over, sheltering us from view of any of the other souls wandering the Underworld.

"You're trying to stop me from making a scene." I stepped away from him into the center of the clearing. I spun around, holding my arms out. "Whoa." I stopped mid-spin, waiting for the clearing to do the same.

"You should probably eat something." Hades caught my hand. "Think of something, anything at all."

I imagined pomegranate seeds and a plastic baggy full of them appeared in my free hand. I put six seeds in my mouth. An owl hooted in the distance.

Hades laughed. "You're going to need more than that. What's your favorite type of bread?"

"I'm a goddess. Do I have to worry about hangovers?"

"Your metabolism will change when you come into your powers. As far as alcohol is concerned, right now you're a human." He suppressed a grin. "Ambrosia gets even gods drunk, so you're in trouble."

I sat down on the cool grass. "Have you ever eaten one of these? They're delicious." I offered him a seed, and he took it, sitting down beside me.

"I've tried everything. I was there when your mom came up with this one." He leaned back, studying the sky.

I followed his gaze. The sky was empty, faintly glowing with the same soft light that filled the Underworld. It was never quite dark here, but never bright enough for my tastes. "You guys really need to get a moon." I tilted my head back further. "Where are the stars?"

"This is the Underworld. The sky is just a decoration."

"Stars are pretty."

"Stars are tragic." Hades turned to face me. "Most of the stars are nothing but reminders of love gone horribly wrong, or men challenging the gods."

"I thought they were gas giants."

Hades waved his hand. "Semantics. The constellations they form are nothing but sad stories. Why would anyone want to have a constant reminder of tragedy hanging above their head?"

I thought about that for a minute, studying the blank sky. "Did you play a part in any of those tragedies?"

He met my eyes and something in them set my heart beating uncomfortably hard. "No."

I smiled. "You're nothing like I pictured you."

"Yeah, let's not go down this road again. If you start talking about how my hair should be on fire, or how evil I should be, I might take Thanatos' advice."

"You're not evil."

"You don't think so?" Hades asked, studying my face. "After what I did to you?"

"You saved me."

"I could have handled it better. I could have taken a second to think, found some way that wouldn't tie you to me." He hesitated. "But when I saw you, there was just something about you . . ." He trailed off and looked at the sky. "Maybe I didn't want to find another way. What if I wasn't just impulsive, what if I was selfish? What kind of a person does that make me?"

I burst out laughing. "Do you always over-think things so much? You saved my life. That's about as selfless as it gets. Being down here isn't convenient, and being married is a little weird, but it's just a few months. It's not like you get anything out of this, and I've been such a brat about it." I shook my head, enjoying the wave of dizziness that accompanied the motion. "Thank you, Hades. For everything. Really." I leaned over and kissed his cheek, giggling at the surprised look on his face. "I owe you, big time."

"I don't think you understand." He reached toward me. I blinked when he brushed a strand of my hair behind my ear. "It's not just a few—"

"Hey, Hades! Persephone!" Cassandra called. She laughed when she found the grove. "Oops, hope I'm not interrupting anything."

"Of course not." Hades stood, brushed himself off, and extended his hand. I lay frozen, hand touching my face where the ghost of his fingers had brushed against my skin.

"Persephone." His voice was gentle. I looked up and grabbed his hand. "We should get back to the party."

Chapter XIII

WAKING UP THE next morning, I was miserable. On top of the inevitable hangover, I also had scratches on my knuckles and a bruise on my right arm. But on the bright side, I didn't remember any nightmares. Maybe I should drink before bed more often. I laughed, and then winced at the sound. Mom would have a fit. She'd probably invented the "your body is your temple" speech. Of course in her case, I guess it kind of was.

I brushed my hair, wincing when I gripped the brush in my hand. What had happened last night? I remembered coming back to my room. Hades had dropped me off like a perfect gentleman.

I glanced down at my knuckles and gasped in surprise. There was nothing there. The skin was unbroken and unblemished. *Must have just imagined it.*

I forced myself through the day, hating the knowing smiles everyone gave me. My headache still hadn't retreated by the time I had goddess lessons with Hades.

"You're not trying hard enough." He set the bowl of M&Ms in front of me. "Charm me into giving you the red M&Ms. They're my favorite."

I looked Hades in the eyes. "Give me the red M&Ms."

"Still not good enough."

"Give me the damn M&Ms," I snapped.

He snickered. "That wasn't very charming."

I winced at the sound. "Please."

"Try harder."

I stood, pushing my chair back and moved the leather ottoman out of the way. Hades raised an eyebrow but said nothing when I touched his shoulders, looking him straight in the eye. "You *really* want to give me the M&Ms."

He pushed his chair back, breaking free of my hands. "It's not seduction, Persephone." He stood, crossing to the window and pushing back the red velvet drapes. "Just look me in the eye and tell me what you want. If you're doing it right, a person would feel compelled to give it to you."

I caught his gaze. "I want Tylenol."

His smile was sympathetic. "That was a little better."

I sighed and tried again.

OVER THE NEXT week I fell into a routine with my lessons and learned my way around the Underworld. On New Year's Eve, I retired to my room early and waited for the clock to strike twelve. There were no cheers and no fanfare. I half expected another ball, but it turned out the dead don't celebrate the passage of time.

In the entire time I'd been in the Underworld, I hadn't felt lonely until tonight. I didn't know why. It wasn't like New Year's Eve was important to me in the living realm. All I would have done was had a sleepover with Melissa, curled up on her couch watching the ball drop while eating cookie dough.

My chest constricted. I missed Melissa so much. Cassandra was turning out to be a great friend, Helen too, but I'd known Melissa since we were born. We'd never been apart this long. There was so much I wanted to tell her.

I crawled into bed, feeling the comforter fluff around me. I didn't want to sleep, I never wanted to sleep again, but I was exhausted. I'd been having horrible nightmares ever since Brumalia. The daily training—physical, mental, and divine—was starting to take its toll. Especially combined with my sleepless nights.

But the bed was so comfortable. My eyelids grew heavier and I began to drift off. With a gasp my eyes flew open. I could see the ceiling, but the edges of my vision were blurry. Tears pricked my eyes, but I couldn't blink. A weight settled on my chest. I couldn't breathe, couldn't move. My limbs were heavy, pressing into the bed. I couldn't turn my head. A scream worked its way through my throat but I couldn't unlock my jaws to let it out.

My throat went raw from my silent screams. My mind was awake but trapped in a body of dead weight. The nightmare had begun. I could never tell if I was asleep or awake when it began. Maybe I was somewhere in between.

The ceiling was white. Flakes rained from it, melting on my frozen skin. My body sank through the snow like a rock. I struggled, but my body wasn't responding.

My thoughts vanished as I heard cold, bitter laughter. Ice crept up my fingers and toes. It snaked along my limbs, the cold biting into my flesh. The wind whispered my name, and I struggled harder.

I felt something warm rise within me, and I latched on to the sensation. My mind flashed back to my few successes during my training with Hades, and the one time I'd made the flower grow. I heard footsteps crunching toward my icy tomb and knew with a quiet certainty that if they reached me I would be doomed. Dream or not, this pain felt real.

The footsteps were closer. I couldn't move my head to see the approaching figure, but the dream had never progressed this far before. I latched onto the warmth within me, and it shot through my body, releasing my limbs and unlocking my throat.

I bolted upright in bed, screaming at the top of my lungs. The sheets tangled around my legs and I frantically tore at them, ripping them in my haste to be free. The door flew open and Hades dashed into the room, motioning for a wide-eyed Cassandra to stay behind him. He looked around the room before his gaze settled on me. My scream died. I took a heaving breath and burst into tears.

"I'm sorry. I'm so sorry. It was just a stupid dream. I didn't mean to wake you up. I'm so sorry," I blubbered through chattering teeth. "I just had a nightmare. I'm sorry."

Hades' eyebrows furrowed together and he knelt beside me on the bed. "You're freezing." He touched my cheek. His hand felt so warm I instinctively leaned into it.

"I'm sorry." I gulped back tears. I couldn't seem to stop repeating myself. My heart pounded in my chest, and I couldn't catch my breath. "I'm really, really—"

Hades shushed me, wrapping a warm arm around my shoulders. With his other hand, he drew the blanket around me. "Cassandra, get Hypnos." His voice had a forced calm to it like he was talking to a caged animal. I didn't see Cassandra leave the room. I clung to Hades, shaking and crying.

"I'm so sorry I woke everyone up." My voice was hoarse.

He shushed me. When I stopped shaking he pulled away from me and looked into my damp eyes. "What did you dream?"

Something in the tone of his voice frightened me. He was trying to sound soothing, but I heard an undercurrent of rage, though I didn't feel like it was directed at me.

I started to shake again. "This is so stupid. It was just snow and ice." I shuddered. "Pretty much exactly what happened that day in the clearing, but this time Boreas was there and—"

Hades' fingers bit into my shoulders.

"You're hurting me."

"Sorry." He let go and rubbed my shoulder.

"N-nothing happened. I don't know why I was so scared. It's just . . . I felt . . ." I swallowed hard. "I couldn't move, and it was just . . . it was just—"

"How long have you been having these dreams?" His voice sounded stilted, controlled.

"I . . . I don't know. Since Brumalia, I guess."

"Why didn't you tell me?"

I looked at him, puzzled. Was he actually upset I hadn't confided in him about my nightmares?

"We're not that close."

He gave me a scathing look, and someone knocked on the door. I jumped.

"It's just Hypnos and Cassandra," he reassured me. "Do you have a robe or something?"

I flushed. It wasn't like I was wearing lingerie or anything, just an oversized Lady and the Tramp T-shirt like the one I had at home. I closed my eyes and pictured a fluffy robe, pajama bottoms, and fuzzy slippers. I was still freezing.

"Come in," Hades called.

"Did you want me to stay?" Cassandra asked me as she entered, Hypnos trailing behind her.

"For what?" I asked, puzzled. "What's going on?" I turned to Hades. "Why did you send for Hypnos? No offense."

"None taken," Hypnos assured me.

"Cassandra, you may go," Hades said.

She looked like she wanted to object but shrugged. "I'm right across the hall," she reminded me.

"Thanks," I replied.

"Hypnos is here to help you set up a mental barrier while you sleep," Hades explained after she closed the door.

I raised an eyebrow. "You guys cure nightmares? That's impressive."

Hades hesitated. "It's not nightmares we're protecting you from. It's—" He broke off, running his fingers through his hair. "Gods can use dreams to communicate with each other and certain mortals. We all have barriers in place, so another god would have to knock, so to speak."

He looked pained. "I'm sorry." His voice was so soft, only I could hear him. "It's been so long since this has happened, I didn't think about having Hypnos build a barrier for you."

Comprehension dawned on me, and I stared at Hades wide-eyed. "That was real? Boreas was in my head?" I started shaking again.

"No," Hypnos replied. "Your consciousness was in a neutral space."

"Nothing was neutral about that space," I snapped, and immediately regretted it. Hypnos hadn't done anything wrong. "I'm sorry." I cradled my head in my hands. "This is just a little much. Attacking people in dreams? Is there anything else I need to know about?"

Hades shrugged. "You forget this is as natural as breathing to us. I'm not used to having to explain such basic concepts."

"There is nothing natural or basic about gods invading your nightmares!"

"May I?" Hypnos approached the bed, holding out his hands. I looked at Hades. When he nodded, I let Hypnos take my hands into his, and felt something click into place in my mind. I shook my head at the unfamiliar sensation.

"You'll need to think of a phrase to say every night before you go to sleep," Hypnos murmured, his eyes closed.

"Not out loud," Hades cautioned.

I closed my mouth with a click, and tried to think of a phrase.

"Just think of that phrase before you go to sleep every night. It's like a lock. If for some reason you want to open yourself to communication, simply think the phrase again. I can teach you more about dreamwalking, if you wish." Hypnos smiled at me. "You may develop a talent for it."

"Thanks." I wasn't sure I could handle another set of lessons, but maybe I could surprise Boreas next time. My mind filled with dark ideas, like tossing Boreas into an incinerator. "I'd like that."

"Thank you, Hypnos," Hades said in dismissal. When Hypnos left, Hades muttered, "I don't get it."

"Don't get what?"

"Boreas shouldn't still be after you. He has to know you're down here with me by now. Coming after you is suicide." He shook his head. "A few thousand years ago, a stunt like he pulled tonight would be grounds for war."

"Are you going to do anything about it?"

Hades shook his head. "Something else is going on here. I need to find out what that is before I act."

With that unsettling thought, he left me to go back to sleep.

Yeah, right.

Chapter XIV

"YOU HAVE ABSOLUTELY no talent for dreamwalking," Hypnos hissed in frustration.

"I'll say," Hades muttered from the divan.

"Maybe if my target was actually sleeping," I snapped.

"I can only sleep so much in a day. If I sleep any longer I'll be in a coma."

"Let's try again." Hypnos took a deep breath. "Hades, sleep."

Hades fell mercifully silent, and I sank into the soft leather couch. The room Hypnos had selected to teach me dreamwalking looked like it should belong to a therapist. Aquamarine curtains covered the windows, casting the room in a soft blue glow.

I closed my eyes and felt Hypnos' powers settle over me, pulling me through layers of sleep. *Hades.* I directed my thoughts. I could sense the energy of other sleeping deities. It was a weird sensation, like catching a glimpse of something out of the corner of your eye only to have it move before you turned your head.

The minds of the gods twinkled in the darkness, reminding me of stars scattered in the vast emptiness. Hypnos had spent the last month getting me to the point where I could sense who was who. It was easier to identify gods I'd met. Thanatos was a guarded cloak of darkness; Hypnos shone like the sun; Hestia smoldered in the night; Charon cast an amicable glow. I found my mother, green and thriving, and Boreas' frozen fortress.

Despite the name, dreamwalking was nothing like walking around. I couldn't keep my distance from gods I didn't like, or get close to another. They all existed, suspended in this disorienting space; the only thing that changed was my awareness of them. If I stopped concentrating on them, they faded into darkness and I could slip into my own dreams without fear of Boreas following me.

Boreas hadn't tried anything since that last awful dream. Maybe Hades was wrong. Maybe Boreas would back off, now that I was protected on all fronts. I doubted he wanted Hades to come after him, but maybe being unprotected in my sleep had been too much for him to resist.

"Persephone!" Hypnos' frustrated voice startled me as it flooded my consciousness. Right. . . . I was supposed to be concentrating.

Since it was the middle of the day, there weren't as many gods to navigate. It was easy to find Hades. He was a bundle of dark energy. I concentrated on sending a small pulse of energy his way. It was a weird feeling, gathering the energy in my mind and aiming it at someone without intention.

To do anything else with my powers, intention was half the battle. I had to keep my mind on exactly what I was doing and what the desired outcome was. It was the difference between planning an arrangement— placing every flower just so to complete my vision—and throwing a flower in the general direction of a vase.

After several tries, I found myself in the library. The bookshelves blurred around me and I rubbed my eyes.

"Thank the gods," Hades said. He was in hyper focus in the center of the blurry room.

"Okay." Hypnos clapped his hands. He looked at Hades and then around the library with an eyebrow raised in question.

Hades shrugged, turning his head toward me. "You did it."

"I did!" I grinned. "Now what can I do?"

"Nothing," Hades and Hypnos said simultaneously. I frowned at them.

"I can continue to work with you if you like . . ." Hypnos sounded less than thrilled at the prospect. "But I have to be honest, you have absolutely no natural talent for dreamwalking. It's not your fault; it's just not in your bloodline."

"Oh." My ego deflated. I'd never been bad at anything before. I always picked up whatever sport or skill I'd been trying to learn like it was second nature. But those were human skills. Divine stuff was different. Even learning to use my own powers was difficult, and dreamwalking was Hypnos' specialty. I nixed my half-formed plan to leave my mind unguarded and ambush Boreas in a dream. He'd had much more practice at this than I had.

"Thank you, Hypnos," Hades said.

"My pleasure. You two should be waking in a few minutes. I'll see you later."

He vanished and I looked at Hades. "He left! What if I get stuck or something?"

"Getting out is easier than getting in. I think Hypnos needed a break." Hades snickered, picking up a book. "I've never seen him stressed. You're really terrible at this."

I sat down on the brown blur of a chair. "Yeah, you told me." I picked up a simple wooden picture frame that I knew didn't exist in the library.

"You've learned enough to protect yourself and to communicate with other gods. That's all you should ever need." His eyes widened when he saw me with the picture frame. "Hey, put that down!"

I stared at the photo in shock. It was me, and yet it wasn't. I was in the clearing, surrounded by ice and snow. I looked radiant and defiant. The image was so vivid and clear that it took me right back to that terrifying moment when I'd first seen Hades.

"Is this how you see me?" I put the picture frame down. The girl in that photo wasn't just pretty, she looked ethereal and confident and completely out of sync with the mental image I had of myself.

"I guess." Hades shrugged at my confused expression. "I don't know what's on that frame. Dreams are weird. Remember, this isn't my mind, it's a neutral space. My mind just decorated it. That picture could have just as easily come from you."

"I doubt *that.*"

Hades turned bright red and snatched the frame. His shoulders relaxed when he saw the picture. I tilted my head to the side. What had he thought was on that frame?

"Rule of etiquette," he explained, setting the frame down. "Never look too closely at anything in the dreamscape if you're using this as a means of communication. It's rude."

My cheeks heated. "Sorry."

"Don't apologize. This actually brings up a good point. There's more to protecting yourself than just creating a neutral space and locking your mind. If you do choose to meet with another god in your dreams, be on guard. You don't want to reveal too much about yourself." In a flash the picture frame was gone. "Did Hypnos show you how to create a dreamscape?" When I nodded, Hades asked, "Could you show me?"

I closed my eyes, and the room shifted to a simple meadow filled with wildflowers. The blades of yellow grass were an indistinct blur with splashes of white, yellow, pink, and green dabbed at random. I didn't have the power to fuel details.

"Good. No personal details to glean here, but not so impersonal it feels like an insult. It makes sense you'd choose a meadow."

"So why choose the library?" I asked, surprised. The room was his sanctuary. I couldn't think of a place more personal to him in the entire Underworld.

"That's not my usual meeting place. I just figured you'd be more comfortable there."

"I think it may be one of my favorite places." In truth it wasn't the library I enjoyed, but my lessons with Hades. They were always the perfect end to a hectic day of breakfast with Cassandra, gardening, dream lessons with Hypnos, history lessons with Hestia, self-defense from Charon, running, and dinner with the group.

Hades and I would banter back and forth for a while, and then he would show me what I was capable of. The worship from the souls gave me just enough of a boost that I could practice. I was still learning the finer aspects of charm, and Hades was showing me things I could only do in the Underworld. Maybe one day we'd get to teleporting.

"My library is your favorite place in the Underworld? Not the gardens?"

Hades had given me free rein over the gardens to practice my ability to make the delicate blossoms bloom. I had a blank slate to create living arrangements in any place I wanted.

Working with the soil reminded me of my mother. I could imagine her sitting on the ground, covered in dirt, tending to some precious sapling. It made me feel connected to her.

I wondered what she would think of all the time I was spending with Hades. I was spending just as much time with Cassandra and Helen, and Thanatos had become my constant companion. But it was different with Hades.

He was watching me, waiting for me to respond, and suddenly I wasn't sure what to say. It wasn't the library or the lessons that made this my favorite place. It was him.

I felt my body waking and the dream faded around me. I sat up. Across the room Hades did the same. I smiled at his disheveled hair. "Nice look."

"Yeah, you too."

My hand went to my hair and my mind flashed to the picture. I couldn't help but wonder how he saw me at this moment. There was an awkward silence as we made our way out of the room. I found Thanatos and headed to the garden.

I DUG INTO THE soil, feeling the energy that pulsed through the packed earth. I focused on bringing new life to this small patch of land and smiled when a dandelion bloomed.

"You're going to be late." Thanatos yawned.

I started in surprise. I hadn't meant to stay in the garden this long. I stood and brushed myself off.

Thanatos laughed. "Here." He reached toward my face and brushed dirt off my cheek. "Can't have you looking like that in court."

"How beautiful!" a voice called out, followed by sounds of agreement.

Thanatos shifted in front of me, and I looked past him to a group of middle-aged women in jogging gear.

"Would you look at these flowers?" A woman in a purple jogging suit let out a low whistle.

The group noticed me and Thanatos, and I heard gasped whispers mentioning the queen.

"Oh, no," I said, approaching them. "Call me Persephone." I held out my hand and a woman wearing pink sneakers shook it.

"Well, hello, Persephone. I'm Gloria."

"We're going to be late," Thanatos reminded me.

"I just love these flowers," the woman said, motioning to the group of dandelions forming a sun design, bordered by bluebells. "I'd just love to have some of these decorating my house, you know, one of those window boxes, but I just can't seem to keep anything alive. Even here!"

The women behind her laughed.

"I could make one for you, if you like."

"Court . . ." Thanatos sounded impatient.

"Later," I amended. "I'll set up a shop in the suburbs."

"Oh, that would be wonderful, dear."

I grinned at her, managing a hurried wave as Thanatos rushed me to the palace.

"I don't know why I even go to court," I admitted, touching my face to check for any dirt.

"You're clear," he assured me. "Why not?"

I fell into step beside him. "I don't really do anything. I just sit there. I'm no help at all to the souls."

"You're a goddess. You can help them as much as Hades could. Maybe more. What do they ask for?"

"To go home."

Thanatos mulled that over. "Anything else?"

I thought for a moment. "They want to make sure their loved ones are safe."

"Well . . . why not help with that? You have people on the surface, right?"

I hadn't thought of that. I'd blindly followed Hades' lead all month, assuming if he wasn't acting, I shouldn't either. That was stupid. He may have more experience, but Thanatos was right. I had far more ties to the outside world than Hades.

And if their people aren't safe? Should I ask Mom to intervene? I considered that. That would be asking my mother to take on a colossal amount of work, and this seemed like the sort of thing that could quickly get out of hand.

We're goddesses. Isn't this our responsibility?

Yes, I decided. As long as I remained in the Underworld, I would do what I could to help the souls. If my mother didn't like it, well, after lying to me for sixteen years, she could get over it.

Chapter XV

"NEXT," HADES CALLED.

I shifted under the gaze of the man who came forward. He was staring at me. I should be used to this by now. The souls stared at Hades and me as if we were . . . well, *gods*, but I wasn't comfortable with the attention.

"Kora?"

I looked at the man again and did a double take. "Orpheus?" I exclaimed in disbelief. "Wha—how did you die?"

"You two know each other?" Hades glanced between the two of us.

"You don't?" Cassandra leaned forward in her seat. "That's only the most famous singer topside right now. You know . . ."—she sang a line from "Mortus Dei"—" . . . that guy."

"Um, thank you," Orpheus said with a modest nod to Cassandra before turning back to me. "What are you doing down here?"

"I can't believe you remember me." I beamed. Hades and Cassandra exchanged glances, and I elbowed Hades. "I met him and his wife backstage at a concert."

"How exciting," Hades replied dryly. "Kora?"

"My middle name." I turned to Orpheus. "You can call me Persephone down here. How can we help you?"

"Your middle name is Kora?"

I gave Hades a look. "And that's somehow stranger than Persephone?"

"More generic, for sure. It's Greek for girl."

I blinked. Mom had named me *girl*? That was pretty generic. No wonder she didn't like me going by my middle name.

Orpheus spoke up. "Last time I saw you, you didn't even know you were a goddess. How did you end up down here? You don't look like you belong with the chthonic group. No offense," he said to Hades.

"Not that it's any of your business, but her parents are Olympian," Hades replied.

"Chthonic? Olympian? What are you guys talking about?"

"Chthonic deities are gods associated with the Underworld. We tend to have darker features." Hades motioned to his black hair. "Olympians were associated with Olympus, and were various shades of blond. The primordials tended to represent their element to the extreme, and the Titans were . . . well, titanic in size."

I blinked. Gods were classified by appearance? I supposed it wasn't relevant anymore with so few of us left, but the whole system seemed strange to me. None of that mattered, though, because Orpheus remembered the last time he saw me! I was sure my face was bright red. Hades sighed, no doubt bored by the whole conversation.

"How I got down here is a long story," I replied. *He wants to know my life story!*

"What can we do for you?" Hades repeated impatiently.

"Well, you see, I haven't died yet."

That news caused stirring amongst the judges. They muttered, glancing at each other. Hades shot a look at Cassandra.

"Then how did you come to be here?" she asked.

"My mother is the muse Calliope—"

"I should have known you were a demigod!" I interrupted. "I didn't know about the eyes thing when I met you, but it was so obvious. I mean, well, if anyone was a demigod it would be you."

"Well—" Orpheus shifted uncomfortably "—I'm human for all practical purposes. I'm just gifted with music."

I sighed. "You sure are." *Oh my God! Did I just say that out loud?* How humiliating.

"Calliope herself is a fairly minor deity," Hades explained, ignoring my faux pas. "Well, sub-deity. She's a singer of some renown herself. You may know her as . . ." He paused. "What does she go by now, Cassandra?"

Cassandra supplied the name, and my jaw dropped. "*She's* your mother?"

Orpheus shrugged. "Yes, but we don't advertise that fact. The lack of age difference would be difficult to explain."

"I was under the impression there weren't many deities left. Is there like a club or something? I'd love to talk to someone a bit closer to my own age . . ." I trailed off when I realized everyone was looking at me.

"You'll be on the surface again then?" Orpheus asked. "You're a psychopomp?"

"A psycho what?"

"A god that can travel between realms," Hades replied. "It's her privilege as my wife. It is not extended to any other mortals, gods, or—" He gave Orpheus a significant look "—demigods."

"My mother showed me an entrance in Italy, in a crater west of Naples, that leads here." He looked at Hades. "I was able to get through. You may want to get that taken care of."

"How were you able to get through Tartarus?" I asked Orpheus, amazed.

"My mother told me only innocents could cross through the river of fire," Orpheus said, shrugging. "Guess I'm innocent enough."

I guess the fail-safe does work if you're alive. Good to know. Cassandra and I exchanged looks. I had a feeling a girls' night was in the works.

"What is so important to you that it is worth traveling through the fires of Hell?" Hades asked.

"My wife, Eurydice. We were hiking, and a snake bit her. I couldn't get help in time. She died." He looked up at us, his eyes glassy with emotion. "I have to get her back."

Hades nodded. "I'm afraid you've come a long way for nothing."

I glanced at Hades. "There has to be something—"

"That's enough, Persephone."

"If you would allow me to present my case in song?"

Hades sighed heavily, but at my excited look, nodded at Orpheus. Orpheus waited a beat, and then opened his mouth to sing a heart-wrenching song begging for his wife back. Coming from anyone else it would have seemed cheesy, but as his voice filled the room, I could feel my own heart breaking for him.

Tears stung my eyes when he'd finished his song. "We have to do something."

"Persephone—" Hades sighed.

I turned to Moirae. "Is it possible?"

She looked startled. "Yes, my queen."

I blinked at the title. For the past month, when Moirae wasn't glaring at me like she'd like to witness my crucifixion, she pretended I didn't exist. I mostly returned the favor.

I smiled at Hades flirtatiously and laid a hand on his. I felt a little silly, but I might as well put that charm to a good cause.

"It would mean a lot to me," I whispered, looking at him through heavy lashes. I was startled to see his face change. He looked completely unguarded. That never happened during goddess lessons.

"Uh . . ." Hades shook his head. "Does anyone know she's dead yet?"

"Just my mother," Orpheus replied, pretending not to notice the scene that had just taken place. "I summoned her when . . . obviously she couldn't help Eurydice. She stayed with her . . . body, just in case I was able to return with her soul."

"Call the soul in question forward," Hades instructed Moirae. "Orpheus, turn away."

Eurydice materialized before us.

"Is this woman judged to be of great good or great evil?" Hades asked.

"Neither, my lord," Moirae responded.

"Very well, then. Orpheus, you must leave the way you entered. There is no other way you can return to the world of the living."

"Is she here?" Orpheus asked. He started to turn.

"Do not look at her!" Hades' voice rang with a frightening authority that froze Orpheus in place. "You two may leave, but you cannot look upon her until she is returned to the realm of the living. Her soul will reunite with her body once you reach the surface, but if you see her in this form she will not be able to return."

She looked the same as she had when I'd seen her alive. I looked at Cassandra.

"There's a difference to humans," Cassandra whispered to me. "Hades isn't trying to make it hard for them; it's just the way it works. If anyone learns of her death before they return, it won't work either. Acknowledgement makes the death final."

"But Orpheus knows."

"The rules are gray when it comes to demigods."

"Thank you!" Orpheus exclaimed. "I will make this up to you, I promise." He closed his eyes and turned toward us, giving an awkward bow.

"Good luck," I called.

"Cassandra, would you please guide them as far as Tartarus? I will arrange for someone to take them from there." Hades motioned for Moirae and the judges to leave the room.

"Of course." She positioned Eurydice behind Orpheus. "Let's go."

Hades waited until Cassandra led the couple out of the throne room before turning to me. "We're alone."

"We are," I agreed, standing nervously.

Hades stood and moved closer to me, pressing me against the wall. I drew in a shuddering breath as Hades leaned closer, his lips almost brushing mine.

He's going to kiss me, I realized. My heart thudded; I wasn't prepared for this. I hadn't thought the whole goddess-charm thing through so well.

"Uh . . . Hades," I squeaked, my lips touching his as I spoke. I swallowed hard. Damn, Hades was hot. My heart was beating a hundred miles a minute and sped up as Hades grinned at me.

"There's something you need to know, little goddess," he whispered, turning his face so his breath tickled my ear. It felt really good. He smiled, and my heart froze. It wasn't a nice smile. "I am much stronger than you. You cannot use your little tricks on me. I am immune, you stupid child. I'll forgive this one transgression, but if you ever try to manipulate my affections again, I will not be so accommodating. Do you understand?"

My cheeks colored in embarrassment. "In practice, I always get you to give me the red M&M's."

"That was a device to let you know when you were using enough charm to affect a human," he snapped. "I got it from a human parenting manual. I didn't think you were stupid enough to believe you could use your charm against me."

My eyes flashed. I remembered mother telling me the only way she'd found to potty train me was giving me M&M's. I was not flattered by the comparison. "Well, that tells me everything I need to know."

He wrinkled his brow in confusion. "About what?"

I shook my head, feeling stupid. "You know, for a moment I thought maybe— Never mind. I know exactly how you see me now. I'm nothing but a child."

"How else would I see you?"

"Get away from me!" I pushed him away. When he didn't budge I glared at him.

"Tell me you will never attempt to charm me again."

I narrowed my eyes at him. Even I knew better than to throw around words like *never.* I could only speak the truth, and future intent got messy when you couldn't lie.

He seemed to realize what he was asking, and shook his head. "Just . . . don't. How would you feel if I could just look into your eyes and make you do something that you didn't want to?"

He was right. I dropped my gaze to the floor. I'd tried to control him, to strip him of his will. "I'm sorry," I whispered. "I won't—"

"Stop," he warned me. "You don't know what the future holds." He sighed. "Helping Orpheus was unusually stupid of you."

"If I can help someone, I will. I'm done watching people suffer."

"You can't save everyone," Hades said, his voice gentling. He drew a deep breath and took a small step away from me. "The sooner you realize that, the better it will be for you."

"I'm not suggesting we return everyone to life, but it was possible in this situation."

"So?"

"So! He literally went through Hell to save her! Her death was a pointless accident. It wasn't fair!"

"Life isn't fair! Why should death be any different?"

"Did you ever stop and wonder if maybe that attitude is why the gods are dead?" I asked. "People don't believe in gods because they can't wrap their minds around the idea of someone allowing all the terrible things in the world to happen."

"Reality has teeth and claws. It's rarely pretty and never fair. Haven't you figured that out yet?"

I clenched my fists. "Why? I get that no one has the power to interfere now, but when the gods were in power, how could they let things get this bad? You're here every day! You hear the stories of murder, thievery, and worse. You see the children who starved to death. This isn't a recent development. Why didn't you stop it?"

"We gave humans free will—"

"That's bull!" I exploded. "If you have the power to stop someone from getting killed and don't, you're just as guilty as whoever pulled the trigger."

"Where do you draw that line, Persephone? There are billions of humans, and a handful of us—"

"Who allowed humans to get to the billions? That was greed, plain and simple. More humans equaled more worship. And really, between the God of Mist, the God of Doorways, and the god of every other useless thing, you couldn't at least *try?*"

"You're angry. I understand. You didn't see this side of the world back in your flower shop. Your mother kept you sheltered. It's a bit of a shock at first, but—"

"But what? Over time I'll get used to it? Used to seeing children in the court of the dead? Used to watching husbands cry over lost wives? Why *should* I get used to it when I can do something *about* it?"

"You can't save everyone. You just don't have that power."

"But you did! You each had the power to grant immortality!" I threw my hands in the air. "Why were only some people given the gift?

My mother has the power to make things grow anywhere. How come people are still starving? Are you all so full of yourselves that you think you're any more deserving of these gifts than any one of those humans?"

Hades took me by the shoulders. The cold marble pressed against my back. I ground my teeth, raising my chin to meet his eyes, trying to catch my breath. "Persephone—"

The door to the throne room slammed open and a dripping wet Charon stormed into the room. "What the hell, Moirae? You can't just zap people out of my boat. It knocked the whole thing off balance—"

He froze when he saw Hades and me.

"Um . . ." He took a step backward. "I'm really . . . I'm going to go."

"No," I said coldly, pushing Hades away from me with all my strength. He rolled his eyes and stepped away. "I was just leaving."

I STORMED OUT of the castle. I'd made my big speech with my big promises, completely forgetting that my big power was making flowers bloom. Like that could help anyone!

Don't forget your awesome charisma. I snorted, walking along the River Styx. To think I'd considered. . . . Hades sucked. I wanted a guy like Orpheus. Orpheus had gone through Tartarus to rescue his wife—*that* was love. Hades probably didn't even know the meaning of the word love.

That was the problem with gods. They could never sacrifice for love like humans did. How could they possibly understand emotions as well as we—

I stopped walking. *I'm not human.*

I'd accepted the fact I was a goddess, but it felt more like my title than my species. I hadn't considered that I wasn't human. Would I be as detached as Hades was in a few hundred years? Was that my future? Would I ever feel the kind of love that would drive me to walk through Hell for the other person if they needed it?

Not from Hades, that was for sure. "How else would I see you?" I mocked, throwing in a heavy sigh for good measure. I didn't know why I cared. It wasn't like I felt anything for him. He was annoying, proud, he sighed all the time, and he was inconsiderate. Well, that wasn't always true. Sometimes he was good, kind, and comforting. Like after I had my nightmare, he'd held me and—

I swore, scowling at my reflection in the crystalline waters.

"Persephone!" Thanatos called. He walked quickly to catch up to me.

I walked faster. "Leave me alone."

"What happened? What did he do?" Thanatos took a few steps at a run over the grass-covered hill until he reached my side.

"I don't want to talk about it, and I don't want company." At his hurt look I softened my tone. "Sorry, I just . . . You said not to think of you as a guard, remember?"

He nodded. "Right. We're friends."

"Then be my friend. Give me some space right now, okay? I can't think unless I'm alone, and I'm never alone here. There's always some-one—" I took a deep breath. "I shouldn't have to hide in my room if I want some space."

Thanatos hesitated. "Okay," he agreed. "I'm going to walk away, I'll be at the bottom of the hill, out of sight, out of hearing range, out of mind, I hope. Take as much time as you need. Just promise to come get me when you're done. And please, don't wander off."

I looked around, surprised to find I was next to the thin ribbon of fire that marked the boundary of Tartarus. I hadn't been paying atten-tion to where I was walking. I'd just walked away from Thanatos.

"Okay," I said. "I'll stick around."

He nodded, but his face was troubled, like he had misgivings about leaving me by myself. But true to his word he walked down the large green hill. He faded from sight and I sat down at the edge of the river of flames and watched them dance wickedly down their slope. It *was* a river, not a wall of fire as I'd assumed in Latin class. I could see clearly to the other side, but there was nothing there. The landscape continued into the distance unchanged. A trick of the eye, maybe? If *I* was sentenced to Hell, I'd stay by the river my whole afterlife in hopes I could somehow escape.

It wouldn't make sense for the good to have to watch the bad suffer for all eternity, I mused, but the other way around would be torturous. What if, on the other side of the fire, I was being watched? There could be someone standing a mere foot from me and I wouldn't be able to see them because of some magic trick.

The river was beautiful; it would be pretty cool to just touch it . . .

Entranced, I knelt by the water's edge and held my hand over the flames. I could feel heat, but it wasn't as blistering as I'd imagined it would be. I touched my fingertip to the flame, grinning when it didn't burn.

"How cool." I took a furtive glance around then stuck my hand into the river. It felt wet. Not like fire at all. I grinned, entertaining thoughts about swimming in the river of flames as I watched them curl over my hand. Something snaked through the river and wrapped around my wrist.

The shock barely registered before I felt a sudden yank. I screamed as I was pulled across the river.

Chapter XVI

I GASPED AS I was pulled through the river of fire and into Tartarus. I didn't get burned, but I felt frozen inside. I stumbled, shocked, and landed on the icy red sand. It was so cold it burned. I was stunned at the sudden change from idyllic scenery to elemental horror. The sky was black, with neon green and bright blue flashes of lightning lancing through the sky, revealing frightening shapes and deformed creatures crawling over the sand.

Someone stood beside me, his hand still gripping my wrist. My mind screamed at me to stop looking at the scenery and face this new threat, but I couldn't move. I couldn't tear my eyes away from the terrible sight. My chest heaved as I struggled to catch my breath. I couldn't seem to breathe here. My skirt dripped tiny flames. The burning cold sapped away my strength. I tore my gaze from the landscape and struggled to turn my head to the side.

"Pirithous!" Adrenaline filled my veins, giving me the strength to scurry away from him with a half shriek that came out sounding more like a terrified squeak.

I took a deep breath, trying to calm myself like Charon taught me. My heart thundered in my chest and every instinct told me to get up and run. I struggled to my feet, eyes widening when I took in Pirithous' changed appearance.

He stepped forward, face gaunt. He looked like a walking skeleton, with cracked and dried skin hanging off his bones. He didn't have an ounce of fat or muscle left on his body. I recoiled when I saw that his eyes were yellow and his hair was falling out in patches.

"What happened?" The question was ridiculous. I shouldn't care what happened to him; I should be running. But the change was so drastic, so far beyond my comprehension, that the question just slipped out. I took a small step backward toward the river, hoping Pirithous wouldn't notice.

"I followed a tip on where to find you, and met a woman named Doso. Turns out she was your mother in disguise. She cursed me with eternal hunger." He laughed bitterly. "I eat all day, and it doesn't matter. I'm starving!"

I couldn't reconcile the image of my loving mother causing a person—any person—enough suffering to look as bad as Pirithous did right now. "My mom made you starve to death?" I asked, taking another small step. My foot brushed against the water, the freezing heat searing my toes.

"Oh, she won't let me die that easily. Luckily, someone else took an interest in me. He showed me this entrance to the Underworld. Didn't know I'd be walking through Hell, but the people here didn't bother me. I guess when you look like this—" Pirithous held up his arm, and I shuddered when I realized I could see the skin between his bones touching. Every vein strained against the gaunt flesh, a landscape of blue bumps. The bones protruded from his paper-thin skin. "—they figure you belong in Hell."

"You came here for *me*?" I needed to keep him talking. If he got distracted enough I could make it across the river. I'd be free as soon as I got onto the shore. I just needed to find the strength to run.

"I couldn't cross the river." His bony fingers dug into my arm. "So I watched and waited. You came." He grinned, the action stretching his skin even tighter across his face. "I knew you would."

I yanked my arm free, rubbing it in disgust. "Haven't you learned your lesson yet? My mother didn't put this curse on you because you asked me out for coffee. This kidnapping thing is never going to end well for you."

"Oh, I don't want you anymore."

Something was draining my energy, but it had to be affecting Pirithous, too. I thought fast. I was weaker than usual but that didn't mean I was at a disadvantage.

"Then what? Revenge? You can't kill a goddess," I said, with more bravado than I felt. Every word I spoke left my lips reluctantly. All I wanted to do was curl up in the sand and go to sleep. Only fear kept me on my feet.

"I found another god interested in your whereabouts. He approached me after your mother cursed me. Said if I could bring you back, he'd fix me."

"Boreas," I guessed, the name sending a fresh flow of terror through my veins. I fought to keep it from showing on my face. I took another microscopic step into the water.

Pirithous' hand shot out to grab me, but I shook him off easily.

Rage danced through his eyes. He obviously knew Tartarus made us both too weak to put up much of a struggle. However, I was mere feet away from freedom, whereas he had an entire dimension of hell to drag me through before reaching the surface.

"What was your plan here?" I demanded. "Drag me through Hell kicking and screaming? You think you have the strength for that?"

"I'm starving," Pirithous snapped. "I'll—"

"Are you going for the sympathy vote here? I couldn't care less whether you live or die. You ruined my life. As far as I'm concerned, you brought this on yourself."

I reached out and shoved his emaciated shoulders, knocking him to the ground. I turned and splashed through the flames.

Pirithous dove for me, dragging me back onto shore with surprising strength. I pushed against him, pulling him through the fire. The fire froze my insides, sending me gasping in shock.

"I'll just have to ask for help!" Pirithous hissed. He turned and yelled at the top of his lungs. "Hey fellas, I've got a live one!"

In a rush of strength, he heaved me onto the shore. I hit the sand and rolled out from under him, springing to my feet. Someone cackled. I turned and saw strange hunched creatures approaching us. They were small, twisted, and bent over to the height of a five-year-old child. Their hairless bodies shuffled toward us, dark eyes glittering with malice. Their skin was bleached, and their noses had collapsed in on their faces. Horror washed over me as I remembered these creatures had once been human.

My blood froze in my veins as I recognized all of the "Bobs" Charon had pulled from Tartarus for my self-defense class.

"Oh shit." Their eyes glittered with hatred when they recognized me. This had to be a huge realm. How could they possibly all be here?

"Well, now, how did you end up on this side of the river?" Bob wheezed, black lips opening to reveal sharp nasty teeth.

I tried to back away, but Pirithous held me in place. I squirmed, trying to get free as more monsters surrounded me.

"This one's got spirit," another one taunted.

"Not for long," one laughed, reaching out to touch my face. I shrieked, squirming away from his hand.

"Now, now," he said. "That's not the way a lady behaves." He slapped me so hard I yelped in indignation.

"Make that noise again," one hissed, salivating. "I liked it."

I squeezed my eyes shut as he stroked my shoulder. My heart was trying to beat right out of my chest. I shuddered at his touch, fear making me hypersensitive to the sensation. *Oh gods, help me!* I felt them move in closer around me.

Another soul touched me and I lashed out. I kicked Pirithous in the shins. The brittle bone snapped when I kicked it. I slammed my head back, smashing in his nose, and drove my elbow into Pirithous' gut. He howled, falling to a heap behind me. The souls surged forward, knocking me to the ground.

"No!" I managed to free one of my hands and throw a punch but they quickly wrestled it back to the ground. I was pinned.

Pirithous smiled his creepy skeletal grin and leaned close to my face. "Not so confident now, are you?"

I lunged forward, teeth tearing at a chunk of his throat. He yelped. His fist drew back and smashed into my face. "You stupid bitch!" His hands closed around my throat.

"Hey, leave her conscious," one of the souls protested. "It's more fun when they struggle." Its hand snaked up my thigh and I twisted, trying to squirm my way free. For a second all I could hear was the souls laughing. Then the wind picked up, whipping around with such intensity that Pirithous stumbled forward.

"Get your hands off my wife!" Hades thundered, appearing in our midst with his cloak flapping.

The dead scattered. Hades caught the squirming figure that had touched me by the throat. "I'm going to send you to a place so horrific you'll think the fifty years you spent here were a vacation." He snapped his fingers, and it vanished.

Hades pulled me close, casting a glare out over the landscape for any stragglers.

"Moirae can deal with the rest. Are you all right?" he asked, concern gathering in his eyes. He untied his black cape and set it gently on my wet shoulders. I pulled it around myself, shivering.

"Forgive me," Pirithous begged, prostrating himself before Hades. "I am desperate, my lord. Grant me death, grant me anything, but make this hunger stop."

Hades looked him up and down. "Demeter's handiwork, I take it?"

I shrugged.

"Very well." Hades snapped his fingers. The Underworld rushed past us in a nauseating whirl. When it stabilized around us I saw we were standing in the banquet room.

"Eat." He motioned Pirithous toward the banquet table. "I'll deal with you later."

Pirithous ravenously shoveled food in his mouth. I stared at Hades in shock. I'd expected him to do a lot of things, but inviting Pirithous to dinner was not one of them.

Hades touched my arm and nodded to the door. "Would you like to get some rest, my dear?"

Dear? "No," I said slowly. "What are you—"

"Cassandra?" Hades called when she peeked into the room. "Why don't you take Persephone and—"

"No, thank you." I clutched his hand. "Could I stay with you for a little while?"

Warring emotions danced in Hades' eyes as Pirithous ate ravenously behind us. "You're freezing." He rubbed my hands between his.

"Please don't make me leave."

He made a motion with his hand, and I could no longer hear Pirithous in the background.

"What just happened?"

"They can't hear us now." Hades watched Pirithous eat. "Are you sure you're okay?" He tilted my chin up, studying my face.

I nodded. "That was—" I took a shuddering breath. "Thank you so much."

Hades nodded, looking distracted. His fingers traced my cheek where Pirithous' punch had landed. A pulse of energy passed through me and every bump and bruise from the fight stopped hurting.

"No, seriously," I continued. "I don't know what would have happened if you hadn't shown up."

Hades stepped back, surveying me with a critical eye. His jaw tightened. "I know *exactly* what would have happened. Cassandra saw the whole thing."

I shuddered at the thought.

Anger burned in Hades' eyes. "What is the matter with you? You were alone for, what, ten minutes? Ten minutes, and you go to the one and only place in this entire realm where you could possibly come to harm!"

"I—" My mouth dropped open as I scrambled for some answer. Where had the man I'd seen a moment ago gone? I wanted the nice Hades back, the one with the look of concern, and possibly even fear, marring his otherwise perfect face.

"What were you thinking? First Orpheus and now this. Have you completely lost your mind? If you have some kind of death wish, I can send you to Boreas!"

"Hades!"

"Protecting you from him is easy, but how the hell am I supposed to protect you from yourself?"

"Hey!" I objected. "How was I supposed to know I could get pulled across the river?"

"I can't always save you!"

"Why do you even bother?" Tears sprang to my eyes. I shivered violently, clutching his cloak tighter around me. "You just think I'm in the way, and all I ever do is screw up. Why don't you just send me to Boreas? It would save you a lot of trouble."

"Why do I bother?" Hades asked, surprised. "You really haven't figured that out?"

I met his eyes, searching for answers. "You were afraid," I whispered, surprised.

"For you," Hades clarified. The heat left his voice, leaving only weariness. "Yeah. You could have been really hurt, and I might not have made it in time." He reached out and grabbed me by the shoulders. "Look, I'm sorry I yelled, but you have to stop throwing yourself into these situations. You could have been hurt."

I nodded, gritting my teeth to stop from trembling. Hades seemed to notice my shaking for the first time and sighed. "I'm sorry I yelled. I just . . . That was terrifying."

I nodded. "Yeah. It was." My voice quavered.

He hesitated, and then pulled me into a hug. I clung to him, taking shuddering breaths, fighting back tears. I was still shaking, still frightened by what had happened in Tartarus, but Hades had saved me.

My grip tightened. "Thank you."

He pulled back, eyes going to the table where Pirithous was eating. "Why don't you go with Cassandra while I take care of something."

His voice was gentle, and there was something in the way he looked at me that made my knees go weak.

I didn't think; I just acted. Quick as a thought I rose onto my tiptoes and kissed Hades full on the lips. He stiffened in surprise, then for a moment he relaxed and kissed me back, hand rising to touch my face.

He broke free of the kiss with a curse. "I can't do this," he swore and took a few steps backward.

"Why not?" I asked breathlessly.

"I'm not Zeus. I don't just go around—" He ran his fingers through his hair, frustrated. "I have standards."

I felt as if I'd been slapped. "I see."

"No! Damn it, that's not what I meant. You're just a child—"

"How else would you see me?"

Hades narrowed his eyes when he recognized his line. "Is that what got you so upset?"

Screw it. I'd already humiliated myself by kissing him. What else did I have to lose?

"Could you just tell me how you feel about me? Do you hate me? Can you even stand me? Because every now and then I see something and I think that you might . . . that you might have feelings for me, but then you do or say something so frustrating and I don't know. This back and forth thing is driving me crazy!"

He laughed. "*I'm* driving *you* crazy? You offer to bring people back from the dead and run off to Tartarus if I say the wrong thing! You're driving me insane!"

My heart sank. "So you *do* hate me?"

"Hate you? No! I—" He broke off, running his fingers through his hair. "I'm in love with you. I've been in love with you since the moment I laid eyes on you in the clearing . . ." He trailed off, looking to the side as if he could see me there. My mind flashed back to the picture in his dream and my eyes widened. "You're beautiful, and kind, and everything I could ever want, but that doesn't change the fact that you're eons younger than me. However much I'd like it to. Pursuing this in any way would be taking advantage of you, and I'm not going to do that."

My mind reeled. I hadn't been expecting that. I didn't know if I was in love with Hades, but I definitely had feelings for him. When I found my voice I said, "Who *isn't* younger than you? People make too big of a deal over age. It's just a number. I'm old enough to know what I want, and—"

"You're not even old enough to know who you are," Hades interrupted. "And you have no idea what I'm capable of. There's no need to rush anything. One good thing about being immortal is that we've got unlimited time to figure things out."

I opened my mouth to respond, but was cut off by a commotion behind Hades. Pirithous was thrashing around on the ground, clawing at his throat. Hades glanced at him and flashed me a dark smile.

"Now here we are." He waved his hand through the air. "Persephone, go with Cassandra."

"What's happening?" I asked as Pirithous' screams became audible.

"Get it out!" Pirithous roared. "Get it out of me!"

Hades shrugged. "I fed him."

Pirithous retched blood and shrieked in agony.

"Would you like some more?" Hades asked as he strode across the wooden floor. Pirithous was lifted from the floor by an unseen force and forced onto one of the banquet chairs.

"No! No! Please, no!" Pirithous shrieked as his hand moved inexorably to his plate.

I watched wide-eyed as Pirithous crammed food into his mouth, sobbing in agony.

"Did you actually believe," Hades asked, picking a pomegranate up from the table and cutting into it casually with a knife, "that you could enter my realm and abduct my wife?"

Hades cut the pomegranate into six even sections. I heard a strange crackling noise and Pirithous' skin began to take on a gray hue.

"The meal you just enjoyed was the flesh of a dear friend of mine who was killed in my realm the last time someone like you entered without my permission."

Pirithous whimpered as his skin hardened, fastening him into place.

"It is fitting that her final act is to put a man like you out of his misery. Indeed, if she hadn't drunk from the Lethe, she would be quite pleased to hear it."

Only Pirithous eyes remained flesh. His mouth opened in a ghastly scream.

Hades ate a pomegranate seed. "Of course you won't really be out of your misery, will you? You'll still be alive in there, still starving. I just won't have to hear about it." He tossed the uneaten sections onto the table. "Now if you'll excuse me, I have some business to attend to."

I stared in horror as a seal with a picture of a head covered in snakes etched its way above Pirithous' clawed fingers.

Cassandra hurried across the room to grab my arm. "Come on. Let's get you out of here."

Chapter XVII

"YOU'RE FREEZING." Helen pried Hades' cape from my fingers.

"And soaked," Cassandra added. She led me through my room, adding onto my bathroom as she walked. The room widened, and a hot tub appeared in the center.

Helen touched my shoulder and I was wearing a green one-piece swimsuit. My feet touched the hot water and I hissed as the heat made contact with my freezing-cold toes. I eased my way into the water.

Cassandra and Helen joined me, keeping light conversation going. I sank into the water, pulling my knees to my chest. They hovered close, not asking me any questions, waiting until I wanted to speak.

" . . . and Hades agreed to give him *another* half-dozen Reapers," Cassandra complained.

Helen shook her head. "Those guys give me the creeps."

"They're not so bad," I objected. I felt like a ball of ice had replaced my heart. I was cold inside, where the warm water couldn't reach. I summoned a glass of hot chocolate and took a cautious sip.

"Are you okay?" Cassandra asked. I looked from her face to the concern mirrored in Helen's and couldn't help but smile.

"I'll be fine. Thank you."

"So what was more shocking? Seeing Pirithous get turned into a statue, or Hades' confession?"

"What confession?" Helen asked.

"Oh, he said he was in love with her."

"How did you know that?" I asked over Helen's gasp.

Cassandra gave me a look. "I *saw* it."

I shook my head. I'd been attacked. I'd just seen some guy turned to stone. And Cassandra wanted to chat about *boys?* "You guys really don't do comfort well."

Cassandra shrugged. "We're dead. We still feel everything, but not to the same degree you do. It makes empathy kind of hard."

I blinked, not sure what to make of that.

"Back up," Helen said. "He said what?"

"He just wants to be friends." I took another sip of my hot chocolate, and the ice-cold feeling in my chest dissipated. I smiled at Cassandra, grateful for the distraction. She had one long pale leg out of the water and was painting her toenails red. I summoned green polish with a shrug. It was better than thinking about what I'd just seen.

"I never realized Hades was that dense," Helen said as she handed me a jar. "Put this stuff on your face, it's amazing."

"He's probably right." I shrugged. "There is a pretty significant age difference. You know, I've got to say, I wish I could redecorate up in the living world like I can here. My best friend Melissa would be so jealous of this bathroom."

Cassandra took the jar of mud mask from my outstretched arm and looked at it skeptically. "If he thought you were too young to have a relationship with, he shouldn't have married you."

I rolled my eyes. "That doesn't count. I'm way too young to get married."

"Oh, Cassandra." Helen sighed. "Put the mask on. Anyway, *I* was married at ten years old. This concern over marrying too young is a completely modern invention."

I nearly smeared the daisy I was painting on top of the dark green polish on my toes. "*Ten?*"

"It's not as though either of you are human," Cassandra pointed out. "You can't play by human rules. Look at all those vampire romance books and movies and television shows. No one makes a big deal about those guys being thousands of years older than the—"

"Actually they do." I sighed, studying my toes carefully. They looked dry; I dipped them back into the warm water, pleased when the polish didn't run. "Just read the reviews, someone is sure to mention it."

"Physically speaking, Hades would be what, twenty? Twenty-five?" Helen asked. "That's not such a big deal."

I imagined coming home from school one day to tell my mom I was dating a man almost ten years older than me and blanched. "Uh . . ."

"My husband was fifty! Surely a paltry ten years doesn't—"

"Times have *really* changed," I explained.

"Whatever, it's still stupid," Cassandra said. "You're too pretty to wait around for Hades to come to his senses."

I waited for the follow-up to that comment, for Cassandra to say I was lucky or some other barb, but nothing came. It was a compliment, pure and simple. I thought back to my conversations with the girls at school and was surprised to realize they didn't have to be like that. Girl talk could just be this. No insults, no guilt trips. I smiled and sank deeper into the warm water.

"It's kind of nice not to be chased after," I admitted. I cheated and imagined a tasteful French manicure on my nails rather than painting them. "For the last few months every guy I've seen has gone kind of crazy."

"Yeah, I know all about that," Helen agreed with a bitter laugh.

"Troy . . ." Cassandra sighed.

Helen nodded. "Daughters of Zeus are nothing but trouble."

"Trouble is right." I shuddered. "I still can't believe what Hades did to Pirithous. I mean, he deserved it, but . . ."

"It's one thing to wish a horrific death on someone. It's quite another thing to witness it." Cassandra scrubbed the mask from her face and rose from the tub, summoning a towel as she walked to the vanity.

"Yeah." I summoned a towel and stood. "What Hades did. I mean Pirithous was—is—in agony!" I couldn't stop thinking of Pirithous screaming in pain.

"He's the Lord of the Underworld," Cassandra pointed out, sitting at a stool in front of the vanity. Helen followed her, summoned two more, and perched on the one in the middle. "You didn't think he had a dark side?"

I sat at the third stool and studied my reflection. I felt like I'd stepped into something way over my head, some world where torture was acceptable—first by my mother's hand, and then by Hades'.

I searched the mirror, looking for the mark of change I felt burning like a brand. I'd seen something terrible. Surely I must look different.

The girl in the mirror remained unchanged. Her eyes were more troubled than usual, but nothing looked out of place.

I jumped as Cassandra's face leaned over mine in the mirror. "You know what we should do?"

"What?"

"I know exactly what you're thinking." Helen grinned.

"What?" I asked again, looking between the two for some signal I was missing.

"We're going to make him regret turning you down," Cassandra announced.

"Makeovers!" Helen said, smiling. "Don't get me wrong, Persephone; you're pretty, but a little makeup wouldn't kill you."

I blushed. I used to love makeup and nail polish and all things girly. Melissa and I used to play in front of the mirror for hours, but eventually snide comments from the other girls had washed away my love for primping. If I put much effort into my appearance and some guy was especially obnoxious, they'd say I was inviting the attention. The girls would glare at me . . . It was just a lot of trouble.

I didn't want attention. I wanted to blend in as much as possible—on the surface. But here . . . here I could be myself again with nothing to fear. Helen and Cassandra weren't going to whisper about me for wearing makeup. No guy down here would dare do more than give me a polite grin. I was marked as the bride of Hades after all. Besides . . . it would be kind of fun to see his reaction.

"What did you want to do?" I asked.

The next half hour was filled with bewildering instructions. "Look up," Cassandra would order, and in the same second Helen would tell me to look down.

"Ooh, that's a lovely color," Helen complimented. "You have to show me how to make my eyes do that doe thing."

"Sure thing," Cassandra replied in a pleased voice. She showed her, then let Helen try it on my other eyelid. Behind closed eyes, I relaxed to the comforting sounds of girl talk.

"So," I said when they fell silent for a minute, "you two knew each other when you were alive, right? In Troy? What was it like?"

The quality of the silence changed. I peeked through half open eyes to see Cassandra and Helen share a long look.

"I'm so sorry," I stammered. I couldn't believe I'd just asked that. "I didn't think about . . . You two must want to forget all about—"

"It's okay," Helen assured me, collecting some pink powder onto an angled brush. "There are days I would give anything to drink from the Lethe." She paused for a second before putting the blush on my face. I closed my eyes instinctively. "I think about it every morning when I wake up. Just forgetting all those horrible things. But all those people died for me. It wouldn't be right to forget them."

"It wasn't your fault," Cassandra said as though reciting a familiar line from a familiar argument. "Menelaus was bound to attack Troy eventually. He was greedy. You were just—"

"A convenient excuse." Helen's voice was bitter.

"What happened?" I asked. "If you don't mind my asking."

"You've heard the stories, I'm sure. You're a daughter of Zeus, so you understand better than most the way people can change around us."

"It's not change," Cassandra said. "You just bring out the—"

"I understand that," Helen replied. "It's still not something ordinary girls would have to worry about. But then we're not ordinary, are we, Persephone? We're lucky."

I looked at her, and she saw that I understood.

"I was taken from my husband and daughter and given to Paris as a prize."

"You had a daughter?" I shook off my surprise, remembering how different things were back then.

"Hermione." Helen smiled fondly. "The last time I saw her was her ninth birthday. I imagine she's down here somewhere, but she probably drank from the Lethe to forget me. They all hated me in the end."

"You were just a scapegoat," Cassandra reminded her.

"I wish they would have just listened to you," Helen replied.

"Even without the curse, my brother was too much of a moron to listen to anyone."

"Who cursed you?" I asked.

"Apollo. I was his priestess, but he wanted me to be a bit more . . ." Cassandra bit her lip, considering her word choice. " . . . *active* in my worship. I refused, so he cursed me with visions of the future no one would believe in life. Death was actually kind of a relief to me." She shook her head. "Forget about us. We're supposed to be cheering you up."

"You don't have to cheer me up. Nothing happened to me. I just—" I sighed, trying to put my feelings into words. I couldn't really talk about my problems to Cassandra or Helen. I was alive. I'd escaped every horrible fate that presented itself to me. They hadn't been so lucky.

"Take a look," Helen said gently.

I opened my eyes and stared into the mirror at their handiwork. "You guys are amazing!" My eyes looked both dreamy and mysterious. My skin glowed, and I finally understood what kissable lips looked like. "What should I do with my hair?" I asked, touching it uncertainly.

"Leave it down," they said in unison.

"Wear this," Helen said, touching my shoulder.

I now wore an off the shoulder peasant dress the precise shade of my eyes. The flowing gown somehow emphasized every curve. "I can't leave the room like this."

"Oh yes you can," Cassandra said, pushing me toward the door. "Go find Hades."

"What am I supposed to say?"

"Guys like gratitude. Say you forgot to thank him for saving your life or something," Helen said, shutting the door behind me.

"Tell us everything!" Cassandra cried from behind the closed door. I walked uncertainly down the hall.

Chapter XVIII

ONCE I WAS OUT of my comforting room, my hands began to shake. Images from the afternoon played before my eyes. I looked down at my dress and snorted in disgust. What was wrong with me? Getting a makeover after watching the man who tried to abduct me get tortured?

I stopped outside of Hades' library. Raised voices made their way through the door.

"I asked you to do one thing! One thing, Thanatos! How could you let this happen?"

"Don't blame this on me! She wanted to be alone. Whose fault was that, I wonder?"

"*What?*" Hades' voice had a dangerous edge to it.

"I heard the way you talked to her after you let Orpheus go. The whole *kingdom* heard the way you were talking to her. You can't treat her that way, like she's some nymph—she's a goddess! Zeus and Demeter's child, no less. She outranks everyone down here but you, and you would never talk to *us* like that!"

Hades replied. I couldn't make out the words, but the quiet fury in his voice had me taking a step away from the door. What did Thanatos mean I outranked him? The only hierarchy I knew of was generational. The further removed from the Titans, the less powerful you were. Was Thanatos further down the line than me, or did this have something to do with being queen?

"She shouldn't need a guard!" Thanatos protested. "She shouldn't even be here! I warned you this might happen. I told you to take her back to Demeter—"

"Demeter is nowhere near as powerful as you remember. She wasn't safe there."

"What you did to that girl wasn't right. She's just a kid . . ."

Their voices faded into quiet murmurs, and I wondered why Hades wasn't using a shield.

"Do you really want to go there, Hades?" Thanatos snapped. "Half your power should be mine. I shouldn't have to beg for more Reapers every time—"

I ducked my head. Hades wasn't using a shield because the library was his sanctuary. He shouldn't have to worry about people listening in. I hadn't known that Thanatos resented his station in the Underworld, but it made sense. He was the God of Death, and all anyone ever talked about, worried about, or prayed about was the afterlife.

I walked away from the door. I shouldn't be hearing this. It was bad enough I'd gotten Thanatos in trouble. I walked to the banquet hall, my steps becoming faster and more erratic the nearer I got. I stopped when I saw the statue that was Pirithous fastened to his chair.

Long minutes passed as I stared at the statue. A door down the hall slammed and angry footsteps filled the hall. I dropped to my knees. I was sorry for all of it. The worry I'd caused my mom, the chaos I'd caused Hades, the trouble I'd gotten Thanatos into, the time everyone down here had invested in me that I'd nearly thrown away this afternoon. And most of all, I was sorry that I was responsible for the torture of a human being, no matter how much he'd deserved it.

The thoughts and fears I'd kept at bay all night rushed through my brain. I didn't know if he could hear me, but I knew he was alive in there, praying for death.

"I'm so sorry," I whispered.

"He doesn't deserve your pity," Hades said from the doorway.

"I know that."

Hades sighed. "I thought Cassandra was looking after you."

"I don't require looking after."

"Clearly."

"I hate him." My breath caught. "I've never hated anyone, but I hate him. I still didn't want this." I gulped back tears. "How could you do this? How could she?"

"Do you want me to undo it?" he asked harshly. "Snap my fingers and put this scumbag back in your path?" He walked across the room with an angry stride. "Let him hurt you? Try to drag you away from me? I could do it, if you wanted. Just say the word."

I was shaking uncontrollably. I opened my mouth to tell him of course I wanted this undone. This was torture, inhumane, wrong. The lie stuck in my throat. I was a monster. Despite my horror, I was relieved that Pirithous was out of the way. A small part of me was furious for all he'd done, and what he'd tried to do. He deserved this.

"I—"

"Yes, Persephone?" Hades asked, his voice dripping with sarcasm.

I had the momentary satisfaction of watching panic cloud his features when I burst into tears. "I did this, didn't I? When I asked mom to do whatever it takes. I knew, on some level I knew what I was asking. I'm a monster."

"It's okay," Hades said, kneeling to my level. "Don't cry." His voice took on a hint of desperation. "Please, don't cry."

I felt his hand rest upon my shoulder, and I had a flash of Hades sitting at the table casually eating pomegranate seeds while Pirithous screamed in agony. I jerked away from his touch.

"Don't be afraid of me," he pleaded. "Not you. I never wanted to hurt you. I'm sorry."

"Of course not, you were protecting me. You and my mom both." I sniffled. "This is what protecting me looks like."

"I shouldn't have let you see."

"You're the Lord of the Underworld," I quoted Cassandra. "You didn't think I knew you had a dark side? You did what you had to. He broke into your realm and tried to take someone under your protection, at the bidding of another god. If you hadn't acted—"

"It would have been taken as a sign of weakness."

"You're not weak. Neither is my mother. You're both capable of more darkness than I'd ever—" I shook my head. "I don't like it, but I'm not stupid. I'm benefitting from your reputation. It's why I'm safe here."

"Exactly."

"If I wasn't so weak, if I was more like you, I wouldn't need protection."

Hades frowned, apparently trying to follow my erratic shift in logic. "No," he said as comprehension dawned on him. "You don't have to be like the rest of us."

"I'm already more like you than I'd care to admit. It's inevitable, isn't it? Right now I'm just some stupid kid, but over eternity . . ." I took a shuddering breath, wiping the tears from my eyes. "I don't want to be rescued or looked after. I want to take care of myself." I looked away from Pirithous. "This is how the gods communicate with each other, isn't it? Shows of force, hurting people? Otherwise you look vulnerable, and right now I'm—"

"No! You don't have to play those games. You don't have to be like us. Everything's different now. You—" he motioned to me "—you're the way we *should* be. You're good, just, and compassionate."

Had I really used those same words to describe Hades only a few weeks before? I laughed bitterly at my naïveté. "Everything's different?" I asked, motioning to Pirithous. "Really?"

"*You* won't have to be this way! Your mother and I will—"

"Fight all my battles? I'll just be a more appealing target." I wiped the tears off my face. "More than I already am anyway. Life's daughter, Death's bride, and a daughter of Zeus to boot. Who doesn't have a score to settle with one of you? I'm not even safe from humans because of my stupid charisma." I spat out the word.

"No."

"Boreas hates her, doesn't he? Her nature intrudes on his winter, life persists during the season of death, and this didn't have much to do with me at all. I'm just the weak link. The way that he can hurt her."

"Boreas has done this before."

"I'm sure he had a score to settle then, too. I'm not stupid. Boreas didn't pop up after hundreds of years because I'm pretty." I looked at Hades, daring him to deny it. "I bet he hates you, too. No one associates winter with death anymore, not really. People are still afraid of you, but he's just a season. I bet he would hate Zeus if he were alive. Lord of the skies, infringing on his winter winds . . . but I'm the weak link. I can't afford to be helpless."

"You'll find your own way. Violence isn't in your nature. You're . . ." He sighed, glancing up at the ceiling as he searched for the right words. "You're light."

I gazed at him uncomprehendingly.

"You're good and pure and—" He sighed. "You're the best part of everything having to do with life. You're strong and brave. More than you know. You stood and fought in Tartarus."

I shook my head. "I'm not brave. I'm just stupid. When something scary or bad happens, my mind shuts off and I act. Believe me, later, when it has time to process, I'm terrified."

"You don't have to be afraid. I can protect you. I just don't want you to be afraid of me." His arm wrapped around my shoulder, and I crumbled against him, clutching him tightly.

"I'm not," I said, looking up at him. "That's what scares me most of all."

Hades brushed a tear from my cheek. I looked up at him, wide-eyed, and his breath caught.

"Hades . . ." I felt myself flowing toward him. I leaned into his touch as his hand moved down to my shoulder.

"Persephone, we can't." He dropped his hand.

I pushed away from him, climbing to my feet. "Because I'm so damn helpless, right? I'm so tired of you, my mother, and random abductors trying to make decisions for me."

"We're not—"

"I didn't want to leave Athens!" I rushed on, scarcely taking time to breath as the jumble of my thoughts took shape into words. He stood, watching me warily. "I didn't want to come here! I'm told what to do, where to go, what's safe, what's not. I can't do this anymore!"

"You're angry—"

"You *think?*" I moved closer to Hades, intentionally invading his space. His back went rigid, but I knew it wasn't in him to back down. "I'm tired of being told I'm too vulnerable, too powerless, too young. I'm a goddess! My father gave me the ability to destroy cities with a smile. My mother gave me the power to create life, and you gave me power over the dead. I may never be able to do that—" I pointed to Pirithous "—to another person, but I shouldn't be defenseless. I'm done running. I'm done hiding. And I'm done letting other people fight for me. I want to go after Boreas."

"Wait. What?" Hades blinked, shaking his head. "And do what? You can't kill a god any more than he could kill you."

"Fine, I can't kill him, but I can make him wish I could." At his surprised look, I grew defensive. "What? I'm going to go all dark-side one day, anyway. I might as well do something so extreme he'll think twice next time he chooses a victim." I paused, considering. "Can gods be castrated?"

Hades coughed. "Uh . . ." He held up a hand, then shook his head. "Persephone, please don't take this the wrong way, but right now you don't have what it takes to go head to head with another god."

"Then teach me." A dull ache crept along the back of my head, and I rubbed at it.

Hades shook his head. "Self-defense is one thing. Teaching you to use your abilities, to protect yourself, and even giving you profiles on all the living gods so you know how to avoid drawing their attention is fine. Great idea, in fact. But I'm not letting you go after Boreas. My only goal in rescuing you was to keep Boreas from destroying you. Teaching you to go on the offensive would be counterproductive to that goal. I'll handle Boreas."

"It's the same thing." My skin was growing uncomfortably warm. It itched like bugs were crawling beneath the surface. I rubbed my arms, trying to regain my train of thought. "Doing something in my name is the same as . . ." I hissed as the ache in my head grew more pronounced, hand flying to my forehead.

Hades touched my temple with his index finger, eyebrows gathering together in confusion. "What the hell . . . ?"

The door to the banquet hall burst open and Cassandra ran in, her face pale. "Hades!"

"Orpheus!" He swore, tilting my chin up so he could look into my eyes. "That idiot."

"What's happening?" I asked around the buzz in my ears.

"Persephone, I need you to focus, okay?" He grabbed both of my shoulders as my eyes glazed over. "Persephone!"

My body stiffened as my mind exploded with pain. I hit the floor, convulsing. The pain grew worse with each heartbeat. Molten glass poured through my veins. I couldn't see the banquet hall anymore. Colors flashed in and out of my vision.

I screamed. Some part of me was aware of Hades and Cassandra holding me down as I writhed back and forth.

"Listen to me!" he yelled in panic. "Persephone!"

I shrieked, fingernails trying to claw into the marble floors. I couldn't think, couldn't form words. I felt as though I could fly apart any minute. It burned; I was being burned alive from the inside out. It felt a thousand times worse than when Zachary had tried to free the soul from my body.

"Do something!" Cassandra shouted.

Hades swore, grabbing both of my hands. "Persephone! Give this to me!" He pressed his hands against mine. "Damn it! She has to consent!"

My wordless wail crescendoed. Hades pressed his hand against my forehead and my body went still. I struggled against the invisible binding. I couldn't move. The pain inside of me begged for some kind of outlet. Hades lifted me and pressed his lips to mine. His voice intruded on my thoughts. *Tell me I can take this.*

It hurts! It hurts! It hurts! It hurts! The only cohesive thought I could form kept screaming through my head.

I can fix this, if you let me.

I struggled to interpret his words through the red fire of pain, but I grasped firmly to the hope he offered. *Please!*

Hades took my hands into his. I felt a pulse of energy sear through me like a burning brand, and then the pain stopped.

My eyes fluttered open and met his. His thoughts and feelings swirled through my head. They were foreign, dark, conflicted, and raw. My mind latched onto them, trying to make sense of them.

With his name on my lips, I sank into blissful darkness.

Chapter XIX

I WOKE UP IN my bed, painfully bright light streaming through my window. I blinked, disoriented, and then the pain hit. It was as though someone had slammed a pick ax through my temple and the seven dwarves were singing "Hi-ho!" at the top of their lungs while tap dancing. I doubled over in agony, grasping my head with clawed hands. The green fabric from the dress was glaringly bright. I squeezed my eyes shut, unable to think.

"I'll let Hades know you're up," Cassandra whispered from the papasan chair.

I winced at her voice but managed a tight nod.

Seconds later Hades burst into the room. I groaned at the noise and Cassandra smacked his shoulder, making a shushing gesture with her other hand.

"What's wrong with me?"

Hades sat beside me and grabbed my hand. "Orpheus has gone public."

I struggled to remember what an Orpheus was.

"Persephone." His authoritative voice brought my eyes to his. "I need you to concentrate for a minute. Take a deep breath." He breathed in deeply, watching to make sure I did the same. "Take all that pain in your head and push it to me."

I stared at him.

"I think she needs you to clarify that," Cassandra said helpfully.

He looked frustrated. "Look, I'm not the God of Poetry or Good Descriptions, okay? Just do it. I'll explain what it means later."

I closed my eyes. Without Hades as a distraction the pain in my head came back in waves that threatened to pull me under. I struggled to hold onto consciousness. I focused on my hand clasped in his. For all his calm demeanor, his tight grip told me he was worried.

I gathered energy in my hands, surprised when they grew warm. The pain in my head lessened as I imagined more filling my hands. For a moment, I held it there, feeling like a stretched out rubber band. Then I released it into Hades.

"That's it," he murmured, releasing me.

"What are you going to use it for?" Cassandra asked.

"A grove of trees near the palace."

"That's the best you could think of?"

"Well, gods, Cassandra, if you've got any better ideas I'd love to hear them."

"My head feels better." I opened my eyes. "What were you saying about Orpheus?"

"He went public."

"Yeah, you said that," Cassandra said. "I think she wants you to elaborate."

"Cassandra!" Hades snapped. "You may leave us now."

My eyes widened. It had not been a request. Cassandra blinked, stunned, and shot him a hurt look.

"*Now*, Cassandra," Hades said through gritted teeth.

"As you wish, *Your Highness*." Her dark hair flared behind her as she spun on her heel to leave the room.

Hades returned his attention to me. "Orpheus has told every major news outlet and his fans about his adventures in the Underworld. He spoke of you in particular."

"Why?" Any other day I'd be flattered that Orpheus was talking about me, but judging by the look on Hades' face it wasn't a good thing. My throat went dry and I swallowed hard. Whatever Hades said next wasn't going to be good.

"Apparently his wife didn't make it. He looked at her as she was stepping out of the Underworld. She's in a coma."

My mouth dropped open. "That's not fair!"

Hades shrugged. "No, but there's nothing we can do about it. Her soul returned to her body, and she's alive enough to where I can't reach her."

"That sucks." I felt sick. He'd gone through hell for her, literally, only to mess up at the last second. I closed my eyes. *Poor Orpheus.* He must feel so guilty.

"Yes. He seems to think you, your mother, or I can help. He's been telling the world about us. He's written his whole experience online, and has been interviewing all day trying to get our attention. Half the people think he's crazy, but apparently some believe him. Or at least they're all talking about us enough to constitute worship."

"Really?"

"Great news for your mother and me. Orpheus most likely meant it as a favor, or tribute, so we would be more apt to help his wife. Unfortunately, it's not good for you."

"Why not?"

"You haven't reached maturity. You're little more than a gifted human at this point, and your body isn't capable of handling worshipers."

"Surely there were child gods."

"Any you've ever heard of?"

I blinked, thinking back.

"That's because we kept them from the public until they were able to handle worshipers. As far as the humans were concerned, they just appeared one day, full-grown."

"Like my mom?"

"We're different."

"I thought you said as queen I would have my own worshipers."

"That's funneled through me. I give you enough so you can practice with your abilities, but not enough to hurt you."

Something in his expression caught my attention. My head was starting to hurt again, but I shoved that aside. "What do you mean you *give* me enough?"

Hades sighed. "That's not important right now."

"I think it is."

He sighed. "When Boreas attacked you and I breathed my essence into you—"

"The kiss?"

He nodded. "I gave you enough of myself so you could come here without harm. Since it's supposed to be an exchange, I had to take something from you."

Vague memories from last night surfaced. "But you needed my consent."

His grip tightened on my hand. "And you weren't being cooperative. More important, I didn't want to take anything from you. What I needed to do to save you was bad enough."

"I see." It was silly to feel hurt. Even I didn't think our impromptu marriage was an ideal situation, but hearing him say it was "bad enough" still stung.

He rolled his eyes. "That's not what I meant, and you know it. Anyway, I took something I could control, that also ensured you wouldn't be hurt. You gained powers, but they couldn't burn through you."

"That doesn't make sense."

"It's bending the rules, but it works. I got the idea from Zeus. It's how he and Hera were bound." His mouth twisted in a bitter looking grin.

"What do gods usually exchange?"

"It depends. Some did whatever it took to become equals. Some exchanged practically nothing so they could retain their own powers. Others completely drained their spouse of all their powers . . ." His voice trailed off, and he looked away. "Like Zeus. That bastard took everything."

I shifted, and he glanced down, looking surprised to see how tightly he was gripping my hand. "Sorry," he said, releasing me.

I rubbed my hand. "So what did I give you just now? What did I take?"

"Whatever your body couldn't handle. I didn't take it, just channeled it through me. That wasn't an exchange. Your power will continue to return to you until the level of worship dies down."

"You were in my head?" I wasn't sure if that part had happened.

He nodded.

"What was that?"

He scratched the back of his head looking embarrassed. "That could become permanent if we were ever to reach equilibrium. Otherwise it will only occur when we're in contact with one another."

I laughed. "So if I bump into you I'll be able to read your mind?" Something in his face made me stop laughing. "What?"

Hades flushed. "Er . . . intimate contact. In this case a simple kiss was able to suffice."

I raised an eyebrow. *Intimate contact.* I gave Hades a speculative look. My cheeks heated when he met my gaze. "Oh. Well . . . uh . . ." I changed the topic. "What would happen if you didn't continue to channel my power?" I swallowed, remembering the agony of last night. "How bad can it get?"

"There aren't words for what would happen to you." He averted his eyes. "It would get bad. Really bad. You could kind of . . . unravel."

"Unravel!"

"I won't let that happen. Come to me when the symptoms start, and I'll take care of it."

I sighed, flopping back in bed. "Yet another thing I need to be rescued from."

Hades frowned. "You could look at it that way, or you could see this as an opportunity to use your powers. I'm simply channeling them. They have to go somewhere."

I looked up. "I could use them for anything I want?"

He chuckled. "Within reason."

"Good. Let's go after Boreas."

He sighed. "You're in no shape to go after Boreas."

"I'm fine," I insisted, swinging my legs off the bed and standing. Black spots swam in my vision and my knees buckled. Hades was beside me in a flash, helping me back onto the bed.

"Give yourself some time to recover. Take it easy today. Okay?"

I nodded. "Tomorrow—"

"Persephone!"

"What is with you?" I demanded. "First you snapped at Cassandra, and now me?"

"Cassandra overstepped."

I drew my eyebrows together in confusion. "She's Cassandra. It's just what she does. You're the one who's acting strange."

He let out a breath and his shoulders slumped. In that motion I saw all the tension he had been trying to hold at bay ease out of him. "Persephone, you could have died." He didn't meet my eyes. "That much power, so fast, before maturity . . ." He made a helpless gesture with his hands. "That could have burned straight through your soul. You could have been destroyed, and it caught me off guard. You've been out for a week, and to be honest, I wasn't sure you would ever wake up."

"You saved me," I reminded him, reaching for his hand. He gripped my hand so hard I was afraid my fingers would break. "I'm okay, and I'm going to be okay, because of you."

"I've been around since the beginning of time, and I've never been afraid until I met you."

I didn't know what to say so I shifted closer. We sat together on the bed holding hands, until I could no longer keep my eyes open.

"I don't want to go to sleep again," I muttered.

"You need to rest," Hades reminded me. "You can't afford to be at half strength."

"Don't leave."

"Wouldn't dream of it."

He wrapped an arm around me and launched into a story about the demigod Arcus, who killed the first werewolf and was reunited with his mother in the stars. I fought to stay awake, listening to his sonorous voice, but soon gave in to sleep, leaning against his shoulder.

Chapter XX

WHEN I WOKE UP a few hours later, Hades suggested it would be good for the souls to see me around the kingdom, if I was up to it. I was ready to get out of my room, and after making sure I was steady on my feet I took off to find Cassandra. She wasn't around the palace, so I decided to head into the suburbs.

I found Thanatos. His eyes looked so relieved when he saw me that I gave him a hug.

"You're okay," he whispered thankfully, hugging me back.

"I'm so sorry. I didn't mean to get you in trouble—"

"You have nothing to apologize for."

I waved to Charon as I walked along the river. He drew along beside me in his ferry.

"Want a ride?" he asked, challenge flickering in his eyes.

"Where are we going?"

"Around. I thought I'd show you the rest of your realm."

I nodded and he helped me into the boat.

Thanatos grinned. "I'll catch up."

"How are you liking the palace?" Charon asked as he pushed off the shore.

"I love it here, though it's not at all what I expected."

He nodded. "There's a dark side to the Underworld too." He motioned to the water. "This river is made of the tears of the souls as they leave the living realm."

I thought of Hades. "I know there's a dark side."

He nodded. "I'm sorry about the souls we used for practice. I dumped them all back in the same place—I just never expected you'd end up over there with them."

I shrugged. "You couldn't have known."

"Yeah, well, Hades has put a stop to that part of our lessons."

I breathed a sigh of relief. Charon rode into the steam made by the river of fire and the river of ice meeting in the marsh. "There's the shore. I'm not picking up any souls right now," he said, answering my unspoken question. "Though with you in here, they may come a bit more willingly."

My cheeks heated, and he grinned at me.

"Hades is a good guy," Charon said after a moment's silence. "He's got a dark side too, but it's nothing for you to be concerned about. He's good. He's not like the Olympians."

"I know."

He stared at me for a moment. "I think you do."

Charon rowed me back toward shore and told one of his stories before dropping me off with Thanatos. I was still laughing as I walked to an empty space on Main Street. Setting up shop in the Underworld was ridiculously easy. Within a few moments, I had a near replica of my mother's shop, minus the fish bowl windows.

It didn't take long for the word to spread. As I created arrangements, souls dropped in to greet me, expressing their concern. They all knew something had happened at the palace, just not what. I assured them I was fine and filled their flower orders. Helen dropped by at midday, pushing her way through the well-wishers to get to the counter.

"When did I get so popular?" I asked her, laughing.

"Since you became Queen of the Underworld."

"I don't think it's that," I said, pushing her behind the counter before she offended anyone. "They aren't asking for anything."

"I didn't mean that. You're our queen. When someone messes with you, they mess with all of us."

"Oh." I smiled. "That's so sweet."

"It's going to make Hades even more obnoxious," Cassandra said, appearing behind Helen. "Feeding his heroic ego and all." She only sounded a *little* bitter.

I smiled at her, unable to find the words to apologize for what had happened.

"You need a crown," Helen mused.

I laughed. "I'd feel ridiculous wearing a crown. Oh my gods, what if people bowed to me? I'd be so embarrassed."

"When did you start saying that?" Helen asked.

"Oh my gods?" I shrugged. "I guess I've been spending too much time with Cassandra."

"Never a bad thing." Cassandra laughed. "Hades would die of embarrassment, too. He's never been into the whole power-trip thing. Still, you shouldn't be too embarrassed. You're the queen." Her tone was light, but I heard an undercurrent in it that made me nervous.

"That's just a technicality. Once this Boreas thing blows over—"

"You'll still be Queen of the Underworld."

Wait, what? That didn't sound temporary. This whole thing was supposed to be over when Boreas was no longer a threat. My mind flashed back to waking up next to Hades. *Do I really want this to end?* "What if Hades wants to marry someone else?"

"He could take a mistress, but marriage is a forever thing in the realm of the gods. You guys don't die, so you never leave your posts."

"He told me marriage doesn't mean—"

"It doesn't. Not in the sense you're talking. You could date other people, and so can he. There could be absolutely no love involved, like Zeus and Hera. Or it could all just be political, but it's still permanent."

I didn't know what to think about that. "So I'm queen . . . forever?"

"You're a good match for Hades," Helen pointed out. She hesitantly touched a white lily. "This is so pretty." She saw me looking at her. "Oh come on, you can't see it? You two are perfect together, aren't they, Cassandra? Life and death. You balance one another."

"Persephone!" A stern looking brunette called from the counter. "What happened to you? The palace has been abuzz with rumors all week!"

"Hello, Gloria," I said with a smile, handing her an arrangement of tulips. She and her band of joggers had been my first customers. I brushed off her questions, unsure what Hades would want me to tell anyone. "How's the husband?"

"Oh, he's doing well, thank you. He went on a fishing trip with the rest of his group. I'm thinking of taking a baking class while he's gone."

"That sounds like fun! I've always wanted to learn how to bake."

We made small talk for a few more minutes. I couldn't believe I'd ever been intimidated by the Underworld. It was just like the living realm. Life went on, so to speak. People were still people, and they continued to do the things that made them happy.

I handed an arrangement of daisies to a Reaper. She smiled and thanked me, leaving the shop with a quick glare in Cassandra's direction. Cassandra narrowed her eyes, then turned pointedly away to talk to Helen.

I rejoined Helen and Cassandra, who were looking at me with amusement. "Baking?"

"What? I think it would be fun. I could make pretty cakes and—"

"Ah, more decorating." Helen laughed.

"You know all of their names," Cassandra observed, after watching me talk to a few more customers.

I shrugged. "It's a flower shop. People talk when they place orders, and you learn a lot about them."

"We need to go to court," Cassandra said. Her voice made it clear she was dreading seeing Hades.

I wrapped a supportive arm around her shoulders. "It'll be fine. He's in a much better mood now." I yelled a quick goodbye to the souls and waved to Helen before walking back to the palace with Cassandra.

"Hi, Moirae." I headed over to my throne. Cassandra took her seat. Hades hadn't arrived yet.

"How are you?" Moirae asked me. Her voice was too close.

I turned my head and jumped when I saw her eyes a hairsbreadth away from mine. "Good, thank you." I smiled at her, unsure whether I was more surprised by her presence or her sudden kindness.

"You handled Orpheus well. The souls could use a compassionate touch."

"Th-thank you," I stammered, looking at Cassandra in surprise. She looked just as shocked as I did but flashed me a discreet thumbs up. Moirae smiled at me and took her seat. A moment later the door opened and Hades walked in, followed by Aeacus and Rhad.

"Ladies," Hades said with a nod.

I smiled at him as he sat beside me. He inclined his head at the judges, and the doors opened, revealing the souls who had recently finished with Orientation.

"Now we're back to the throne room," Minos said cheerfully. "You've met Moirae, of course, but now allow me to present the rulers of the Underworld: Lord Hades and Queen Persephone."

We stood, and the souls awkwardly chose whether they would bow or nod. Modern day customs didn't allow for much exposure to royal etiquette. I grinned at them and they relaxed visibly.

"Welcome," Hades greeted them in his booming voice. "We wish you a happy afterlife."

I resisted the urge to roll my eyes. He'd taken my corny sendoff from my first nerve-wracking day at court and run with it, using it at every court.

"If anyone has any questions or concerns, my fellow judges and I would be more than happy to assist you while we get you settled."

"May I speak to the queen?" a woman called from the back of the crowd.

"Of course."

Minos led the remaining souls from the room. Only a handful chose to stay and have concerns addressed by Hades or me. I was intrigued by this woman and leaned forward as Hades motioned her to the floor.

"Miss—er, Your Majesty—"

"Persephone is fine," I assured her.

She nodded. "I died in my sleep." She paused as the gravity of that statement caught up with her. "I, um, died in the middle of the night." She blinked back tears as I murmured my condolences. "I had a baby three weeks ago, and she's still in my house. No one knows that I'm—" Her voice caught. "She's all alone. Please, is there some way I could go back?"

Hades shook his head solemnly. "No. I'm sorry."

"Please! I don't have family in the area, and I don't have many friends. Her father was killed during his deployment, and if I don't get back she could die before anyone finds me!"

I nodded. This was exactly the sort of situation I could handle. "Moirae will take all your information down. We need your address, phone number, and if you have a spare key hidden anywhere that would be helpful. I will send someone—"

The woman blanched and I hurriedly continued. "Alive. In the living realm, to collect your daughter immediately. We will get her to your family safely."

"There's no one else." She broke down sobbing.

"That's okay. She'll be in good hands." I told her about my mother and her priestesses, ending with, "She may even get a chance to be blessed with immortal life."

The woman took a second to process this. "I would never see her again?"

"That will be up to her."

"She won't remember me," she said, blinking back tears. "I want what's best for my daughter, but I just wish I could hold her again. Why was I taken from her! We had three weeks—" She broke off as the tears overwhelmed her.

I wanted to hug her, or offer some sort of condolences, but what could be said in a situation like this? It sucked beyond description.

The woman collected herself and gave Moirae the pertinent information. Then she left to be reunited with her husband.

"How bittersweet," Hades said after we contacted my mother. "Reunited with one love while another is lost forever."

I nodded, blinking back my own tears. What right did I have to cry over this?

"Is that why gods view immortality as a curse?"

Hades shrugged. "Mostly when people were cursed with immortality, it was done in anger. The cursed would live, alone, and watch everyone they came to care for die over time. No one used it like your mother does. She formed a community. She's always been different from the others." He smiled at me. "Come on. It's time to go to dinner, and then do your training."

Chapter XXI

OVER THE NEXT week, Hades began training me to use my abilities in earnest. I had to burn through my power before it burned through me, so every night after dinner I met with Hades in his library, I had my lesson, and then he would channel the residual power away so I could sleep without fear of exploding or something.

Tonight was no exception, even though I was exhausted after the Valentine Ball. It had been different from Brumalia because Cassandra had been distant since Hades had snapped at her.

I couldn't blame her for being upset. She had been acting as the Queen of the Underworld for who knew how many hundreds of years before I came along. She'd always been at Hades' side in court, public events, planning the events, and running a thousand minute day-to-day activities at the palace. Then I came along.

I didn't want the job. Cassandra could do it all, for all I cared. I'd grown to love the Underworld, but I didn't want to rule it.

I missed Cassandra.

"You're not focusing." Hades sighed.

His constant sighing didn't grate at me like it once had, but it didn't stop me from feeling a pinprick of annoyance for my interrupted reverie. I tried to empty my mind like Hades instructed. I'd been excited about today's lesson. He was finally teaching me how to teleport. It would probably only work in the Underworld, but it was possible I might be able to do something similar in the living realm. That would be a great resource if I ever needed to escape—or sneak up on—someone. Though I wasn't sharing that revelation with Hades.

Then we started the lesson. Hades used a lot of phrases like "empty your mind," "visualize a place," "focus your energies," and whatever. It all felt New Age to me.

Still, every now and then everything would snap into place, and I would feel things starting to shift. Then Hades would stop me and make me do it again.

I emptied my mind and tried to focus my energy. I could feel it buzzing through me, resonating from the plants I grew in the library and humming through Hades. I visualized myself standing behind him and gave a little *push*.

The world shifted around me, and I felt myself being pulled apart and thrown back together in a whir of sickening motion. I landed behind Hades with a *thud*, stumbling against his chair and nearly falling into his lap.

"I did it!" I exclaimed, laughing.

"Good. Let's stop for tonight." Hades caught my arm and stabilized me.

"But I just got the hang of this!"

"You're straining too hard. You need to back off before you burn yourself out." He led me back to my seat and gave me a little push. I frowned at him and sat.

"Fine. I'll go to bed." I stood, or tried to. My knees gave way beneath me and I sank back in the chair, exhausted from using my abilities. Hades gave me a sideways glance as he returned to his chair, wisely saying nothing.

"Why can't we lie?" I asked. The question had been weighing on me ever since the words to save Pirithous had stuck in my throat. "Humans can, so why can they do something we can't?"

"It's a fail-safe we implemented after we created them and made the world a more suitable place."

"How do you mean?"

"When a god speaks, the words have power. Speaking an untruth could change the nature of the thing we're lying about. Since creation was a collaborative effort, we took away our ability to change our creations without the other gods present."

"Oh." I glanced around the library, searching for a way to change the topic without making it obvious I'd pushed myself too hard to make it down the hallway. "You don't have to keep those. I can plant them outside." I motioned to the flower pots scattered around the room.

Wait a minute. They weren't scattered. I leaned forward. Three tiny flower pots decorated the windowsill. One sat on a table, and a pair of tall pots flanked a set of bookshelves. Hades plucked the flowers we'd been working with today off the table and set them on his desk, shuffling the papers to make room.

Hades was decorating. With something of mine. The library was his most private, personal space, and something I'd made belonged in it. This was big.

"You draw on them for your power. It leads to better practices."

I frowned, shoulders slumping. *Or there's a perfectly logical explanation.*

Hades shrugged. "Also, they smell like—" He cut off and busied himself in sorting his papers. "They smell good."

Me? Did they smell like me? My mind flashed back to the throne room. He'd said he was in love with me, but. . . . I glanced at the flowers again.

Holy cow! He was. He really was. "Hades?"

He turned from the desk. "Yes?"

My mind went blank. "Um . . . you have a lot of books." The instant the words left my mouth I felt stupid. But I hadn't known what else to say. *I've known this whole time that you can't lie or anything, but I didn't* really *believe you until I saw the flowers?* That sounded stupid. Besides, I knew where the conversation would lead. *Stupid age difference.*

"Reading is a passion of mine."

"Ditto." I smiled, thinking of a few of my favorites.

His eyebrows rose in surprise, but I was used to that reaction. I was admittedly not the brightest crayon in the box, so people seldom thought I was the type of person who would sit around on rainy days and read books. Granted, I was more likely to be reading the latest supernatural romance novel in the Dusk series than I was to be reading Jane Austen.

"Don't look so surprised," I snapped, moving to stand.

Hades laughed. "I've just never seen you with a book. I've seen you here before, but never reading anything."

I pulled my phone out of my pocket. I wasn't getting service, but I could still access my books, music, and movies.

"All my books are on here." I opened the application. "Less clutter."

He took my phone and started flipping through the small screen. "You read whole books on this?"

"All the time. They have a big version, but Mom says it's too expensive." We'd see about that when I got back from the Underworld.

Hades snorted. "These aren't books, these are—" He paused. "Dusk? Seriously?"

"What? It's good!"

"I considered creating a dimension of Tartarus that forced souls to watch the movie based on this book for all eternity. Complete with shrieking harpy fan girls in the audience."

I snatched my phone back. "Have you even seen it?"

"Cassandra made me watch it." Hades shuddered.

"It's a great movie and an even better book!"

"It's ludicrous. What is with this recent human obsession with vampires?"

I sat up in my chair. "Were there ever any vampires?"

"Well, there was Hecate's daughter, Empusa. She would seduce men and drink their blood as they slept. Poseidon's daughter, Lamia—"

"Like the Midnight World books!"

"What?"

I scooted my chair closer to him and pulled up the book on my phone. "Born vampires are called Lamia, and made vampires are called—"

"Yeah, sorry I asked. Anyway, Lamia was Poseidon's daughter. She had an affair with Zeus and had several kids. Hera found out about it and forced her to devour her children—" I gasped and Hades paused. He looked as though he was going to say something, perhaps to defend Hera, then shrugged and continued with the story. "Afterward, Lamia continued to drink the blood of mortal children until Zeus took pity on her and removed her eyes."

"How exactly was that supposed to help?"

"It makes it harder to catch the children."

I shook my head. "That's . . . you know what, there are no words."

"There were also Striges, or Strix, which were birds that fed on blood, and there was that island of the blood dri—"

"Okay! I'm sorry I asked." I held up my hands in surrender. "I meant—" I pointed to my phone "—vampires like these."

"Refined gentlemen who occasionally drink blood? It's a complete myth."

I thought it was ironic to hear that from Hades while sitting in the Underworld, but refrained from pointing that out. "What's your favorite book? Oh, let me guess. *Inferno*."

Hades laughed. "No. It's hard to say a favorite. I enjoyed everything by Alexander Dumas. Have you read his work?"

"I've seen the movies."

"The books are much better." He stood and pulled a few from the shelf. "Here, you should read them. In print."

I laughed and stood to accept them. "Thank you." My hand brushed his when I took the books and I suppressed a smile at the thrill that went through me.

Hades cleared his throat, and I realized I'd frozen in place, but then he hadn't moved either.

The door to the study burst open and I jumped guiltily away from Hades, as if I'd been caught doing more than just standing there. Hades remained where he was and raised an eyebrow at the intrusion.

"Yes, Cassandra?"

"I need to talk to you," she panted. I wondered if she had run all the way here. "Alone."

I gaped at her. She'd been distant but never rude. She couldn't be ignoring me completely now, could she? I ground my teeth together, hurt. I'd never been good at confrontation. I wished I knew a way to make this right.

Hades frowned. "Cassandra—"

"Hades, I mean it," she snapped. "I'm sorry," she said quickly. "This can't wait."

"You've had a vision?" Hades asked, and Cassandra nodded. The two exchanged a look I couldn't read. Hades let out a tense breath and turned to me. "Persephone, you should—"

"Don't finish that sentence," I warned him, and turned to Cassandra. "Why don't you want me to know what you saw?" I asked Cassandra, panic rising. "My mom? Did something happen to my—"

"No," she assured me. "Your mother is fine."

"What then?" I demanded. "What happened?"

She looked at Hades, appealing to him with her eyes.

"Persephone . . ." Hades whispered.

"No! I am not leaving until I know what she saw!"

Cassandra looked apologetically at Hades. "Boreas has taken Melissa."

Chapter XXII

THE AIR WHOOSHED out of my body and I sat with a thud. Has taken. Not will take. Whatever she saw, it was something that would be done now that Boreas had taken Melissa. A thousand possibilities competed for attention in my thoughts, each worse than the last. Hades was talking, but I couldn't hear him. All I could think about was my friend in the hands of that monster.

"Why didn't you warn us?" I advanced on Cassandra. She must have seen something in my eyes because she shrank back.

"I can't see everything. There's been a lot happening on the surface. Her kidnapping must not have been chaotic enough to draw my attention."

I narrowed my eyes. What *else* had happened that I wasn't told? I forced that thought to the background. It didn't matter right now. I had to rescue Melissa. "You have to help her," I told Hades.

"Boreas is only doing this to draw you out," Hades reminded me. "I can't let you go after her, and I can't leave my realm unprotected."

"You can't *let* me?"

"I can't risk you for a mortal. No. I'm sorry." He cut off my protest with a wave of his hand. "I know this is hard for you, but if it's any consolation, I don't think he's going to go to the extremes with her that he did with Oreithyia. He only chose her to draw you out. Once he realizes we're not coming he'll simply kill her, and then you'll be reunited with her down here."

Cassandra's inward hiss of breath was the only warning Hades got before I flew at him.

"You *bastard!*" I shrieked, my fists flailing, all of my self-defense lessons completely forgotten. He caught my wrists easily, dodging a knee to the groin. "Coward! You would just let her die!"

"Persephone!"

I tried to twist my wrists from his grasp, but he was too strong.

"Let me talk to your mother, okay?" I tried to wrench free, and he raised his voice. "Let me talk to her! I can't just step in, Persephone!

That is her realm and the daughter of one of her priestesses!"

The words penetrated the red haze clouding my mind. I went slack in his grip, breathing erratically. My mom could fix this. She would rescue Melissa. Mrs. Minthe was her priestess. Mom had arranged for Melissa to be born so I would have a priestess. Boreas had chosen his victim well. Melissa mattered too much for us to let her die.

I was not in the room for the conversation with my mother. For some reason Hades was afraid I might try to attack him if the conversation didn't go my way. I lay down on my bed and did my best to rest. I needed to be at full strength, and Hades and I'd just spent the last of my powers.

After endless hours, Cassandra updated me on the situation. Boreas was holding Melissa hostage, and the price for her release was me. He promised no harm would come to her until next Saturday, when the exchange could be made.

That seemed like a long time, but it made sense. He'd no doubt burned through his powers kidnapping Melissa. He'd need ample time to get them back.

Of course, both my mother and Hades agreed exchanging me was out of the question. Their goal was to find Boreas as soon as possible and rescue Melissa. That was fine with me. I had a backup plan if necessary.

Over the next week I threw myself into my training. I was careful not to tip off Hades to my plan. He approached my goddess lessons warily but couldn't deny them to me. It was too dangerous not to have them. He seemed relieved when I chose to focus on teleporting. I could practice everything else on my own time.

Charon was more blunt. "You're not going to do something stupid if I teach you this, are you?"

"How exactly could I use pressure points against Boreas?" I asked in a dry voice. I wiped my sweaty palms on my black exercise shorts, shifting my feet to see the indentions they made on the blue mat.

"You couldn't. You know that, right? If you get this close to him you're as good as dead."

"I know that."

Charon met my eyes. "He'd come after you sideways, using the elements at his disposal. You'd want to be fast on your feet and prepared to break the ice. Watch under your feet, watch for flying icicles, and remember, your plants don't react well to his ice."

I kept my eyes level with his. "Thank you."

He sighed. "Has Hades taught you how to make shields?"

I shook my head. There were different kinds of shields. Hades used shields for privacy as opposed to defense. There were shields to prevent you from being seen, or heard, but there were also shields for physical protection. For the next hour I practiced throwing up a shield when Charon tossed dirt clods at me.

I focused on keeping him off balance, alternating my shields with making vines twist up around his feet.

"Hey! You don't need the thorns here!"

"Sorry!"

We kept it up for another few minutes before calling it quits. I stood, breathing hard.

"It won't be enough," Charon muttered on his way out the door.

"Why not?"

"I don't want to hurt you. He does. He really, really does. Please, Persephone. Don't do anything stupid."

He didn't wait for me to answer before he left. He knew I couldn't lie. After that lesson, Thanatos followed me like a shadow in and out of the palace. He was unusually silent about the whole thing. My feelings were a little hurt. I'd been counting on his support. He might not help me, but I knew he'd understand. Without him to talk through my plans, what could I do?

I shot him a frustrated look before I knocked on Hypnos' door.

Hypnos answered, face falling when he saw it was me. "Persephone."

"I need to learn how to get into human dreams to tell Melissa how hard we're trying to find her. Maybe she knows where she is!"

"It's not possible. She hasn't been given immortality yet. She hasn't been altered in any way. We can't enter every human's dreams. Just a select few."

"Melissa's my priestess. Shouldn't she be one of the few?"

Hypnos shook his head. "I already tried. Your mother hasn't done anything to alter her yet. She's probably waiting for you to stop aging before cursing her with immortality."

"What about Boreas; can't you spy on him in his dreams?"

"His defenses are too good."

"Better than you?"

Hypnos hesitated. "Actually, yes."

"*How?* Hades and my mom said there was no way he had much power left. How is he pulling all of this off?"

"That's a good question."

When no answer was forthcoming, I gritted my teeth. "What if I leave myself open? If he came to me, how could I get information from him?"

Hypnos' face closed of all emotion. "I'm not going to help you if you're going to do something foolish. Goodbye, Persephone." He closed the door.

When I could sleep, I left my mind unguarded. Boreas didn't take the bait. I felt like I'd hardly blinked when Saturday arrived. I summoned my keys and wallet and shoved them in my book bag. I pushed it under the bed, then I went to wait outside of Hades' chambers, as I had every morning since Melissa's abduction, while he conferred with my mother. I jumped when the door opened.

"I'm sorry," he whispered. "She couldn't find him, but she's not giving up. She's searching everywhere. We know exactly where he's going to be this afternoon. If she can catch him off guard before . . ."

I knew what he meant. If they could rescue Melissa before he realized that I was not coming . . . otherwise she would be dead.

Tears weren't hard to call up, and I flung myself into Hades' arms. He hugged me, and I muttered something about my bedroom, sniffling for good measure. He led me back to my room where Cassandra was waiting.

"I need to change," I said as though dazed. I plucked at the top of my white dress, indicating the stains from my mascara running.

Hades held out a hand, blocking Thanatos from entering my room.

"I'll wait out here," Thanatos said with a shrug.

The door closed. I made a show of sniffling while I changed into jeans and a thick velvet shirt. When Hades' footsteps faded down the hall, I stopped crying. Cassandra turned to face me, eyes wary.

"Interesting choice," she noted as I pulled on a sweatshirt.

"I'd do the same for you." I reached under the bed and grabbed my bag.

Comprehension dawned in her eyes. "I can't let you."

"I don't suppose that, since I'm your queen, you have to obey me?" The sentence came out garbled, the thought half formed in my head, but the indignant look that flashed through her eyes told me she understood what I was getting at.

"Humans have always had free will. I've known Hades much longer than I've known you. If you try something, I will go to him. I can't let you do anything stupid."

"I've got free will too." I grabbed her arm. "It's not in your power to *let* me do anything."

"Thanatos!" she shouted.

I acted without thinking, otherwise it would have never worked on Cassandra. When I opened my eyes, we were looking down at the palace as the Lethe sparkled becomingly in the distance.

"What did you do?" Cassandra wrenched her arm free. "Where are we?"

"Olympus."

"You can't! No one can teleport past the rivers!"

"No, *you* can't," I replied, as though I'd known this would work. "I'm queen of this realm, remember?"

"Persephone!" she gasped. "You can't do this. I can't cross the Lethe."

"I can't have you telling Hades," I replied, watching mournfully as our friendship died. "I'll be back for you, but if I don't make it back, it won't take Hades long to find you."

"Thanatos had to have heard me!"

"Then I'd better hurry."

"No! Persephone!" She grabbed my arm. "Please don't leave me here. Anywhere else, you can leave me anywhere else and I'll stay, I promise I'll stay. Please don't leave me here." She sounded close to tears, her voice was panicked, and she was breathing hard.

"Why?"

"Please," she begged, tears dripping down her face. "Don't leave me where the other gods could find me. You wouldn't understand. You didn't grow up when they were in power. They aren't like you or Hades."

She was shaking, and too late I remembered how she had been cursed with visions.

"I won't leave you in Tartarus." I shuddered. "I couldn't put you through that."

"I won't tell him, I promise. Please don't leave me here, please." She searched my face and saw I didn't believe her. "Take me to the other side of the Styx," she suggested. "You know Charon won't reach it until this afternoon. You know his schedule as well as I do. You can do that."

I grabbed her arm and we vanished. When the Underworld materialized around us we were standing on a rickety pier, sticking out into the black water. I remembered the water was made of the tears of those leaving the living realm and wondered if any of those were Cassandra's.

She collapsed on the pier, shaking and crying.

"I'm sorry," I whispered, feeling terrible that I needed to leave her in this barren landscape. A thick mist shrouded the pier, leaving me with the feeling of being smothered in darkness.

"Just go." She shifted away from me and faced the river.

I vanished. When my feet touched the ground again, I was standing in Tartarus. The ground hissed beneath my feet, and I heard a bent figure snuffle, feet dragging the ground as it shuffled my way.

I shuddered, remembering being surrounded by those once-human twisted beings. I flicked my fingers, and a thorn bush sprang up around it. The wretched creature hissed and snapped its jaws, spittle flying from its decayed and bent mouth. I circled it, making sure it was secure.

"You're going to take me to the nearest entrance." I watched as the thorns grew into its thrashing body. "Now."

I released it, and the creature stumbled. I expected more of an objection, but the creature led me to a small passageway. It eyed me hopefully. I grimaced as I touched its shoulder. "I wouldn't bring you with me if I could."

I teleported him to the edge of the river of fire. If I got back, I wasn't sure I'd have enough energy left to defend myself, and I didn't want to risk him waiting for me at the entrance.

I adjusted the backpack on my shoulders, took a deep breath, and stepped into the narrow crevice between the stones.

Chapter XXIII

I EMERGED FROM the earth with a confused frown. I should be in Athens, not the Arctic! Snow and ice covered the ground. A splash of red against the frozen wasteland caught my eye. I slid across the snowy surface. I bent my knees, touching my hand to the ground to slow to a stop when I approached a giant snow-covered tree with long icicles weighing down its mighty branches. A carpet of poppies surrounded the base, somehow unaffected by the snow towering around them.

My breath caught, and I surveyed the landscape with new eyes. It wasn't possible. I'd never seen more than a few inches of snow in Athens in my entire life! There should be a lake in the distance, and a road. I didn't bother looking for my car; my mother would have picked it up shortly after the attempted abduction. The blanket and the pomegranate would be long gone, but surely an entire park couldn't be obliterated by snow!

I closed my eyes, envisioning Five Points. Hades hadn't been sure if I could teleport in the living realm, but the theory was sound. The earth was my domain, shared by my mother. I should be able to move about as freely here as I could in the Underworld. With a sickening lurch, the land whipped around me, and I found myself standing in Earth Fare's parking lot, the organic grocery store across from my mother's flower shop.

Five Points was deserted. Every store was closed tightly against the icy invasion. I picked my way across the street until I reached the window of our shop. Empty. Everything was empty. No one was walking down the street, and no cars waited at the intersection.

Fingers clumsy with cold, I reached into the bag I'd prepared in the Underworld and pulled out the shop keys. It was no warmer inside. I flipped on the heat and perched on the wooden stool by the register. Unwilling to deal with the shop's slow computer, I pulled out my phone, loading the webpage for the Banner-Herald. Story after story filled the screen. For the first time in written history snow covered the ground worldwide. Meteorologists were scrambling for answers.

Here and there I could see touches of my mother's work to keep the world afloat: Plants inexplicably unharmed by frost, electricity that had remained on throughout the blizzard, women—my mother's priestesses—coming to the aid of stranded motorists. While I'd been making my impetuous demands, the entire world had been freezing.

Mention of Orpheus' new cult slammed the brakes on my thoughts. Orpheus had been careful not to mention Boreas, so as not to lend him power with belief. My mother's name was used frequently as someone who could help during this time of peril. The mysteriously helpful women were identified as belonging to something called the Eleusinian Mysteries or the cult of Demeter. At the base of the cult was a heartfelt tale of a woman trying desperately to be reunited with her lost daughter.

This blizzard couldn't have been going on since my abduction. Orpheus and his wife had been hiking before she died. My fingers swiped across the screen, looking for the first of the stories. They began days after Orpheus had begun to make headlines.

I breathed deeply. It wasn't as bad as I'd thought, but it was far worse than I'd been told. All of my updates for the living world came from Cassandra. I laughed out loud; Cassandra, the most trusted soul in the Underworld, *could lie*. My hands shook in anger.

Stop, think, I commanded myself with a deep breath. I could guess at their reasoning. They didn't want me doing something stupid. Unforgivable perhaps, but I had bigger fish to fry. What did this mean for me?

Boreas was stronger than I'd thought. Winter and its elements would be the first thing on everyone's mind right now. He would be gathering strength from that.

Why was he doing this? This had to be bigger than me. However powerful Boreas had become, he still couldn't hold a candle next to Hades or my mom. If this was a pride thing, or revenge against my mother, why hadn't he tried something like this before?

I glanced at the clock. Ten-thirty. Boreas would be at the park at noon for the exchange. Hades could discover me missing at any moment, and this would be one of the first places he would look for me. It was time to move on to the second stage of my plan. But first, warmer clothes. I'd underestimated the bite of the cold.

I debated saving my powers, but my head was already aching. I needed to burn more power if I hoped to be able to stay on my feet in the clearing. I closed my eyes and teleported to Masada Leather. I quickly searched through the racks and found a thick leather jacket. I pulled it on. I couldn't find anything warmer than the jeans I'd summoned in the Underworld, so I searched until I found a pair of winter boots that didn't have a crazy heel and kicked off my sneakers. I tossed the price tags on the counter with the appropriate amount of money, and then teleported to the university's greenhouse to wait out the next hour. I couldn't go to the clearing early; there was too much of a chance I'd be spotted by my mother—or even Hades, once he found Cassandra—and I needed to practice.

AT NOON I APPEARED under my tree in the clearing. I made sure I knew exactly where the entrance to the Underworld was and breathed a little easier with the knowledge that I could return to safety where Boreas couldn't follow. To my left, I saw my mother, tight-lipped and pacing the clearing. She looked furious. My feet crunched in the snow and she glanced up, eyes widening when she saw me.

"Persephone—"

Ice shot up around the clearing, forming a thick wall between us. Boreas materialized in the center of the clearing, holding a struggling Melissa. Her eyes met mine.

"No!" she shouted.

I glared at Boreas, finally able to put a face to my fears. He was tall and broad-shouldered. He wore a white toga, which blended perfectly with his snow-white skin. A white mustache and beard worked together to hide his lips, leaving the only color on his face his ice-blue eyes.

He gave me a cold smile and widened his eyes. "This is a surprise."

His voice sent shivers up my spine, but I forced myself to stand tall as the wind whipped my hair around.

"Cut the theatrics," I snapped. "You're not impressing anyone."

He laughed. "As you wish." The wind died down. Sunlight returned to the clearing, but the ice wall remained. I frowned. He shouldn't be able to keep my mother out.

"I am releasing your friend," Boreas announced with a strange grin. He shoved Melissa toward me, and she ran the remaining steps until she reached me. She threw her arms around me in a quick hug before turning her attention back to Boreas.

"Are you okay?" I asked her.

"Are you *insane!*" she snapped. "What are you doing here?"

"I swore your friend would be unharmed until I released her to you. Would you say I have kept my bargain?"

I looked at Melissa. "Did he hurt you? At all?"

"My wrist is a little sore from him yanking me around," she grumbled, "but no, he didn't hurt me."

I took a deep breath and looked at Boreas. "You've upheld your end, and I'm prepared to uphold mine."

"Good."

Without batting an eye he sent an icicle hurtling toward us. I shoved Melissa away from me and in a flash of power the tree's branches shot around us in a protective shell.

"Enough of that," Boreas said coldly. "I only have to deliver you alive. He didn't otherwise specify in what condition."

He?

Boreas' footsteps crunched along the snow. "You have been a thorn in my side for too long, you and your bitch of a mother."

"Run!" I shouted to Melissa. "It's me he wants!"

"I'm not leaving you!"

"You have to!"

The tree shattered and I hit the ground, hands covering my head. I threw up a shield, rolling away from the daggers of ice. Vines shot around Boreas' ankles.

"Persephone!" Melissa shrieked. I blindly groped for her hand. The second my skin made contact I teleported, calling up the image of Five Points.

My breath whooshed out of me when I hit a solid wall of ice. I fell to the ground, Melissa tumbling after me. I gasped in pain, unable to draw breath into my lungs.

"Persephone!" Melissa shook my shoulder. "Persephone, you have to get up. Move! Persephone—" She hiccupped.

Ignoring the blinding pain, I turned to face her. It was a struggle to make even that simple movement. She slouched above me, her face frozen in shock. A red icicle emerged between the two middle buttons on her blouse, and I frowned at the incongruous image.

"Melissa?" I wheezed. She collapsed on top of me, her blood vivid against the white snow.

Chapter XXIV

COLD HANDS GRABBED at my throat, dragging me up through the icy snow. I dug my feet into the snow and clawed at his hand. His foot caught me in my ribs, and I felt something snap. Boreas released my throat and yanked me to my feet by my hair. His lewd gaze took in my struggling form, and he smiled.

No. Not happening. My wordless howl erupted through the clearing. The scream unleashed something deep within me, and I felt the power I'd been holding at bay explode through my body. What did it matter if it burned through me? Melissa was dead, and anything would be better than what Boreas had planned for me.

A bright flash filled the clearing, and for a split second every detail in the clearing stood in stark relief against the light. Boreas howled and dropped me. My feet hit the ground and the snow melted beneath my feet, giving way to newborn grass.

I looked at Boreas and narrowed my eyes. Vines shot through him, growing from within his struggling body, holding him aloft in the air.

"What are you *doing* here?" Thanatos asked behind me. "Hades is going to—"

"You can't take her." My voice was so feral I didn't recognize it. I met his eyes and saw his pupils widen.

I drew back in surprise. I wasn't supposed to be able to charm gods!

"My lady," he gasped. "I have no desire to offend you, but a soul was lost here today and a soul must be collected."

"Any soul?"

He hesitated, and I stepped aside. Thanatos drew in a sharp breath at the sight of Boreas. The vines looped around his body, squeezing and tightening their grasp. Boreas made choking sounds as the vines crept out of his mouth, working their way out of his throat.

I met Boreas' eyes and watched his pupils widen. When I was sure he was charmed, I commanded, "Speak."

The vines shot out of his mouth and loosened from around his neck. Drops of frozen blood soaked into the grass beneath him.

"I am sorry," he breathed, entranced, "to have angered you. I will do anything to make it up to you."

"Why me?"

"You're beautiful and strong and—"

"Why did you come after me!" I demanded.

"I would have chosen you amongst thousands of others. All others pale in comparison to you—" I narrowed my eyes at him, and he swallowed hard. "I was asked to retrieve you by my master."

"Who is your master?"

"Long has he been in hiding, building his strength. When he discovered he still had a daughter in the mortal realm, he instructed me to—"

My head whipped forward in surprise. "*What?*"

"Zeus lives." He gasped as the vines tightened around him in response to my surprise. "I will tell you anything you wish. I will do anything."

I didn't want anything from him. I wanted Melissa back. Tears pricked my eyes and I spoke without thinking. "I wish you were dead."

Boreas disintegrated into snow and ice.

I blinked. Gods weren't supposed to be able to die either. What was going on?

Doesn't matter; you have a soul now. Maybe you can still save Melissa.

"There's your soul," I told Thanatos, like he had a choice in the matter. I wasn't sure if this was possible, but it was worth a shot. "Melissa stays."

"Yes, my lady," he said reverently. He stared at me, and I shifted uncomfortably. Thanatos was a friend. Manipulating him like this was wrong.

"Go get Cassandra. She's at the entrance to the Underworld. Return her safely to the palace. Only then may you tell Hades where I am."

He vanished, and I breathed a sigh of relief.

Melissa stirred. I knelt beside her and placed my hand on the icicle, watching it melt away. Her flesh knit itself back together. My head was buzzing, the flesh on my hands tingling uncomfortably. I released a final surge of power, shattering the ice wall.

The world spun around me. Dimly I heard footsteps crunching in the snow. My mother's voice. Strong arms wrapped around me and Hades whispered in my ear before I fell into a blissful slumber.

Chapter XXV

I WOKE UP, AND every bone in my body ached. *Hades.* I looked up at the ceiling, felt my cotton sheets, and knew I was home. The realization filled me with a crushing disappointment. The feeling shocked me. Only a few months ago, I'd been in tears because I couldn't come home. Now all I wanted to do was go back to him.

"Mom?" I croaked hoarsely.

She was beside me in an instant, fussing over me until I finally got a word in edgewise.

"What am I doing here?"

She looked surprised. "Where else would you be?"

"The Underworld."

"Honey." She fluffed my pillow and adjusted my blankets. "You destroyed Boreas. Why would you need to go back?"

I frowned at her. "That actually happened?" When she nodded I asked, "Melissa?"

"She's fine. You saved her." My mom fidgeted. "How did you kill Boreas?"

"I don't—" I paused. "Was Hades here?"

"He helped me get you home." Mom touched the back of her hand to my forehead. "But he went back a while ago. Do you remember what happened to Boreas, sweetie?"

"I'm not certain. What day is it?"

"March twenty-first." She smiled at me. "Happy birthday, sweetheart."

"The spring equinox," I murmured.

A smile broke through her worried features. "I've missed you so much." She gave me a hug.

I breathed in the familiar and reassuring scent of damp earth and newly-grown plants.

"I missed you too." Tears sprang to my eyes.

We spent the rest of the afternoon catching up. I told her about my time in the Underworld, and she told me about her struggles through the blizzard. She was visiting Orpheus' wife in the hospital daily, trying to restore communication between her soul and her body. Between his cult and the new additions to her priestesses I'd sent her from the Underworld, she was quickly gaining ground on Hades as far as powers were concerned.

She'd cursed Melissa with immortality. She'd hoped to do it when she was older but was afraid Thanatos would come to his senses and return for her soul.

"He wouldn't do that," I told her. "You didn't have to curse her yet."

"Persephone, I have no idea what happened in that clearing, but I'm not going to risk Melissa again. You won't be aging for much longer, especially with your powers surfacing so young."

"I don't want to lose her any more than you do."

She frowned at me. "Speaking of your concern for Melissa . . ."

"Mom, I'm sure you have a long lecture all stored up about how I came to be in that clearing, but it's going to have to wait."

"Excuse me?"

I gave her a look. "Hades will be just as worried as you were, and they're doing this whole equinox thing tonight . . ."

"Persephone—"

"Mom, I'm linked to the Underworld for the rest of my life. Boreas being gone doesn't change that."

"I know, but you need to prepare yourself for the possibility that you aren't wanted there anymore."

"What? *Why?*"

"Persephone, what you did in that clearing was terrifying. From the little we could gather from Thanatos, you charmed and killed a god, which shouldn't be possible. I'm just saying be prepared for some . . . apprehension."

She gave me a strange look. I nodded, feeling lightheaded. "What is it?"

"You've changed," she said, tears glittering in her eyes. "You've blossomed. I feel like the last time I saw you, you were this little girl, and now you're all grown up."

I THOUGHT ABOUT that while I drove to Melissa's house. I didn't feel grown up. I felt small and uncertain in the face of all that had happened. I had to see Melissa before I returned to the Underworld. I had to see with my own eyes that she was safe.

Mrs. Minthe opened the door. "Persephone!" She pulled me into a comfortable hug. "Thank you! Thank you so much for bringing Melissa back to me."

Tears dampened my hair, but I didn't mind. She ushered me into the house and offered me cider and cookies. "Your mother did her best, but I just knew—" She drew a shuddering breath. "But you rescued her." She smiled at me. "I will never forget that."

"Mom?" Melissa called from down the hall. She emerged carrying a laundry basket overflowing with jeans and T-shirts. She saw me and set it down with a smile. "The hero returns."

I smiled back at her, relieved not to see any apprehension in her eyes. "For a bit. I'm heading back down under for a few hours. I want to see how Hades is taking all of this."

A plate crashed in the kitchen, and I turned to see Mrs. Minthe reaching for a broom. "Slippery fingers." She waved a hand. "Sorry if I startled you."

"You're going back?" Melissa motioned for me to follow her to the laundry room. "Why?"

I brought her up to speed on my time in the Underworld, telling her all about Hades while Melissa sorted her laundry. "So you see, I need to at least try to apologize to Cassandra and Thanatos and work out some kind of schedule with Hades. That is if he's not all scared of me like my mom seems to think."

The sound of the news in the background caught our attention, and we peered around the door to see the television in the living room.

"And I told my son, Billy Bob. I says 'Billy Bob! You get out there and shovel that there dern snow!' And he says, 'I can't, Maw-Maw, it's ice.' I couldn't leave my trailer! I ain't missed church in fifty years, and I couldn't get out of my dern trailer."

The camera cut away from the obese woman with the stringy brown hair and yellow teeth to a put-together blond woman in a power suit. "And there you have it," she said sadly. "Residents were trapped in this trailer park for over a week . . ."

"Where do they find those people!" I gasped.

Melissa laughed, peering around the corner for her mom and shoving all the laundry into the machine. "Every time Georgia makes the national news, I swear reporters look for the nastiest rednecks they can find. But back to the subject, your mom thinks Hades is scared . . . of *you?*" She giggled.

My face fell. "You didn't see what I did in that clearing, Melissa. *I'm* a little scared of me." I took a deep breath. "I am so sorry! It's my fault he came after you, and then he actually *killed* you. Now you're sixteen forever and—"

"Seventeen," she reminded me. "Happy birthday to us, and I'm not mad. Well, okay, I'm a little mad," she amended, "but only for you actually being stupid enough to come after me. None of what happened was your fault. It was all Boreas'. No one else was responsible. Although," she said, raising her voice, "you'd think turning seventeen and dying would be enough to get you out of chores for a day!"

"Had you finished your chores yesterday, you'd have the day off," her mother called in a sing-song tone.

I suppressed a smile. "Melissa, can I ask you something?"

"Of course."

I followed Melissa into the living room, careful to keep my voice low. "About being a priestess . . . did you have a choice?"

She shook her head. "I was born into it. But I think I would have chosen it. You're my best friend. It was hard being away from you this winter. Every time something happened, I wanted to tell you about it, and without you there it wasn't real."

We'd been born hours apart. My mom had always made it sound like she'd met Mrs. Minthe in a prenatal yoga class. I remembered my mom telling me the story about how her water broke when she was in the goddess pose.

Of course I got the joke now.

"Was anything real?" I asked, thinking back on the endless play-dates and sleepovers, how we were always in the same clubs, classes, and sports. I'd never thought anything of it before, but now it seemed so manufactured.

"Everything's real," Melissa reassured me. "You're my best friend, Persephone. I mean, you saved my life—"

"You wouldn't have been in danger if it wasn't for me."

She shrugged. "Wasn't your fault."

I sank into the plush leather couch, relieved she still called me her friend. There were Mrs. Minthe's famous vegan cookies and cocoa sitting on the worn cedar coffee table. I snatched a cookie while I searched for my righteous indignation.

"I can't believe you knew about me this whole time."

"I wanted to tell you." She sat beside me. "You have to believe me, Persephone. I wanted to tell you but I couldn't. Your mother wouldn't let me. She bound me to secrecy when I was born."

I considered that for a moment. "So do you have to listen to her? To me? Is that part of being a priestess?"

"You're gods. You can bind anyone to anything if you wanted to. It has nothing to do with me being a priestess. That's just an antiquated title. I'm not going to perform any ceremonies, or pray to you, or anything weird. I just believe in you. You choose how you want your followers to show their devotion."

"What do Mom's priestesses do?"

"My mom and the others honor her by working with the earth and growing things. They also give her a bit of everything they grow, but I think that's more about friendship than tithing."

I thought back on the jars of jam, fresh baked breads, and fruits and vegetables my mother's friends were always bringing over and had to agree. They would come bearing gifts, and the women would retreat to the back porch and gossip for hours. That didn't seem like worship to me.

"They're all her followers, aren't they?" I realized. "All of her friends."

Melissa nodded.

I shook my head. This was too much to process, and I had more important things to worry about. "I'm glad you're okay. I'll drop by again when I get back from the Underworld. We should do something normal. Like go to a movie."

"The new Dusk movie is out."

I grinned. How had I forgotten about that? I left Melissa and headed back to Memorial Park. I parked my car and ventured into the clearing. It looked so different today! The clearing was drenched with life. The grass was a vibrant green, and wildflowers had burst into bloom. The tree was gone, but several saplings had already sprung up in its place. The sun was starting to sink in the sky when I ducked into the Underworld. My feet barely touched down in Tartarus before I teleported to my bedroom in the palace.

I walked across the hall and knocked on Cassandra's door. She opened the door and then she drew away from me apprehensively. I looked behind her and saw Helen on the couch.

"What are you doing here?" Cassandra asked coldly.

"Persephone!" Helen exclaimed. She ran to me and gave me a hug. "Thank the gods you're okay!"

I smiled at her. "Cassandra, I'm so sorry."

She waved her hand, distrust still in her eyes. "It worked out."

"You're not going to the Equinox celebration in *that*, are you?" Helen asked.

I looked down at my floral patterned skirt and pink top and shook my head. "I was kind of hoping you'd help me with that."

Cassandra sighed. "Come on in."

Chapter XXVI

THE PARTY WAS in full swing by the time Helen declared I was ready. I gripped their hands tightly as we walked to the ballroom. What if my mom was right? I hadn't really meant to surprise Hades like this. I just needed to see him, to talk to him, and hear that everything was going to be okay.

Helen had outdone herself on my dress. It was a beautiful full-length strapless yellow taffeta gown. The material gathered around my stomach, enhanced by clusters of diamonds forming daisies. Corset strings tied the dress in the back, starting just beneath my shoulder blades. My hair was down, and the same diamond daisies were sprinkled throughout, forming a loose crown. I wore a matching bracelet.

"Hades can take care of the ring," Helen joked.

The door to the ballroom opened and Thanatos stumbled out, laughing at something Charon had said. They both stopped when they saw me.

"Whoa," Charon said, giving me a once-over before pulling me into a quick side-hug. "It's good to see you're okay."

"Thank you." I looked at Thanatos. "I'm so—"

"I was honored to help you." He clasped my hands. "You were incredible out there."

"Are you still . . . ?"

"No," he assured me. He glanced at Helen, Cassandra, and Charon. "Could I talk to you in private for a moment?"

The blood drained from my face. "Melissa?"

"Is beyond my reach. I just needed to ask you something about Boreas. His . . . unusual death has made his soul difficult to classify, and I'd like to get this sorted out before I go."

"Can't it wait?" Cassandra asked.

"It will only be a moment," Thanatos promised.

"You guys go ahead," I said with a smile at Helen and Cassandra. "It's probably best we don't all show up together. Hades may not be too thrilled with me after what I did."

Cassandra shrugged and grabbed Helen's hand, pulling her into the throne room just as the music shifted to a slow song. Charon nodded at me and set off in the opposite direction of the dancing girls.

My heart sank when they didn't argue. Charon couldn't lie, but I would have welcomed false platitudes from Cassandra or Helen.

"Are you going somewhere?" I asked Thanatos.

"Vacationing on the surface for a bit. You won't be needing me for guard duty down here, will you?"

"No. I'm probably going to be spending most of my time on the surface from now on."

Thanatos nodded. "Boreas died human, somehow. He didn't have an ounce of divinity left. Do you know what he did with his powers before he died?"

"No, but I bet it had something to do with Zeus. Have you told Hades what Boreas said about him?"

Thanatos shook his head. "He needed to know you were okay before he could handle news like that. He's not happy you snuck off, but he really does worry about you."

I smiled. "Well, I hope you enjoy your vacation. I hope telling Hades about Zeus doesn't mess it up for you."

"I'm not really all that useful to Hades." Thanatos looked down at the marble floors, scuffing his black shoes back and forth. "Have you told . . . anyone that you charmed me?"

I frowned, thinking back. I'd told my mother and Melissa about the fight with Boreas, but between witnessing and then committing a murder, charming Thanatos wasn't all that memorable. I studied Thanatos. It was memorable for him. His face was flushed, his hands were gripped tightly together, and he wouldn't meet my eyes.

He's embarrassed. I remembered him saying I outranked him, and as far as bloodlines went, I did, but knowing that and having his will overpowered by a goddess who hadn't even come into her powers couldn't feel very good.

"I haven't told anyone."

"Is there any way . . . I hate asking you this, but could you promise not to tell anyone anything about me? It's just that I'd never live it down if anyone ever found out I'd been charmed."

I smiled at him. "I promise. I can't promise Hades won't figure it out, but he won't have any help from me."

A grin broke out across his face. "Thank you."

"It's the least I can do. I'm really sorry I used you like that. It wasn't right."

Thanatos shook his head. "Just don't do it again, okay?"

I opened my mouth to agree, but the door opened, smacking me in the elbow. "Ouch," I muttered, rubbing it. I got out of the way as a group of souls left the ballroom, laughing among themselves.

I glanced through the open door and saw Hades in the center of the room. His eyes met mine.

"I'll be going now," Thanatos said. "Bye, Persephone."

I nodded, my mouth going dry, and walked through the door. The ballroom had been redecorated for the Equinox. Flowers covered every corner. Halfway into the ballroom the floor gave way to grass, and the ceiling changed to open sky, with randomly placed stars decorating the sky. Souls smiled at me, but I only had eyes for Hades.

My pulse hammered in my throat. "Can I have this dance?"

He pulled me close to him, putting his hands stiffly at my shoulder and waist. "I wasn't expecting to see you again."

"I'm not going to apologize to you. I would do it all again if I had to."

"That's a terrifying thought. How *did* you manage to kill Boreas?"

"I'm not sorry," I said quickly. "He deserved it. He deserved worse! He killed Melissa and who knows how many other people during that blizzard. Not to mention what he had planned for me. I'm not sorry."

"You don't have to be." Hades' voice was soft. "You don't have to explain that to me."

I looked up at him. "I'm not sorry." My voice shook. "I'm not. That doesn't make me a monster. I know you're disappointed or whatever, but if I had—"

"What?" He titled my chin up so he could study my face. "What are you talking about?"

"You wanted me to be different . . ."

Hades shook his head. "You defended yourself. I don't think any less of you for that." The song changed and we swayed with the music. "I just want to know how you did it."

"I told him to die." I swallowed hard. "And he crumbled."

"He was charmed, I presume?"

I nodded.

"That shouldn't be possible." He looked at me warily. "Don't ever try to charm me."

I glared at him. "Did you know Zeus was still alive?"

He stumbled, stepping squarely on my foot.

"I guess not," I muttered.

"What are you talking about?"

"Boreas told me when I charmed him. He said he was working for Zeus." I shrugged. "He wants me for something. But Zeus is dead, isn't he?"

Hades' face hardened. "I'll get to the bottom of this. But at least this explains how you were able to charm and kill Boreas. He'd sworn fealty to Zeus."

"What does that mean?"

Hades glanced around the ballroom, then took my hand and led me outside. "A god can swear fealty to another god, and it transfers all their worship and power to that god. In return they can be given more strength than usual, but they aren't themselves anymore. They're bound to that god. They have to follow their will." He gave me a level stare. "It's practically signing away your divinity. When you asked him to die, he probably willed the rest of his power to Zeus."

"Why would Boreas do that?"

Hades shrugged. "Who knows what Zeus promised him? In any case, Boreas would only be vulnerable to Zeus or his offspring."

"He did all that," I grumbled. "And now he's living the high life on Olympus."

"Actually, his soul is in Tartarus. He died without divinity. He was judged as a human would be." Hades gave me a smile so dark it sent chills up my spine. "After I had a long talk with him."

"And he didn't tell you about Zeus?" I didn't agree with torture, but I'd figured if Hades did . . . whatever he had done in that talk, it would yield results.

"I didn't think to ask if a god had somehow managed to come back to life." Hades sounded defensive. "We'll have to have another conversation. But in any case, he's in Tartarus, so be careful coming and going from the Underworld."

"I'm glad he was judged as human." I looked Hades straight in the eye. "Gods shouldn't get special treatment when they're judged."

Hades gave me a bitter smile. "Then we'd all go to hell. So your mother doesn't mind you coming here?"

I shrugged, not appreciating his implication with that particular change of topic. "It's not her favorite thing, but she'll get over it. I *am* queen here, aren't I?" He gave me a look I couldn't decipher, and I exhaled impatiently. "You didn't think I knew this was forever?"

His eyes darted to the floor. "I was going to tell you, but I was looking for a way to reverse—"

"I don't want you to."

He looked up.

"I love it here. I feel like I belong here."

"Then why didn't you just stay?" His voice was gruff. "If you love it so much, why run to danger?"

"Because Melissa needed me, and she means more to me than any other human being in either realm. And I'm glad I was able to stop the suffering of the people in the living realm, because I care about them just as much as I care about the souls. They didn't deserve to freeze for me, and yeah, on a more selfish note it was really nice to see the sun again. I belong on the surface just as much as I do here." I touched a hand to his cheek. "If you still want to find a way to undo it, go ahead. But not on my account."

He smiled at me. "I couldn't ask for a better queen."

"I love you." The words left my mouth of their own volition. I gulped at the empty air, trying to take them back.

He froze.

"I'm not one hundred percent sure," I babbled. "Well, I guess I kind of have to be if I actually said it, but I'm not stupid. I know I've only known you for, like, three months, and the age difference is kind of colossal. But I know you feel the same way."

"Persephone—"

I held up a hand to stop him. "You're about to remind me that you don't want to take advantage of me, but we're kind of *married*."

"Marriage doesn't mean anything to gods."

I moved closer to him, standing on my tiptoes until our lips were inches apart. "Maybe not, but it means something to you."

"You're hardly the first woman I've shown interest in," Hades scoffed. His eyes sparkled with challenge. He wasn't going to shrink away from me. He leaned closer. "There was Minthe, and Leuce, and—"

"Minthe?" I interrupted his list. He looked at me quizzically and I shook my head. It was just a strange coincidence. "Never mind. You didn't *marry* them."

"They got turned into plants," Hades grumbled.

"I love you," I said firmly. "That might change over time, but for right now, you're the first person I think about when I wake up and the last before I go to sleep. When I'm happy, I want to tell you, and when I'm scared or upset, I know you're the only one who can make things right. We may never work as a couple, but we're linked for the rest of eternity. And I don't know about you, but that's too long for me to wonder 'what if.'"

"Persephone—"

"There's no pressure to do anything about it. I just thought you should know. I—"

Hades kissed me, hands cupping my face. It was a soft kiss, but not a quick one. With regret I broke the kiss.

"Unfortunately, I've got a curfew. See you later this week?"

"Later this week?" Hades asked, his hand still touching my face.

"Mmm, court," I reminded him, leaning into his touch. "You'll have to reschedule it, though. I've got school."

"We'll work it out."

A thought occurred to me and I stepped out of his grasp so I could pursue it without distraction. "I could only charm Boreas because he'd sworn fealty to Zeus? There's no other way?"

"With enough power, you might be able to charm me, since we're bound together, but anyone else?" He shook his head. "Not to my knowledge."

My heart began to pound. "It's not about power? I channeled *everything* I had to charm him. I felt like I was about to blow up or something."

Hades gazed into the distance, thinking. "The Titans had enough power to charm the minor gods. Zeus often managed with some of the lesser deities. So theoretically, it's possible to have enough sheer power to overwhelm another god, but you don't."

He would know. He'd been channeling my power for weeks.

"Why?" Hades asked.

I opened my mouth to tell him my horrible suspicion, but the words wouldn't come. *Oh gods, I promised I wouldn't tell.*

Thanatos had sworn fealty to Zeus. He'd been working for him this whole time. He'd left me right by the river of fire. What had he done after that? Pirithous wasn't just in the right place at the right time; he'd been led straight to me. Thanatos hadn't interfered with my escape from the Underworld, even after Cassandra yelled for him. He'd known I was going to Boreas. I thought back on every conversation we'd ever had. The words suddenly seemed twisted and manipulative.

"Oh gods," I whispered. Tears gathered in my eyes.

"I know you're scared of Zeus." Hades misinterpreted my panic. He gave my shoulders a squeeze. "But you don't have to be. I can protect you." He grinned. "Not that you can't protect yourself."

I tried to correct him, tried to explain myself, but the words wouldn't come. I willed myself to speak the words. *Thanatos is working for Zeus.* My head felt light, blood roared in my ears, and my stomach twisted. I couldn't breathe, couldn't think.

I *had* to tell him. Thanatos was a psychopomp. He could come and go from the Underworld anytime he wanted. I looked into the ballroom, blood running cold at the sheer number of Reapers mixed in with the crowd. Sucking in the light around them.

I couldn't speak. My hand seized at the very thought of writing. I searched frantically for some kind of loophole but couldn't think of anything.

"Are you okay?" Hades asked, eyes wide with concern.

"I'm tired," I whispered.

He nodded. "It's been a rough couple of weeks. Come on. Let's get you home. You said something about a curfew?"

I nodded, numb as he lead me away. I couldn't bring myself to smile at the souls I passed. They were all in danger because of me. Because I'd been an idiot and allowed myself to get locked into a promise.

Some queen.

RETURNING TO school was strange. The campus, which had once felt so large to me, seemed minuscule now. I hadn't missed much. School had been closed through the blizzard. The weather was warm again, so Melissa and I ate lunch outside on our picnic blanket and quizzed each other for our human anatomy test next period.

"Well, look who's back," Rachel said in a snarky tone as she walked by. Her face pulled into a mask of fake sympathy. "I heard you were . . . traveling."

I smiled at her, for just a moment reveling in the knowledge that I could charm her into jumping off a cliff. I knew all about the rumors circulating the school.

My mom couldn't lie, so she'd told the main office I'd had a rare opportunity to do some exploring out of the country. Which was true, in a manner of speaking. We'd spent the weekend teleporting to all of her favorite places in Greece and Rome before I returned to school so I'd actually have something to tell the teachers. It had been fun until I realized I'd have to pull an all-nighter to write my reflections of a winter full of travels before school started.

"I had a great time," I answered, looking her straight in the eye. "We got caught in some snow, though, which was weird. I heard it got pretty bad here too?"

Her pupils dilated and retracted. She looked at me, confused. "Uh, yeah," she replied, sitting on the blanket. "It was so scary, we couldn't go anywhere . . ."

I smiled at Melissa while she talked. School was much nicer since I'd gotten a handle on my charm. It was taking time, but I was working on releasing the students I'd unknowingly had in my power. With any luck, Rachel would be more like she used to be.

I drew six pomegranate seeds from my plastic bag. My hand froze halfway to my mouth, goose bumps rising on my flesh. A cool breeze tickled my hair, whispering my name in the wind. I stood, glaring into the stand of trees in the distance.

Someone was watching me.

The End

A Sneak Peek at the Exciting Sequel to *Persephone*

Daughter of Earth and Sky

I'D BEEN HERE before. My bare feet glided down the leaf-strewn path, unharmed by the rocks and twigs crunching beneath me. Massive live oaks draped with Spanish moss created a canopy above me, transforming the forest path into a tunnel of speckled sunlight. The air was heavy with humidity. The moist heat pressed against my skin and stole the breath from my lungs.

A memory tugged at my mind, but I was unable to place it. My Eeyore nightshirt clung to my skin when I reached the path's end.

"Dungeness," I whispered, coming to a halt when I recognized the sprawling ruins of the ancient ivy-covered brick and stone manor. Athens Academy had taken my class on a weeklong trip to Georgia's coastal islands freshman year. Cumberland Island had been a major highlight because of the sea turtles, wild horses, and these ruins.

"But how did I get here?" I knelt to pick up a smooth, white stone. The weight of it in my hand felt reassuring.

I turned, hoping the path held some answers, but it was no longer there. I stood on the shoreline looking out to sea. In the distance, a girl stood thigh-high in the ocean, clad in a gown of strategically placed sea foam. Although her back was to me, I could tell she was perfect. The curly ringlets of hair cascading down her flawless creamy skin matched the intense orange of the sky as the sun sank into the sea.

She glanced over her shoulder, aquamarine eyes meeting mine. I was shocked to hear Boreas' cold voice roll off her tongue. "Zeus lives."

My mind screamed against the onslaught of images that raced through my head: Cumberland Island, two sunsets, lightning crackling in the sky.

Dasvidaniya. I forced myself to think the word, closing my mind to the invasion of images bombarding my mind . . .

I bolted up in bed with a gasp. A weight in my hand made me look down. I unclenched my fist, revealing the white stone from Dungeness. That had been no ordinary dream.

Gods used dreams to communicate with each other, but an un-guarded mind is ripe for attack. To protect myself, I was supposed to think the word *dasvidaniya* before bed, closing my mind to other deities. But it had been months since Zeus had sent Boreas to abduct me, and nothing had happened since that horrible day in the clearing. I'd grown complacent.

That's no excuse. I glanced at my phone and saw it was almost three in the morning. With a groan I flopped back into bed, took a deep breath, and closed my eyes. *Hades.* I directed my thoughts to him. I could sense the energy of all the other sleeping deities, both alive and dead. It was a weird sensation, like catching a glimpse of something out of the corner of my eye only to have it move before I turned my head. It was easier to find gods I knew. I could sense Hypnos' energy right away, flickering like a strobe light beyond the horizon. He was always the easiest to find because I'd learned to dreamwalk from him in the Underworld.

I found Hades next, a bundle of dark energy guarded like a fortress. I sent out the mental equivalent of a knock and found myself in the Underworld, standing in his library.

"This better be good," he grumbled, sitting in his usual oversized leather chair. The library faded into muted reds and browns, fuzzy and unfocused. Hades, on the other hand, was in hyper-focus, the sharp angles of his face almost too real in this strange setting.

My heart leaped at the sight of him. His dark curly hair fell into his bright blue eyes. His lips curved in a smile despite his grouchy tone. He loved me. How long would that last when he realized what I was hiding from him?

A few months ago, Thanatos, the God of Death, tricked me into promising that I wouldn't reveal he was working for Zeus. Actually, I'd promised I wouldn't tell anyone anything about Thanatos, and that Hades would have no help from me learning about his betrayal.

I was stupid like that sometimes.

I'd tried everything I could think of to break my word, but gods can't lie. My promise was ironclad.

"It's good to see you, too." I leaned down and kissed his forehead, letting the images from my dream flow into him. I tried to slip thoughts of Thanatos through the kiss, but my mind rebelled at the idea, and I only managed to convey a troubled feeling. Given the nature of my dream, Hades wouldn't think much of me feeling worried.

His eyebrows shot up. "When did this happen?"

"Less than a minute ago." My hand trailed off his shoulder.

He gave me a disapproving look, but didn't waste time lecturing me about leaving my mind unguarded. He could sense I was kicking myself enough as it was.

"What did it mean?" I perched on the arm of his chair. I usually have a better sense of personal space, but Hades was the only thing in this room that looked real and solid. Staying close to him made me feel grounded. I frowned, comparing the nauseating swirls of unfocused furniture coloring this room with my dream. "Whoever sent that message put a lot of energy into making it feel real."

"It had Poseidon's signature all over it. He considers himself to be quite the artiste." Hades waved his hands in the air. A dark, mocking smile played on his lips.

"Poseidon's still alive?" I wondered if he could be working with Zeus.

Hades nodded. "He won't be working with Zeus, either. They didn't—I mean don't get along. From what I could gather from your dream, something is happening in two days at Cumberland Island. I don't know what the girl means, but she did mention Zeus."

"This is the first lead we've gotten," I murmured, linking my hand with his. We hadn't learned anything new since Boreas' earth-shattering revelation that Zeus was alive and looking for me.

"I can handle this." Hades' eyes met mine. "You don't need to come."

"Yes, I do." I leaned down and gave him a slow kiss.

He broke the kiss, gripping my shoulders gently. "How much time do you need to talk to your mother about leaving?"

I took an inward hiss of breath. I hadn't thought of that yet. "Thirty minutes?"

"See you soon." He smiled and pushed me out of his dreams.

A Bonus Read!

Medusa

WHAT HAD ONCE been my hair now shifted and writhed atop my head. Athena's punishment turned me into a monster. I squeezed my eyes shut and buried my head further in my arms doing my best to ignore the augmentations my body endured. My tears hissed as they touched my flesh. They burned, but my skin healed before the pain could register.

I was ruined. Huddling against the cold marble wall, I hunched over my knees and did my best to tune out the gods discussing my fate in the other room. What did it matter what happened to me now?

"Why did you call me here?" Hades' voice rang out from the other room, laced with ill-disguise rage. Everyone was so angry with me. How very unfair. "My responsibility is to the dead.   The girl still lives."

"I would like you to fix that." Athena's voice sounded calm in comparison to the Lord of the Underworld, yet it still rang off the vaulted ceilings. They were not speaking very loud but volume had never much mattered in this temple of cold cut stone.

I could picture the goddess studying Hades with dispassionate grey eyes, dark hair wound back so tight it pulled at her skin. She always wore her robes in an unflattering, shapeless cut. Athena was beautiful; anyone with eyes could see that, but she buried her beauty under a layer of harshness like a weakness that needed to be armored.

I was beautiful once. The fairest in my village, I've been told. A distinction I gave little thought to since my sisters and I devoted our lives to Athena. We were desperate. Our mother died while birthing my youngest sister, and my father took to the bottle and traveled down into the depths of despair, where we could not follow. But we'd still had Athena. Temple girls always had food, shelter, and protection.

And there I thought gods could tell no lies.

"What did that pitiful creature ever do to you?" Hades demanded, bringing me back to reality.

"She and Poseidon defiled my temple."

"She was raped." Hades' voice had gone low and dangerous, the tenuous candlelight in the temple flickered in response to the darkness within his tone. "Hardly a willing participant in this petty little feud between you two. Striking at her because you cannot strike at him is reprehensible and—"

"Petty feud?" Athena gasped. "The naming of this city is life and death for me, Hades. We were not all gifted a realm. I have seen the base of Olympus, and it crumbles. According to Apollo's prophets, this city could outlive us all. If my name survives the fall of Olympus then I survive—"

"Pray you do," Hades interrupted. "Because if this is how you treat your worshippers, I have no intention of letting you anywhere near mine."

I closed my ears to the rest of their conversation. Athena was supposed to protect me. I recalled the relief I felt when I managed to crawl to the temple steps after the rape, bruised and battered, inch by painful inch. But she did nothing to avenge me. Instead she screamed at me and her words became curses. My hair shifted and hissed in response to my anger.

The hissing intensified, and I jumped when a hand touched my shoulder. Hades drew back, hands held up in a gesture of surrender, eyes closed. Obviously, even gods could not bear my ugliness. "I have no intention of harming you." He spoke in the careful, precise, yet vague way of the gods, unwilling to promise to cause me no harm, should it come to that. Neither did he elaborate on his definition of harm.

Needless to say, I was not comforted. "Are you here to kill me?"

Hades' lips quirked up in a subtle smile at my question, and he shook his head without opening his eyes. He looked nothing like Poseidon. Strange since the two were brothers. "No." He crouched beside me, keeping his distance. "But I suggest you accompany me home before your patron gets her wits about her."

Home? The Underworld. I believed in the legends of the gods. It's difficult not to, when you attend to one every day, but surely the land of the dead was just a bedtime tale, meant to inspire fear or hope. The dead were gone and buried, every trace of life snuffed from their hollow shells. Preparing my mother's corpse for burial taught me that. Nothing, not even the gods, could rekindle that spark.

But looking at the man before me, with hair so impossibly dark it would make the darkest midnight seem to dawn, I found myself a believer. Power emanated from his statuesque frame, filling the room with fear and finality. Athena was awe inspiring, but Hades . . . he was something else entirely.

Athena! I looked around the room of the temple, pulse pounding, but she was nowhere to be seen.

"She's gone," Hades assured me. "And you need not fear her . . . " he hesitated. "Directly. My kind can no longer kill you." He waited for that to sink in. "Neither will old age."

I struggled to wrap my mind around what he seemed to be saying. "Am I immortal?"

"Not quite." He rushed to clarify, leaning forward a bit on his hands. "You can be killed, but not easily. Athena granted you quite the defense system."

Granted me? He made it sound like a favor. "Can you reverse the curse?"

The smile faded from Hades' face. "No. If it were within my power, I would change you back. But I can promise you that she will regret what she's done."

I can hurt them, I realized. That was why he wasn't looking at me. Whatever she did to me made me dangerous to the gods themselves.

Hades seemed to sense the directions of my thoughts. "I realized you have a lot to think about at the moment, but this bears repeating. You do not want to be here when Athena realizes what she's done. I can take you somewhere that should be safe. Will you come with me?"

I didn't have to think very hard before I said yes. This temple held my home, my sisters, and my friends. My entire life was contained within these walls, and I was no longer welcome here.

Drying my eyes, I climbed to my feet. Hades blindly held out a hand to help me, grazing my shoulder as I rose. I flinched at his touch. A muscle in his jaw twitched, and I worried my reaction offended him until I saw the red welts swelling upon his hand. They rippled, healing in an instant, but I was shaken. What would my touch do to a human?

I already knew what happened to a mere mortal who so much as looked upon me. Hearing my horrified screams as Athena's curse took root, a villager had rushed to my aid. Poor man. I would never forget the look of horror in his eyes as his skin hardened to stone. A shudder went through me. I was, indeed, a monster.

I could not risk saying goodbye to my sisters, so I closed my eyes, conjuring up a mental image of them, Stheno and Euryale. They were so young. In memory, I rubbed a hand over their dark hair and kissed their foreheads. Please be safe without me. Surely Athena's wrath would not extend to them.

I followed Hades down to a large cavern just outside of the Underworld. Cracks in the stone glowed red with magma, but Hades assured me it was safe. There was a large chamber and several smaller caves within the structure, all furnished comfortably. I'd never lived in such luxury in the world above. However, my new home held no mirrors, no glass, nor anything reflective. From this lack, I gathered that at least part of my curse could be used against myself. Or perhaps not. Every part of me was poison. My blood, my flesh, the snakes that writhed atop my head. All deadly, yet I remained standing. Perhaps Hades just wanted to spare me from seeing what I'd become.

As the weeks passed, Hades continued to visit. He could not have known how much his frequent visits meant to me. How it felt to speak to another living being after days of solitude. Thanks to him, I never wanted for conversation long. Especially given that he knew what I could do to him. The sheer trust he put in me every time he walked into my cave with his eyes closed was astounding. We talked of everything and nothing. The Lord of the Underworld brought me books to read, new clothing, anything I asked for, never asking for a single thing in return.

I had just begun to settle into my new life when the first of the heroes showed up.

"Hello?" he called, venturing into my cave.

At the sound of his voice I ducked behind a stalagmite. I had no wish to turn this young man to stone. "Who are you?" I demanded. "What are you doing here?"

"A woman?"

The hero sounded surprised. He crept deeper inside my cave then straightened up, tugged on his reflective breastplate, and slicked his fingers through his hair. In a deeper voice than before he called, "Fear not, fair maiden! I will rescue you!"

A pang went through me. I'd been fair once, a maiden too. No longer. I shook off my melancholy, knowing full well that dwelling on my past would not resurrect it. "I fear I am past saving."

"Nonsense," The hero declared, chest puffing in pride. "For I am Hercius!"

I tilted my head, frowning as I tried to place his name.

As though sensing my confusion, his chest deflated a bit. "Once I finish my task all will have heard of me. I shall be famous! I will become immortal in the pages of history!" His confident voice rang through the cavern.

"I do not need your help," I said firmly.

The hero really was handsome. His hair, eyes, and skin had a golden hue that seemed to almost glow in this dark cave. He looked strong, and he was quite tall. Of course he was nothing compared to Hades, but he was still pleasing to look at. I watched him curiously. After all, he couldn't see me, so it wasn't as if he knew I was being improper.

"Are you sure you do not need to be rescued from the gorgon?" he asked, squinting into the shadows where I stood.

"Gorgon?" I moved forward just enough for my shadow to edge into his vision, hand resting on the rock in front of me. "That is my father's name."

"No, not Gordon," Hercius laughed. "Gorgon, the monster with snakes for hair and terrible, grey-cast skin. Why I heard it can turn a man to stone just by looking at him." Hercius tilted his head. "Heh, perhaps that is why you have not been affected. You are a woman." He seemed surprised at this insight, as though he was unused to the sensation of thought entering his mind. Perhaps it tickled.

"What do you intend to do with this gorgon when you find it?" I asked.

"Why, chop off its head, of course."

I gave a little gasp. "You must be so brave."

He grinned and polished his sword. "Yes."

"And strong."

He flexed his muscles. "I've been told so."

I sighed. "Oh, you sound handsome. Are you handsome? I cannot quite see you."

"Well . . ." He preened and stepped closer, into the light. "How about you come a little closer so you can tell me what you think?"

"Too bad you're not very bright," I mused.

"Huh?" He looked confused as I stepped out from behind the stalagmite.

I watched without flinching as he turned to stone.

Oh, but he made such a lovely statue.

They were not always as foolish. More came within the next several months, but I persevered. Soon my new home had many new decorations. I posed them around the cave. Sometimes I spoke to them, not as if they were enemies intent on vanquishing me, but gentlemen who had come calling. One day I feared they might answer me and wreck my illusions of kindness.

When Hades next visited, he took in the statues with raised eyebrows.

"I could seal off the main entrance," he offered. "Then the only way in and out will be through Tartarus. That won't stop the demigods, they can enter my realm, but it should weed out all but the most persistent of them."

I had feared rebuke. For all intents and purposes the heroes had been murdered by my hand as sure as if I had stabbed them with a knife. But he did not seem particularly concerned about their welfare. Only mine. Knowing he would not turn and catch my lingering gaze made me bold, and I studied him without reserve. Gods, he was wonderful to look at. He was tall and strong, and his dark hair fell onto his angular face. For a fleeting moment, I wondered what his eyes looked like. But of course I could never know.

I would run myself through with a sword before I allowed harm to come to Hades.

"Well?" He asked, turning his head so it almost seemed as if he were staring straight at me.

I started in surprise, my mind replaying our conversation. I had never answered his question. "I cannot enter Tartarus."

He nodded, his expression shifting to one of sympathy. I wondered how he managed to convey so much emotion without his eyes open. His whole persona seemed to alter. "I would never keep you here against your will, but it is safer."

Sometimes it was tempting to leave, but then I risked disappointing Hades. He was all I had. The only living being who would mourn my passing. I made up my mind to never do anything that would earn the cold regard he'd given the heroes.

"I know I am safer here." I sat down on one of the plush chairs he'd provided. "And I never intend to leave, but the idea of actually being trapped here with no way out . . . " I shuddered.

He nodded. "I understand. I've shielded both of the entrances the best I can, but Athena's giving them all kinds of tools to work around it."

I felt a flash of anger. Why wouldn't she leave me alone? It would have been a kindness to strike me dead that day; instead she chose to make me into this . . . thing. To change her mind now was just cruel. "Don't bother." I shrugged at his surprised look, then remembered he couldn't see me. "I have no wish to hurry my death along. But your Underworld sounds lovely. And when I die..." I looked up at him, "I won't be like this forever will I? If I die—"

"You will return to your mortal form," Hades confirmed.

I let out a sigh of relief. There was hope. I would not be a monster for all eternity. "And if I drink from the Lethe?" I asked, referring to the river of forgetfulness in the Underworld that allowed souls to forget their lives.

"It is aptly named. You'll forget you were ever anything else but Medusa—"

The sound of my name spoken from his lips set my heart beating fast. "I have no intention of doing anything foolish to bring about my death, but . . . "

"You won't try too hard to prevent it either." He finished my sentence for me, sounding sad. I hoped I had not offended him. It never occurred to me he might be hurt that I was willing to forget his friendship. But surely . . . he was a god, and I was a monster. I couldn't mean much to him. Certainly not as much as he meant to me.

"Have you met Cerberus yet?" Hades asked, shifting the subject to something more pleasant.

I blinked. The three-headed monster guarding the entrance of the Underworld? "No . . . "

"He's the smartest dog. I'll have to bring him up sometime. Do you like dogs?" When I nodded, Hades launched into a story, and I leaned back in my chair. I loved his stories. He was so animated when he spoke. His hands moved, punctuating his speech. I glanced down at my grey hands, clasped in my lap; my nails were sharp like talons, my fingers bent and bony. It was a mercy he could not look upon me. I was a monster. And yet he continued to visit me and entertain me with his tales, making the long stints between the attacks of the heroes almost bearable.

I could tell the next hero was different, right away. Oh, he looked like the rest. He had the same golden features I'd since learned marked him as a demigod, the same brawny looks, but he had less bluster. This hero did not burst into the cave like he owned the place, shouting challenges. He snuck in, moving between the statues, eyes glued to his shield with his sword at the ready. I would have to be careful how I handled this one.

I crept behind him, ducking behind stones when I could. If I could surprise him into looking up at me for just one second he would be doomed. Another statue for the collection.

The hero paused when he reached the statue that was once Hercius and made a small noise in his throat as if he recognized him. Well, this was different. He was the only hero to show fear. His hand clutched so tight to his sword that his knuckles turned white. Was his hold so tight to stop his hands from shaking?

"I won't harm you if you leave now," I promised him.

His head snapped up, and I ducked behind a column before he could see me.

"Are you Medusa?" His voice shook.

"Yes, and you?"

"Perseus." He let out a deep breath. "I . . . I have no choice."

"You seem to have walked into this cave of your own volition." I tried to keep the anger out of my voice. He had no idea what it was like not to have a choice. "You can turn around and walk back out."

"She'll die." His voice cracked.

I closed my eyes. This was not fear; it was desperation. Someone he loved was at stake.

His words echoed throughout the cavern, and he seemed to draw strength from them. The hero had a purpose. He darted in my direction, heaving his sword. I stepped out of reach.

A flicker of movement in his shield drew me up short. My face reflected in the shiny metal. I froze, horrified. She had left my face unchanged. The snakes writhed and shifted atop my head. My skin was an ugly, mottled grey from the neck down. But my face was still my own, untouched by the curse that had been laid upon me. Somehow, that was worse.

The hero's eyes met the reflection of mine. "I'm sorry. I'm so sorry," he said. The high-pitched sound of metal sang through the air as his sword swung toward my head.

Acknowledgments

I'd like to acknowledge all the members of the Athens Area Writers Group and my friend Amber Floyd. If it weren't for them, my book wouldn't be half as interesting.

About the Author

Kaitlin Bevis spent her childhood curled up with a book and a pen. If the ending didn't agree with her, she rewrote it. Because she's always wanted to be a writer, she spent high school and college learning everything she could to achieve that goal. After graduating college with a BFA and Masters in English, Kaitlin went on to write The Daughters of Zeus series. Visit her at KaitlinBevis.com.